Woods
And shame the devil.

And
Shame
the Devil

A RINEHART SUSPENSE NOVEL

A RINEHART SUSPENSE NOVEL

And
Shame
the Devil

✦✦✦✦✦✦✦✦✦✦✦✦✦✦✦✦✦✦✦

Sara Woods

✦✦✦✦✦✦✦✦✦✦✦✦✦✦✦✦✦✦✦

HOLT, RINEHART AND WINSTON
New York   Chicago   San Francisco

Any work of fiction whose characters were of a uniform excellence would rightly be condemned—by that fact if by no other—as being incredibly dull. Therefore no excuse can be considered necessary for the villainy or folly of the people in this book. It seems extremely unlikely that any one of them should resemble a real person alive or dead. Any such resemblance is completely unintentional and without malice.

**O! while you live,
tell the truth and shame the devil!**

—KING HENRY IV, Part I, Act III, Sc. i.

And
Shame
the Devil

A R I N E H A R T S U S P E N S E N O V E L

In Sir Nicholas Harding's study the first fire of autumn had died to a heap of glowing cinders, leaving the room pleasantly warm. Antony Maitland, coming in quietly, went of long habit to prop his shoulder against the mantel and waited patiently enough until his uncle pulled off his spectacles and looked up from the foolscap pad on the desk which was covered, incomprehensibly, with a tangle of figures.

"Having trouble with your income tax?" he asked then, with sympathy.

"At the moment, no." Sir Nicholas frowned, and glanced at his watch. "I thought you'd gone to the theater," he said in a complaining tone, as though the failure to implement his announced intention placed the younger man in some way at an unfair advantage.

"Jenny went, she hasn't got back yet. I've been with Chief Inspector Sykes." Antony paused for long enough to watch the faint spark of interest light in Sir Nicholas' eye. "He wants my help," he added, and deliberately kept both face and voice without expression.

"That sounds extremely unlikely." Sir Nicholas' attention had been held for the moment only. The gleam faded, and his eyes went back to the scribbled figures under his hand.

"Not for himself. That wrongful-arrest case . . . *you* know, Uncle Nick."

"I've read about it." The admission came grudgingly.

"He asked if I'd take it on, defending the two police officers. What do you think about that?"

Sir Nicholas was heard to murmur, without looking up, something about the mammon of iniquity.

"No, really, sir, whether you mean me or them, that's hardly fair comment."

1

"Don't you think so?" He pushed back the pad with every appearance of loathing. "With your facility for stirring up trouble whenever you come into contact with the force it might be useful—"

"This isn't the local chaps, sir. Nor the C.I.D."

"No, of course. Somewhere in the north, as I remember. Do you really want to go to Leeds Assizes?"

"Arkenshaw, to be exact."

"It's the same thing," said Sir Nicholas gloomily. "What do you know about—er—the totalisator?"

"About what?"

"The totalisator. A device, I understand, which shows the number and amount of wagers placed—"

"Yes, but—"

"I find myself at a loss." Sir Nicholas spread his hands eloquently. "However, it occurs to me that in your misspent youth you might have acquired the knowledge I am seeking."

"I couldn't afford to misspend it at the races," said Antony, and added rebelliously, "As you jolly well know."

"A pity. My client," Sir Nicholas told him, "is alleged to have worked out a system for defrauding his bookmaker—"

"Clever chap. But where does the tote come into it?"

"Something to do with the—er—the odds at which the bets were laid. As for your comment, I'm inclined to agree with you. I have been endeavoring to master the principle involved, but so far, I admit, without success."

Antony shifted his position a little. "Well, I don't see how you can expect help with that."

"I don't."

"The thing is . . . about this case of wrongful arrest—"

"Don't touch it!" said Sir Nicholas with sudden energy.

"That's what I said to Sykes. Heads you win, tails I lose."

"To make matters worse," said his uncle, obviously following his own train of thought, "the plaintiffs are both from Pakistan . . . if I remember rightly."

2

Antony nodded. "The inference the prosecution will invite us to draw is that there's racial prejudice mixed up in it somehow."

"How do you think that will affect the jury?"

"Well, you know, sir, however they feel about it, however they'd act themselves in any circumstances that arose involving the color question, they'll be all for fair play if the hint of victimization arises."

"Are you so sure that nothing of the kind has occurred?"

"I'm not sure of anything. How can I be?"

"Then, if you want my advice—" He broke off, eying his nephew rather fixedly. "But you don't, do you? You've made up your mind."

"I can fit it in all right," said Antony, on the defensive. "The Epworth business has been postponed—"

"How does Sykes come to be involved?" asked Sir Nicholas, resigning himself.

"He isn't, really. He was at school with Sergeant Duckett."

"One of the defendants?"

"Yes."

"A sympathetic character, no doubt."

"Not precisely." ("A hard man," Sykes had said. "Stubborn. And—it's not a bit of use denying it, lad—he doesn't like foreigners.")

"I see," said Sir Nicholas. It was probable that he did see, quite clearly. "I can't think why you're bothering me with all this."

"I wanted your opinion."

"Why? You never act on it," said his uncle grumpily, but with some truth.

"It's interesting," said Antony, abandoning pretense. "But tricky . . . don't you think?"

"Not nearly so 'tricky' "—Sir Nicholas repeated the word with an air of distaste—"as the workings of this preposterous machine."

3

"I don't see why you need to understand it, but Derek might be able to help you. Have you tried him?"

"He's still away. However . . . it's an idea," Sir Nicholas conceded. He picked up his pencil and began to sketch, idly, on the blotter. "It means 'going special,' " he said, reverting to his nephew's problem, "and it occurs to me to wonder, just why does Sykes want you?"

"I asked him that." Maitland was encouraged by this sign of interest. "He just smiled in that sedate way of his, and didn't answer."

"It wasn't as an advocate," mused Sir Nicholas. "Not that I am denying your eloquence; indeed, I have suffered from it myself on occasion."

"We both know half a dozen fellows on the circuit who'd talk the hind leg off a donkey, given a chance," Antony agreed.

His uncle looked pained. "Might it have been," he suggested gently, "because of your known tendency to meddle in things that are, strictly speaking, none of your concern?"

"Sykes would be the first to condemn any interference."

"It isn't his case," Sir Nicholas pointed out. "And as far as the Arkenshaw police are concerned, they have already, presumably, done all they can. Did he give you any indication—?"

"Now I come to think of it," said Maitland slowly, "he was careful not to express an opinion as to the rights and wrongs of the affair."

From Sir Nicholas' expression it was obvious that he did not think much of this. He put down the pencil with careful symmetry across the corner of the pad. "And yet he succeeded in arousing your interest."

"Well, yes, I suppose he did."

"How?"

"For one thing, there's a direct conflict of evidence—"

"Between plaintiffs and defendants? That is to be expected."

"Yes, of course, but between two of the witnesses as

well. In the main . . . you know what people are, Uncle Nick—"

"Unhappily."

"It's all pretty vague. But these two are positive, no chance of an honest mistake; and one of them is lying."

"Not necessarily the plaintiffs' witness, however."

"I realize that. The other thing . . . well, why is the case being brought at all?"

"I should have thought that was sufficiently obvious."

"That's what the jury will think: why is the case being brought, unless it's true? It gives the plaintiffs a built-in advantage, don't you think?"

"And possibly a valid one." Maitland raised his hand suddenly in a vague, dissatisfied gesture, and Sir Nicholas' tone sharpened a little. "Can you be quite sure, Antony, that in taking this brief your own mind is clear of prejudice?"

Antony took his time to consider that. "I can be sure, at least, that I have no feeling against the plaintiffs because of their race," he said at last. Sir Nicholas scowled at him.

"That is not what I meant, as I think you know. Why should you think it odd that the action is being brought?"

"Well, look at it, Uncle Nick. Here are two chaps accused of burgling a suburban home. The police seem to think there's a good case, but they're acquitted. Wouldn't you think that would satisfy them? They can't possibly hope for substantial damages; they can't even be sure of their costs."

"In the interests of abstract justice—"

"I admit, if the case was rigged, they'd be sore," said Antony with a trace of impatience in his voice.

Sir Nicholas had opened one of the drawers of his desk and was scrabbling in it in an ineffectual way. "If you would be content to accept your instructions on their merits," he remarked, "I should feel no anxiety at all. But these civil cases . . . you realize, I suppose, that if you identify yourself with an unpopular cause your reputation is bound up in it to a far greater degree—"

Maitland had straightened himself as his uncle was speaking. He selected a box of matches from the cache behind the clock, and strolled across to the desk to place it on the blotter. "Your cigars have been kept in the bottom drawer for the last thirty years," he said helpfully. "I don't suppose Gibbs has moved them now."

Sir Nicholas looked at him with more exasperation than gratitude. "If you're going to add mind-reading to your other accomplishments, life will hardly be worth living," he said disagreeably. "It so happens I was looking for something else." But he made no further protest when Antony produced the box and placed it at his elbow, and a few minutes later his hand went out to it in an absent-minded way.

I

No one, set down unexpectedly in the center of Arkenshaw, could mistake it for a moment for anything but what
it is: one of the smoke-grimed cities of the industrial West
Riding. In fact, it is a little removed from its sisters in
Airedale and Calderdale, with a cold sweep of moorland
insulating it from its nearest neighbor; and the King's
Cross to Arkenshaw express has been whittled down to a
mere two carriages by the time it reaches its destination,
having been segregated at Leeds and shunted off into what
is undeniably a branch line. It may be because of its re-
mote situation (for surely it cannot be because of its im-
portance as a center of population); it may be for some
strange, historical reason, long forgotten; but for whatever
cause it enjoys its own assize.

Antony Maitland, alighting from the train there in the
dusk of a November evening, found nothing for encouragement in the vast cavern of the Midland Station, and
still less in the chilly wind that followed him up the plat-
form. There was a handful of passengers only: businessmen for the most part, a group of women who had probably been shopping in Leeds, a girl who had refused the
offered services of a porter, though her case looked a
heavy one. It wasn't that she appeared hard up; an inde-
pendent turn of mind, perhaps, and most likely there'd be
someone to meet her. He put down his briefcase and
scanned the little group of people beyond the barrier while
he fumbled for his ticket. That anxious-looking young
man in the dark overcoat, he'd be the one. But the girl
passed by without a glance and went on resolutely toward
the booking hall.

He found his ticket, surrendered it to the collector, and stood a moment to get his bearings. As he started off again the young man, abandoning his anxious scrutiny of the few remaining passengers, turned and said doubtfully, "Your name doesn't happen to be Maitland by any chance?"

The absurdity of the query invited comment, the worried air forbade it. Antony said seriously, "Well, yes, it does." And then, "I wasn't expecting—"

"I'm Chris Conway."

"I see." His instructing solicitor, younger than he'd expected, but that didn't explain . . . "It's very good of you," he said.

"I thought . . . well, you might have difficulty getting a cab."

Maitland, translating freely, decided that it was reasonable enough, after all, for his companion to want to have a look at him. "I was going to give you a ring," he said, "as soon as I got to the hotel."

"Have you some luggage? An Austin eleven hundred," he added to the porter who appeared just then with Antony's suitcase. "I'm parked in the taxi rank."

"I want to see our clients," said Maitland, falling into step beside him. He wasn't quite sure if he was being sidetracked.

"Yes, of course. Tomorrow morning—"

"With the case due to be called at any minute? I'm sorry I was delayed, but I really think I must see them tonight."

"But I'm—"

"You've got a previous engagement. I realize I'm putting you to a great deal of trouble." His tone was polite, but held no suggestion of compromise. Conway laughed suddenly and said: "Oh, well! I'm due at the Ducketts' in half an hour anyway."

"In that case—"

"I'm taking Star to the pictures."

"Star?" said Maitland vaguely; but his sidelong glance at his companion was not vague at all.

8

"Sergeant Duckett's daughter."

"I see," said Maitland again; and again his tone conveyed polite bewilderment. They had reached the car now, and he waited until Conway had unlocked it and the porter had left them before he added with a grin, "That's very convenient. You can make your apologies in person."

"You mean . . . take you with me?"

"I do indeed." Their eyes met for a moment, and then Conway shrugged resignedly and climbed into the car.

"If you insist," he said.

Maitland tossed his briefcase onto the back seat. "I'm sorry." There was amusement as well as sympathy in his tone. "I realize you think I'm being high-handed, but it really is important, you know."

"Then, wouldn't you rather—?"

"I'd rather come with you." He got into the car and slammed the door, and turned to look at his companion. Conway had obviously been prepared for the unconventional, but seemed to think this was carrying things too far. "In the circumstances," Antony added consolingly, "it is obviously the most convenient thing."

Conway was backing out of his parking place. "There's Constable Ryder as well," he said. "Or had you forgotten?"

"We'll see him afterwards," Maitland told him cheerfully; and added, after the briefest glance told him that the other man's face had set into rather stubborn lines, "If it comes to that, what about Bushey? Is he at the hotel?"

John Bushey was the member of the North Eastern Circuit who was to act as his junior.

The car was edging out of the station yard now, with a caution that was perhaps disproportionate to the flow of traffic. "No, he lives in town," said Conway. "He said he'd be in if you cared to phone him."

"I'll do that, later on." Again there was the sidelong look at his companion, and for the first time he embarked on something that might be taken for an apology. "The

9

brief was admirably prepared, you know. I couldn't have asked for anything better."

Something of the rigidity went out of Conway's bearing. "Then why—?"

"Don't you think in a case like this it is especially important to know your clients?"

"To see if you believe them?" Oddly, he seemed to find the idea confusing. There was a pause, which might only have been because he was involved in the delicate enterprise of passing a tram car, and then he added, with a faint trace of bitterness, "I didn't think you'd care about that."

"You'd be surprised," said Maitland lightly, and sat back in his seat and looked out at the passing scene. Here in the center of the town it was nighttime already, with the buildings crowding in upon you, and the street lights and shop windows glaring their defiance of the dark hills which—so far as he remembered—surrounded Arkenshaw on every side. But though he affected an interest in what he saw, mentally he was assessing Chris Conway: still in his twenties, probably . . . it was hard to tell. His manner was that of an older man, but there was also at times more than a suggestion of immaturity. He was of medium height, with dark brown hair that might easily have been red if it had never seen a bottle of hair oil, gray eyes, and regular features. The worried look might be indigenous, or again it might not. What was quite certain was that he was taking his responsibilities seriously.

They had been brought to a halt by yet another tram. Maitland found himself staring at a fountain with a group of nymphs whose draperies might be suitable enough for water sports, but which he considered quite inadequate for so cold a night. He removed his gaze and looked instead at Conway's reflection in the windscreen. "Have you known the Ducketts long?" he asked.

A man with a long pole was maneuvering the tram's arm from one overhead cable to another. Conway might have been fascinated by the operation; in any event, he made no attempt to answer until it was completed and the un-

10

gainly vehicle had swung away down the left arm of the fork. Even then he had to wait for the lights to change before he was free to take the right-hand road. There was less traffic now, and they could make a better pace. He said, as though unconscious of the pause, "Since I took his instructions."

There didn't seem to be anything to say to that, though it didn't go any way at all toward answering the questions that were in Antony's mind. "You hadn't done any work for him before," he hazarded, feeling his way.

"I don't suppose he'd ever needed a solicitor. No, we came into it when they knew the writ would be issued. Duckett and Ryder, that is. They asked us to accept service, and the matter was referred to me. I'm the junior partner," he added, and Maitland had a private smile for the inconsequent tone, because the statement was so clearly relevant. . . .

"The plaintiffs," he said. "Who's appearing for them?"

"The solicitors are Jones and Ashby, a very reliable firm. As for counsel, the local chap's Martin Roberts; he handled the defense at the first trial." Conway paused a moment, his eyes intent on the road ahead. "This time, Kevin O'Brien is leading him."

"Bringing on their big guns, are they?" asked Maitland, and saw in the windscreen that Conway was amused by the note of surprise in his voice.

"I'm afraid they are. That's why—" He broke off, and for the first time ventured a sidelong glance of his own. "I only know O'Brien by reputation, of course," he said.

"He's just about as good as they say," Antony told him. "Which means, in this case, too good by half."

"You don't think we've an adequate defense, then?"

"Do you?"

"People have been acquitted before without the police being regarded as liable—"

"Yes, but . . . someone's lying, aren't they? I mean, you can't just dismiss the whole thing as an unfortunate mistake."

"No," said Conway. The idea seemed to depress him. After a moment he added, still gloomily, "We're nearly there."

They had left the center of the town behind, and the mean, dreary streets that immediately surrounded it. Here, facing on to the road, were orderly terrace houses of blackened stone, with a glimpse as you passed the turnings of more modern dwellings of stucco and brick. But they came to another crossroads before the car turned to the left, and then right almost immediately into a narrow lane with a high wall on one side ("Waterworks," said Conway) and open ground on the other. About three hundred yards from the turning there was a long, gray house, a one-time farm most likely; Conway drew in on the grass verge, close beside the wall. "Here we are," he said, and waited for Maitland to get out, and then slid across the seat to follow him.

There were lights ahead, a block of flats from the look of it. But here it was dark and silent, and the wind from the moor was cold, so that Antony realized for the first time that they had been climbing steadily ever since they left the town behind; and thought—also for the first time— that perhaps there was some sense after all in the heavy overcoat Conway was wearing. The old farm seemed marooned amidst the evidences of progress, but that wouldn't last, of course. "It's a dilly of a position," said Conway, leading the way across the road. "All this is scheduled for a golf course." He hesitated a moment with his hand on the gate. "Don't forget," he added, "this was your idea."

Antony was pondering this remark as he followed down the flagged path to the front door. Chris Conway seemed a self-possessed young man, not the sort to be daunted by a sergeant of police, however formidable. There was, of course, the complication of the girl, which he had tried so unsuccessfully to probe. For himself . . . well, why the devil should the fact that Sergeant Duckett had given his daughter a revolting name like Star prejudice his counsel in his favor, before he had even met the man?

12

It was the girl who came to the door. "Come in, Chris, you're early." She didn't add, "How nice!" but the sentiment was implicit in the warmth of her tone. Her voice was low-pitched, her accent a little broader than Conway's. Antony took a moment to wonder, while the solicitor was explaining himself, how long it would be before his own instinct for mimicry overcame him, which it had been known to do from time to time in similar circumstances, and generally with embarrassing results.

He had followed Conway into the hall, which smelled strongly of furniture polish and by daylight would probably have dazzled the eye. The girl turned to greet him, seeming to take his presence for granted, and he found this reassuring. She was a little thing, with a cloud of dark hair. In the dim light of the hall her eyes looked dark too, but later he had every opportunity to observe that they were a clear hazel, and very direct. Meanwhile, he found himself wishing that she would smile, but she had a grave look as she said, "You'll have to wait a little while, I'm afraid. But I don't think he'll be long."

Maitland embarked on his own apologies, but was interrupted almost immediately by a voice from a room on the right which said in a peremptory way, "Don't stand out there, wasting the electric." Conway began to look positively haggard, but he obviously knew the drill and made for the light switch, plunging the hall into darkness a moment before Star pushed open the door of the room. "All right, Grandma," she said. She was still serious, but the smile seemed to have got into her voice.

The best description of the big room would be that it was a combination of living room and kitchen. There was an old-fashioned range with an open fire, and a hideous Victorian sideboard with an array of willow pattern, a bowl of fruit, and a bunch of chrysanthemums in a vase with dragons careering fiercely across it. The mantelpiece had a frill all around—brown chenille with bobbles; and the marble clock was flanked by two severe-looking nymphs—obviously relations of the ones he had seen downtown, but at least in here there was no chance of their catching cold. The table was spread with a white cloth, and laid for a meal.

In a high-backed Windsor chair to the left of the hearth, old Mrs. Duckett sat enthroned. She was a stiff-backed lady of ample proportions, with creamy-white hair drawn into a tight bun, blue eyes, a roseleaf complexion, and an uncompromising manner. She was still grumbling at her granddaughter as they trooped in. "It's that young man of yours, I suppose. Whispering in corners, you ought to know better, the pair of you." But she broke off when she caught sight of Maitland, and beckoned to him imperiously, completely ignoring the introduction which Conway and Star had commenced in chorus.

"When were you born?" she demanded, and gave him a piercing look.

As an opening remark it had at least the merit of originality. Antony said, "July the fourth—" and broke off at a loss when she remarked "Hmph!" It sounded as though her worst suspicions had been confirmed, but after a moment, "You don't look like Cancer," she said, as though the words were an accusation.

"Well, I . . . I don't think—"

"The Crab," said Conway behind him, with a great air of helpfulness.

"She means your horoscope," Star explained. "The sign you were born under."

"Oh, I see," said Antony, relieved to have so much at least made clear.

"Scorpio . . . perhaps," said Grandma Duckett judiciously. "Or even Taurus. I don't *see* you as Cancer," she added in a discontented tone.

"Unless someone went to great trouble to deceive me," said Antony, "I'm afraid we'll both have to make the best of it."

This time he was in no doubt as to the fiery nature of the look she gave him. "You wouldn't be laughing at me, young man?"

14

"No, indeed." Maitland, who had prodded the reluctant Conway into bringing him here from a simple sense of duty, was now beginning to enjoy himself. "It's really very interesting. Our friend Conway, for instance—?"

"Oh, him. Pisces!" said Grandma, lowering her voice as though she were speaking of some nameless evil. She looked at her granddaughter and shook her head. "I warned her, you know, but would she listen?"

Conway was moved to protest. "No, really, Mrs. Duckett, you know you told me I should find my best friends under Capricorn, and Star—"

"I may have told *you* that," said the old lady with spirit, "but I never told her to associate with you. That's different. Pisces!" she said again with loathing.

"Well then, who should he—?"

"Capricorn, or Taurus, or Virgo. But that isn't to say *they* should have anything to do with *him.*"

"Then, who—?"

"Nobody," said Grandma with relish. "So far as I've ever been able to find out." She gave Antony a glare. "It's no laughing matter," she told him.

"I wouldn't dare." There was a strong feeling in the room of time reversed, so that at any moment, he felt, they might all be back in the nursery. But he couldn't resist a glance at Chris Conway, who managed to look guiltier than ever. "A sort of moral leper, I suppose. You know, I wouldn't have thought it." Conway grinned sheepishly, and Star, who evidently felt the visitor's behavior was getting out of hand, raised her voice a little and said clearly: "Mr. Maitland is waiting for Dad."

"Then he'd best sit down." The old lady indicated the chair opposite her own with a regal gesture. "Fred will be in any moment, and then . . . have you had your supper?"

It was on the tip of Antony's tongue to say he had dined on the train, but somehow the lie remained unuttered. "Then you'll have it with us," said Mrs. Duckett with a sort of grim satisfaction. "Both of you," she added.

"But I've already—"

15

Conway's protest was cut off short. "You've had your tea, I suppose, and seeing as how you're not going to the pictures, you can have your supper now . . . like a Christian," she added obscurely. "Soused herring it is, which is good *and* economical. And don't you go forgetting that, my girl."

Star had gone across to the cupboard, and was composedly taking out fresh cups and saucers. "I think I heard the car," she said. "Shall I make the tea, Grandma?" Conway cast a despairing glance at Maitland and was at once relieved and irritated to see that he had settled himself back comfortably in his chair and that his expression conveyed nothing but a sort of pleased expectancy. He was a tall man, dark, with a thin face and a casual, almost diffident manner that Chris was finding a trifle confusing, having already decided he had been a trifle foolhardy in conjuring up so recklessly an associate who knew exactly what he wanted and meant to get it.

Mrs. Duckett had cocked her head, listening. "Aye," she said at length. "He's in the scullery now, washing his hands. You can mash it now, there's a good girl, and give it time to draw." And as she spoke, a door that led toward the back of the house opened and Sergeant Duckett came in.

He was a powerfully built man, with rather fierce blue eyes, mouse-colored hair plentifully streaked with gray, and a fine, sandy moustache. His mother said, "Here's Mr. Maitland to see you, Fred," and he nodded to Antony as he came across the room, but addressed himself to Conway.

"I thought that was for tomorrow."

"Well, you see—"

"It seemed important that I should see you." Maitland spoke quietly, and Conway's sentence trailed thankfully into incoherence.

"Well, and why then? Didn't he give you the facts?" Duckett jerked his head expressively in the direction of his solicitor.

16

"Oh . . . facts!" said Antony vaguely. "Of course he did. I have also read the transcript of the evidence at the original trial. But there are still a couple of questions—"

"I've always done my duty," said Sergeant Duckett truculently. "If anyone wants to make anything of that."

"I shan't keep you long." Maitland's tone was pacific, but he was wondering with carefully concealed amusement just what his uncle would have made of so belligerent a client. "The plaintiffs, now"—he pulled a ragged envelope out of his pocket and stared down at it blankly for a moment—"Ghulam Beas and Chakwal Mohamad, if I've got the pronunciation right—"

The sergeant swore. He did so in a completely unemotional tone, and with great profanity, and Grandma surged up out of her chair. "We'll have none of that here, Fred Duckett. And none of that heathenish talk either," she added, turning an admonitory eye on Counsel. "Not till we've had our suppers." Antony smiled at her, and meekly took the place she indicated to him at the table. His client might be—what was it Sykes had said? a hard man?—but quite clearly Mrs. Duckett was in full control of the household. If she had delegated the pouring out to her granddaughter, it was probably because she found it difficult; she managed well enough, but he noticed now that both her hands were twisted with rheumatism.

The tea was strong enough to skin the roof of your mouth, but the soused herrings were surprisingly good. Presumably they had died happily. Grandma took her obligations as hostess seriously, and discoursed amiably enough on a variety of topics. Fred Duckett had relapsed into silence, but he obviously took the presence of a stranger at their board very much for granted. Chris was silent, too, except for sporadic—and ineffectual—protests over the refilling of his plate. Star was eating her supper with the self-possession that seemed to be natural to her; she spoke only when addressed, but that seemed natural too, and once she raised her head at some remark of Maitland's and her eyes met his with a distinct flicker of amuse-

17

ment. Only when the teapot had been drained did Grandma push her chair a little away from the table and say in her forthright way, "Now, then, if you want to get down to business—"

Maitland looked at his host. "Perhaps we could—" His gesture was indeterminate, but clearly suggested retirement. He was thinking regretfully that it would be a pity to leave the warmth of the kitchen.

"You can have your talk here. What can't be said in the light of day," said Mrs. Duckett, killing Maitland's protest dead before it could be uttered, "didn't ought to be said at all. Besides which, there's no call to be lighting gas fire in t'parlor."

The sergeant seemed to regard his mother's orders with a certain fatalism, but had energy enough left for a small show of authority. "No reason why you shouldn't be sidening t'pots, Star," he said, and waved impatiently to the two younger men to sit down again when the girl got up obediently.

Antony subsided, and began absentmindedly to pile together whatever plates were within his reach. Between them, they'd made a pretty clean sweep; for all her talk, Grandma's economies, it seemed, did not extend to the supper table. Fred Duckett had pulled a pipe out of his pocket and then laid it down, with ostentatious virtue, beside his cup. "The plaintiffs," said Maitland, raising his head. "Did they ask for legal aid?"

Star reached past him to remove the pile of plates. Her father said slowly, "They did when we had them up in summer; and got it, too." He sounded puzzled, and looked at Chris Conway almost doubtfully. "Not this time. At least, I don't think—"

"We'd have known if they'd made application," said Conway, nodding.

"Yes, of course. Were the solicitors—Ashby and Jones, did you say—were they acting for them before?"

"No, they weren't. It was a chap called Walters, I remember that."

"The thing is, you see, I'm not at all clear why they're bringing the case."

"Spite," said Duckett. He sounded more confident now. "That chap Beas, he's a troublemaker. Always was."

"I see." He had pulled out the envelope again, and laid it on the tablecloth before him, but this time he did not make even a pretense of consulting it. "A journalist," he said, and looked inquiringly at Conway.

"That's right. Rather a chip on his shoulder, I'd say."

"Who's backing him, then? The local paper?"

For some reason Conway looked startled. "Well—" he said. "He's by way of being a protégé of theirs. They're certainly backing him up, but not backing him financially, so far as I know."

"Local prejudice?" asked Maitland quickly.

"There wasn't a thing in the damned article—sorry, Mrs. Duckett!—that you could complain about."

Star paused halfway across the room with a tray of crockery. "They said, 'The ugly specter of racial prejudice is showing itself in our midst,' " she quoted. Her voice had an indignant quiver. "I don't call that nothing."

"Speak when you're spoken to," said Grandma, without looking around; and Sergeant Duckett, keeping his end up, growled, "Get on wi't'job, lass." Conway kept his eyes on Maitland's face and said doggedly: "There wasn't anything to tie it in with the case, you see."

"No, I suppose there wouldn't be."

Star had reached the scullery door, but still seemed to be hesitating. She said at last, "You know what they say, Dad. They say you don't like foreigners."

"No more I do!"

Maitland was momentarily startled by the violence of his client's tone. "I can see you're going to get me into trouble," he protested.

"And what might you mean by that?"

"If you blow up in court at the mere mention of the plaintiffs—"

"And why wouldn't I? Tell me that!" The sergeant's fist

19

crashed down on the table with sufficient force to set what was left of the crockery rattling. "Coming here and taking a man's character—"

For the first time Maitland was fully aware of the bitter anger under Duckett's composure. Anger, and a sort of confused resentment at the turn events had taken. He said steadily, "If you happened to be wrong when you brought the charge against them—"

"We weren't wrong."

"There was that other time," said Star, coming back from the scullery with the empty tray.

"And we weren't wrong then, neither," said her father fiercely.

Old Mrs. Duckett had been clicking her tongue in unheeded reproof. She said now firmly, "Don't you take on so, Fred. Not but what I didn't tell you no good would come of it. When Uranus is in Virgo—"

"Now, Mother!" said Sergeant Duckett uncomfortably.

Antony fought down a strong temptation to inquire further into Uranus' doings. It all sounded vaguely improper. "All the same, I'd like to hear about that 'other time,' " he said.

The sergeant threw a furious look in his daughter's direction. "It were nowt."

"Another case where the defendants were acquitted?"

"Yes. Well, it was only one man."

"A Pakistani?"

"It was." He paused, scowling. "Bag-snatching, if you must know. A clear case."

"But the jury didn't convict."

"Here, now! What is all this?" Sergeant Duckett looked around a little wildly. "Think you can cross-examine your own witness, hey?"

"What happened?" persisted Maitland, unimpressed.

"He proved an alibi," Conway put in quickly, perhaps under the impression that his client was about to suffer an apoplexy. "And the judge said—"

"Never you mind about that," said Duckett, controlling

20

himself with an effort that was alarming to watch. Conway shrugged and relapsed into silence, but Star—still going about her duties with that odd air of detachment—took up where he had left off.

"The judge said the case should never have been brought."

"Just you wait, lass," said Sergeant Duckett venomously. He turned to Maitland and added, "If you must know, they sprang the evidence on us. But judge said—it was this chap Gilmour that's sitting on this assize—he said we ought to have investigated proper. That's all!" His mouth closed with a snap.

"Then, to get back to the present case, Sergeant, and accepting the fact of the plaintiffs' guilt of the charge you originally brought against them, you've mentioned Beas, but what about the second man?"

"Mohamad. A nice enough young fellow on the face of it," said Duckett grudgingly. "Medical student, some sort of scholarship, but his home's here."

"And the family are known to be hard up," put in Star. She removed a second trayload of china to the sideboard and gathered up the cloth by the corners.

"And who told you that?" asked her father aggressively.

"It's what they say." Her face was expressionless. The sergeant shrugged helplessly, but Mrs. Duckett was not so easily appeased.

"Now, if you've been listening to uncharitable talk, my girl—"

"Oh, Grandma!" Just for a moment there was a hint of exasperation in her tone; then she smiled. "Information received," she said lightly. "You can't grumble at that, luv, and me a policeman's daughter."

The smile was all that Maitland had hoped it might be, and Chris Conway was visibly shaken by it. The sergeant said gruffly, " 'Appen not for long." He sounded depressed, but less censorious than before. Grandma sniffed and said disagreeably, "None of your sauce, now!" Star took the tablecloth and disappeared with it into the scul-

21

lery. "There's Capricorn for you," the old lady added, and glared at her son as though it was all his fault . . . which, in a way, it was.

"'A nice enough young fellow,'" said Maitland thoughtfully. And added unnecessarily, "Mohamad, I mean. Not so likely, then, to be motivated by spite."

"Led astray," said Grandma with relish and a fine inconsistency, before the sergeant could get his wits together to answer. "Led astray by evil companions."

"He's twenty-three." Duckett sounded half-apologetic. "T'other chap, Ghulam Beas—he's in his thirties."

"Thirty-five," said Chris.

"So you think he's the moving spirit? The older man."

"Stands to reason, doesn't it?"

"Yes, perhaps. Well, if they're lying, their reason's obvious enough. The witnesses, now—" This time he did take a look at his envelope. "Barlow, Thompson, Jowett, Lawford, Randall, Marshall, Ward," he muttered, and raised his head again. "This boy, Martin Ward—"

"What about him?"

"He says quite positively he saw Beas and Mohamad coming down the path from the front door of the Barlows' house. This is in direct contradiction to—what's her name?—Miss Garrowby's evidence, so naturally I'm curious."

"What do you want to know?"

"Family background . . . age . . . record at school." Maitland was vague, even a trifle diffident.

"Respectable," said the sergeant heavily. Considering that the boy was one of his own witnesses, he was oddly unwilling. "Father's chief cashier at the district branch of the Northumbrian and Wessex—"

"Gemini," said Grandma in a deep voice, "most unsuitable."

"—and the mother's a busy type of woman, Red Cross, that sort of thing. Martin's sixteen, a clever lad from what they say. Mr. Samson at the Grammar School, he speaks

22

well of him. An only child." He glanced at the scullery door before he added, "Like our Star."

"Well, then," said Maitland, declining to be diverted, "why didn't they believe him?"

"Because he *is* only a boy. A teen-ager. Unreliable," said Duckett, slapping the table again but this time with less force. "*And* we've had plenty of trouble with the kids around here," he admitted, "but that's not to say young Martin's telling a lie."

"His evidence, I understand, completely confirms your own." Maitland's face was expressionless, but something in his tone made Duckett glance at him sharply.

"*And* Constable Ryder's. There was two of us there, think on."

"I'm not forgetting Ryder. That brings us then to the plaintiffs' witnesses."

"Konat Iskander. Another of these foreigners," said the sergeant scornfully.

"Pakistani?"

"Yes, of course." He seemed surprised at the query, and it occurred to Antony that in this part of the world the two words were almost synonymous. "He backs them up about the time they left the pub. Which is only to be expected. And Art Saddler . . . I thought better of Art; not but what he's about as vague as our lot."

"But Miss Garrowby"—he looked down at the envelope again—"Miss Emily Garrowby."

"A nosy old maid," said Duckett viciously.

"You agree, then, that she was probably looking out of her window?"

"For aught I know. But when she says those two were 'walking along the pavement,' " said the sergeant, his voice rising dangerously, "I say she's a liar."

Antony glanced at Conway, who shrugged his shoulders resignedly. No point, then, in again indicating the unwisdom of so much vehemence. He said, "We'll leave it there, then," and saw with amusement that the words brought Duckett down to earth with a bump.

"Why . . . is that all?"

"That's all. I had very complete instructions from Mr. Conway, you know. Unless, on reflection, you can tell me why they're prosecuting."

"Well, I can't," said Sergeant Duckett rather sulkily. "Not unless it's spite, which is what I said and what I stick to."

"All right, then. I shall see you in the morning, of course." He turned to smile at Grandma, and got a glare for his pains. "It was very kind of you, Mrs. Duckett. I hope I haven't upset your evening too much."

"Hope's cheap," she told him cryptically. And then, relenting a little, "Can you do *owt* about all this, young man?"

"I can try."

"Don't be expecting too much, that's all." Her voice took on again its sibylline quality. "When Saturn and Mars are in conjunction—" He didn't say aloud that he was more concerned with the unknown Miss Garrowby's testimony, but perhaps she saw it in his eye. "Well, you think it's all nonsense, I suppose, but don't be too sure about that. If you'd been Scorpio, now, or even Taurus like Fred here, it'd be different. But Cancer . . . I don't know."

She was still shaking her head over the problem when Maitland had said good night to the sergeant and followed Star to the front door with Conway at his heels. This time there was no loitering; she shut them out into the cold night with the briefest of farewells.

II

Neither of them spoke until they were in the car again, driving along the dark lane toward the lighted block of flats. Then, "A most redoubtable old lady," said Maitland in a reflective tone. "You might have warned me."

24

Conway, his eyes on the road, spoke unguardedly, "As a matter of fact, I was hoping—"

"That she'd annihilate me," said Antony without rancor. "I know!"

For the first time Conway lost his worried look. "You ought to see her with Mr. Ogden," he remarked appreciatively.

"Who's he?"

"Methodist minister. He feels it his duty to point out to her that star-gazing is hardly consistent with regular attendance at chapel, but as Grandma is just as militant about Christian principles as she is about her wretched horoscopes, it doesn't leave him with much to say."

"And neither of her preoccupations has taught her resignation."

They had slowed for the turning; right, and then right again, back toward the town. "She's a holy terror," said Chris in gloomy agreement.

"A proper caution," said Maitland absently. Conway never noticed the lapse into the local idiom, but he did hear something very like admiration in the other man's voice and said with renewed resentment: "It's all very well for you."

Maitland turned quickly. "Miss Duckett's a charming girl." He would have been the first to admit that as an apology the statement was inadequate, but even so he was hardly prepared for the note of fury in Conway's tone as he replied.

"It's a mistake to become emotionally involved in what ought to be only a job of work. Go on . . . say it!"

It was the last thing he'd be likely to tell anyone, having heard the reproach only too often himself. "Who told you that?" Antony wondered. The answer, when it came, was completely unexpected.

"Sergeant Duckett," said Chris. He sounded sullen, and after a moment Maitland laughed.

"At least you must admit the advice was disinterested. And if you want to know what I think—"

"Well, what?"

After all, it wasn't easy to put into words. And why should he feel that Conway was in need of reassurance? "You can't afford *not* to become involved," he said, "if you're to stay alive at all." Chris stalled the engine as he drew up at the crossroads, and said "Damn!" petulantly. "If you stop caring, you might as well be dead," Maitland went on, raising his voice to compete with the driver in the car behind, who was blowing his horn in an overwrought way. The Austin moved off again, jerkily.

"And so—" said Conway; his voice, at least, was calm.

"You said to me earlier you 'didn't think I'd care' whether the defendants were guilty or not. Did you mean that? Or did you mean, you hoped I wouldn't?"

"I . . . well, of course . . . I only want the truth."

Not a fair question, perhaps. Conway wanted to win the case, was quite desperately anxious for a favorable verdict, and that was understandable enough. But at the same time it was only too obvious that he was firmly convinced of his clients' guilt. "That's all right then," said Antony. "We both want the truth. Let's find it."

"I suppose you think that's easy."

"No."

"Well, anyway, I don't see what we can do."

"Go and see Constable Ryder, for a start."

"That's where we're going. But—"

"I suppose you realize that, as things stand now, we shall lose."

"You can't know that," Chris protested.

"Grandma Duckett would agree with me, and I bet she'd have reached the same conclusion without Uranus if she'd put her mind to it. I needn't point out the consequences for our clients, because quite obviously you've thought about that yourself."

"It isn't only them."

"No. The disgrace would involve their families, who would also be affected by such mundane matters as their loss of job, loss of pension—"

"You say all this is inevitable," interrupted Conway bitterly.

"An Arkenshaw jury acquitted Beas and Mohamad. If nothing fresh comes to light—"

"Yes, I see."

"And if you're right, and Duckett and Ryder cooked up a plot between them to shop those two unjustly—"

"I never said—"

"No, but the thought is sticking out all around you like an aura," said Maitland cheerfully. "If they did that, they'll get what they deserve, and there's nothing you, or I, or anyone else can do about it. If they didn't . . . well, maybe we can prove it, and maybe we can't."

The car came to a halt as he spoke, and Conway pulled on the hand brake. "This is where Constable Ryder lives," he said, and, turning, found his companion's eyes fixed on him with some sympathy and a good deal of amusement. There was something about his smile that Chris found disturbing, some quality in Maitland that he envied, even while he resented it. "You're making me nervous," he said, and was immediately angry with himself for speaking with so much candor. He got out of the car and shut the door with a slam.

By the time he reached the pavement Maitland had alighted too. "Believe me," he said earnestly, "I'm the soul of discretion." Chris didn't say anything, but his expression conveyed very accurately his disbelief.

Constable James Ryder was a large, amiable, and bewildered young man. Not being a native of Arkenshaw, he lived normally at the station house, but he had come to lodge with relatives in one of the dark little streets near Comstock's Mill until the case was over. "Seemed like it was the best thing to do," he said, and eyed Maitland uncertainly, as though hopeful of approval but not expecting it. He had a slow way of speaking, and whatever his feelings were, he wasn't going to give them away.

They were in the parlor of a small, stone terrace house ("What they call a 'through,'" Conway had said as they approached the front door). Stiff net curtains; a tall bamboo stand supporting an aspidistra whose shiny-clean leaves testified to the loving care with which somebody regarded it; a suite not more than fifteen years old—strangely modern-looking in those surroundings—with low-backed chairs and a sofa whose magenta upholstery shrieked wordlessly at the crimson carpet; a whatnot, with artificial roses carefully arranged in a bright blue bowl (and how did they manage to keep *those* free from dust?); a wooden clock with Westminster chimes, as presently became apparent; and a television set with a lace doily protecting its glossy veneer from a silver-framed wedding group, vintage 1935. In the midst of all this splendor Constable Ryder looked clumsy and unsure of himself. Conway made for the sofa and sat down with a let's-get-this-over air, and Maitland followed his example until he saw their host perch himself on the edge of one of the chairs; then he got up again with a murmured apology, and began to prowl.

The constable seemed undisturbed by his restlessness; in some odd way it seemed to reassure him. His brown eyes followed Maitland's tall figure across the room and back again. "You say you've seen sergeant. What can I tell you then?"

Antony halted his pacing. He said abruptly, "What happened that evening last March?" and Conway's brows drew together, because after the interview with Duckett he hadn't been expecting this kind of question, and he couldn't quite see . . .

"I made my point with t'sergeant." Ryder seemed to take the inquiry as the most natural thing in the world; or perhaps he was beyond being surprised by the vagaries of the legal fraternity. "Corner of Badger's Way, that was. We walked down the street together—"

"Had you anything to report?"

"Nothing to matter. Nobbut routine."

"And what sort of a night was it?"

"Bitter cold, and windy."

"Yes, I see." (Already the phrases of his opening address—to be modified heaven knew how many times—were weaving themselves in his mind. ". . . and as it was a cold night they were walking down the road together, rather than stand talking on the corner. . . ."). "What time was this?"

"Not so long after the half-hour."

Maitland let that pass. "You were on the same side of the road as number nineteen, weren't you?"

"That's right. So as we came up to it there was someone yelling from an upstairs window. 'Help! Thieves! Murder!'" A slow grin disturbed the cornstable's gravity. "Proper silly he sounded."

"Yes. No doubt. And then—?"

"Well, we hurried. And there they were, just coming out of the gate."

"Who were?"

"The two foreigners, of course. So sergeant said, 'Hold hard,' and then he said, sharp like, 'What are you doing here?'"

"They didn't try to get away?"

"No, well, you see, it wouldn't have been much good. The older one's a stiffish sort of chap, but short; five-foot-three or -four, I'd say. And young Jackie—"

"Young—who?"

"Mohamad," said Conway. "Chakwal Mohamad. That's what they call him hereabouts."

"Oh, is it? A sort of term of endearment, I suppose," said Maitland sarcastically. Ryder ignored his tone and said in a pleased way: "Aye, that'd be it. Everyone likes Jackie."

"And is—what's-his-damn'-name?—Beas also a popular favorite?"

"No, I wouldn't say that. But if you're a writer," said the constable tolerantly, "there's always some as won't like what you have to say."

"Has he written anything to displease the police, for instance?"

29

"I don't think—" The question seemed to take Ryder out of his depth, and he glanced at his solicitor as though appealing for his support.

"Nothing like that," said Conway.

"What, then?"

"Better conditions for his people, a more lenient immigration policy. That sort of thing."

"I thought there'd been a very large intake from Pakistan in this part of the world."

"There has. There was also, at first, a good deal of exploitation, and housing is always a sore point. On the whole, though, it hasn't worked too badly. Of course, if two chaps get into a scrap that's a race riot—according to the papers. And Beas being one of them would naturally see their point of view."

"That's what Duckett meant when he said he was a troublemaker?"

Chris hesitated. "Something like that." As he spoke, Antony became aware that Ryder was scowling, but when he allowed his glance to become a stare of open inquiry, the constable only shook his head and muttered something.

"If you've anything on your mind, Mr. Ryder—"

"Nay, then, it's a worry . . . all this."

Maitland found himself puzzled. An unimaginative man? . . . Perhaps. A stupid man? He didn't think so. But a man who wasn't being completely open with him, without any doubt at all. The question was, why?

"You'd better go on again, then, about that night," he said. "You say the accused didn't try to get away. Did they say anything?"

"Well, Jackie, he looked kind of shamefaced like. And Beas started to—to bluster," said Constable Ryder after a moment's search for the word he wanted. "And then Sam Barlow came running out of the house, saying, 'Stop them! Stop them!' And a fair clip he looked, too," added Ryder reminiscently.

"What was his story?"

"He said he heard someone moving about, and looked

30

over the banisters, and saw the two men crossing the hall."

"Did he identify them?"

"When it came to the point, he wouldn't. Not definitely. Two colored men, he said. But you see, sir, they were on the path when we first saw them, hadn't even reached the gate—"

"Yes, I remember. Did Barlow say if anything was missing?"

"He hadn't taken the time to look. But then as we were going back to the house he saw his wallet, half under a bush; behind it there was something white, a handkerchief screwed up, and sergeant said to leave them there but I'd best stay on watch."

"And when they got back into the house," Conway put in, "Sergeant Duckett looked at his watch and it was ten-forty-three. So we estimate it was twenty to eleven when they all met at the gate."

"Does that fit in with the time it took for the others to walk from the pub? Assuming their story was straight."

"It fits pretty well. Beas is the only one who will venture an estimate. He puts it a couple of minutes later, but that could easily be to keep on the safe side."

"Good." Maitland looked again at the constable. "Mrs. Barlow, of course, backed up her husband's story."

"Afterwards, she did. That night she nobbut got halfway down the stairs when he was shooing her back again. There's a glass panel in the front door, I could see them through that. Didn't want us to see her in her nightie, I expect. Quite an eyeful, she is," said Ryder, who seemed to take a good deal of pleasure in the recollection, "and in one of those pink, frilly things—" Here Conway cleared his throat loudly, and the constable broke off, looking abashed.

"Well, yes," said Antony, "we mustn't shock the judge. While as for the plaintiffs' counsel," he added, improvising freely, "he's notorious for his puritanical outlook."

"Oh, come now, sir, he's an Irishman," protested Ryder, recovering his spirits.

31

"I must have been thinking of somebody else."

"But you don't know Gilmour," said Conway, declining to be cheered. "He asks questions. Yes, I thought that would shake you," he added, seeing Maitland's look.

"A bit dim, is he?" said Antony, showing a singular lack of that respect which is due from counsel to the bench.

"Awkward," Conway told him.

"Heaven and earth!" He looked again at the constable, who was still grinning. "Mrs. Barlow confirmed her husband's evidence afterwards, and—"

"Mr. Barlow looked and said his coin collection was missing," broke in Ryder eagerly. "That was what was wrapped in the hankie."

"Exactly where did you find it?"

"There were some rose trees and such, bordering the path. And this holly, an ugly thing it was. I suppose it was the best they could do for a hiding place when they saw me and sergeant."

"The coins and the wallet were under the holly bush?"

"That's right."

"Was the handkerchief ever identified?"

"No."

"Woolworth's," said Conway. "Washed at home." Maitland turned on him a strangely impersonal look.

"Fingerprints?" he said.

"Nothing to help."

"And the two men who were picked up—?"

"It was quite reasonable that they should be wearing gloves," Chris assured him.

"Ah, yes, a cold night. I don't suppose, Mr. Ryder, that the Barlows were left alone while you took the prisoners to the station."

"Oh, no, sir. Sergeant phoned from t'house. But when we did get down to t'station and they turned out their pockets in the charge room, blowed if there wasn't one of the coins in Mohamad's pocket."

"Part of the collection, you mean?"

"That's right. Set great store by them, Mr. Barlow did. Said they were valuable, too, and this one being gold, perhaps he wasn't so far wrong."

"What did Mohamad have to say about that?"

"Nothing at all."

"Nothing!"

"No, sir, they neither of them said nothing. Once sergeant had asked them, formal-like, to accompany us to the station, Beas kept mum; and when Jackie started to say something, he shut him up quick."

"I see. But your story of seeing them come down the garden path had some backing, hadn't it?"

"The schoolboys . . . well, only one of them had noticed. And when that Miss Garrowby got up and swore—"

"Why should she have been lying?"

There was a queer little silence. Maitland heard Conway catch his breath and thought (as he had thought before, when he was talking to Sergeant Duckett), he doesn't like me asking that. Ryder seemed merely puzzled, and said after a moment's thought, "Beats me. I was fair capped when they called her." He returned counsel's rather hard stare with apparent candor, and it was Maitland who turned away at last.

"That'll do for now," he said, and was suddenly aware that he was very tired. But what had he expected, after all? Two clients—decent chaps on the face of it—who might, or might not, be guilty of a particularly mean piece of chicanery; and the men who were accusing them, so far unknown quantities in the equation, for whom he was already beginning to feel a sneaking sympathy as strangers in a strange land.

"Sorry you came?" asked Chris when they were back in the car again. When Maitland did not reply at once he added carefully, "I rather like Ryder myself."

"Oh, so do I. Or was it his setting?"

"The house?" said Conway, puzzled. "The room?"

"The parlor," Antony corrected him with an air of satis-

33

faction. The word seemed to please him. "There's something honest about it, don't you think? Ryder himself has . . . reservations."

"Don't we all?"

"I'm afraid so. For instance, no one will tell me—and I'd still like to know—who's paying for the prosecution."

"I've been wondering about that. Don't you think it's just the sort of case O'Brien might take without a fee?" Conway asked. And added with a touch of impatience, when Maitland was silent, "Did you ever know an Irishman who wasn't agin authority?"

Antony was thinking that the suggestion showed more penetration than he'd been giving Conway credit for. All the same . . . "If that's the case, who interested him?"

"I don't know," said Chris. There was no doubt now about his irritation. "And I can't see," he added, slamming on his brakes and coming far too violently to a standstill as the traffic light changed to red, "what the hell it matters anyway."

Antony slid down more comfortably in his seat, and the movement seemed in some way to dissociate him from the moment's problems. "Perhaps it doesn't," he murmured pacifically. "On the other hand . . . perhaps it does."

III

Back at the hotel he phoned John Bushey, and arranged a meeting early the following day. Afterward he went down to the bar mess, where dinner was long since over. He paid his respects to the president, was provided with a cup of muddy coffee (which made him think more kindly of Grandma Duckett's black brew of tea) and a liqueur, which he saved up to take the taste away. He knew several members of the circuit, and others he had heard of; an hour passed pleasantly before he remembered he had an early start tomorrow and decided it was time to retire.

As he crossed the hall, the desk clerk hailed him, and

handed over a long manila envelope, well filled with papers. Maitland stood a moment, weighing it in his hand. Something Chris Conway had forgotten? He heard his name spoken, and turned to find Kevin O'Brien at his elbow.

O'Brien was a tall man, narrow-shouldered and with a thin face that had, in repose, an impassive look. But his voice was rich and mellow, and could be most persuasive, and when he smiled, all hint of austerity was gone. He knew just when to use that smile, thought Antony without envy; a superb tactician who had, at the same time, a coldly brilliant brain.

"I hear we meet tomorrow," said O'Brien. He had his enigmatic look; but he knows, of course, thought Maitland, on whose side the gods are fighting . . . and the planets for that matter . . . and the stars in their courses. . . .

"So I hear. Have you just got in?"

"No, I arrived about three o'clock. I had a dinner engagement. Are they still in session?" O'Brien asked, jerking his head in the direction of the door from which Antony had come. "I ought to report in, I expect."

"They're still there, and Anderson is telling the story of Mr. Justice Kingford and the ballet dancer's suit for slander."

"Then I think, perhaps—" O'Brien's gesture was eloquent of his disinclination to hear that hoary tale again. "There'll be plenty of opportunity to renew old acquaintance, we'll be here for some time, I should think." He shot a look at his companion, half-amused, half-appraising. "It promises to be an interesting business."

"Very," said Maitland, not committing himself.

"I don't suppose you agree with me, at all. No scope for your particular talents, is there, now? No excitement."

Antony let that one pass. A big man, bulkier than ever in a heavy overcoat, came out of the cloakroom at the far side of the hall, waved good-humoredly to O'Brien, and plunged at the revolving door with so much energy that it seemed likely he would be borne around by it a second time. It wasn't surprising, of course, that O'Brien should have acquaintances in Arkenshaw who weren't members of the bar . . . or perhaps it was the plaintiffs' solicitor he had been dining with. Whoever it was, Maitland was conscious of an air of well-being about his learned friend that argued a more convivial evening than he himself had enjoyed. They moved together toward the staircase, and started to go up slowly, side by side.

"Have you been here before?" O'Brien was asking.

"Only once, a long time ago."

"I was born here," said Kevin, and was obviously pleased when Maitland looked surprised. (Did that invalidate Conway's surmise? On the whole, he thought not.) "That's a long time ago, too; and a long time since I left. There's none of my family here now. What do you think of our fair city?"

"So far, my main impression has been one of cold."

"We must remedy that. They're a hospitable bunch, *that* doesn't seem to have changed. But I thought you must have some connections here."

Antony was oddly cheered by the realization that O'Brien was as curious about his briefing as he had been about the plaintiffs' choice of counsel. That seemed reasonable enough now, but it left unexplained the other question that was troubling him.

They parted at the door of Kevin's room; Antony's was farther down the corridor. He went in, discovered with some surprise the envelope which he was still holding, tossed it onto the bed, and settled down to put through a call to London, where he and his wife had a flat at the top of Sir Nicholas Harding's house in Kempenfeldt Square. Presently there was Jenny's voice, saying sleepily, "It's terribly late, darling. Have you been carousing?"

"That's a foul slander. I dined on soused herring . . . which is economical, and good," he added reminiscently. He wasn't finding it difficult to remember the herring.

"Then I'll try it on Uncle Nick next time he comes to dinner—"

"No, really, Jenny!"

"—not forgetting to tell him it was your recommendation."

Antony decided that perhaps she wasn't so sleepy after all. "I don't believe you even know what it is. As for beverages, I have had three cups of strong tea, one cup of coffee, heavily laced with sand, and one *small* liqueur."

"Such virtue!"

"At the call of duty . . . I say, love, what sign of the zodiac were you born under?"

"I'm not sure. Virgo . . . I think," said Jenny doubtfully. And then on a rising note of indignation, "Did you wake me up, just to ask me that?"

"I want to know whether it was a good idea for me to marry you," Antony explained, and heard her chuckle at the earnest note in his voice.

"It's a bit late to be thinking about that now."

"Not a bit of it. I'm sure Grandma would say it was better to know the worst."

"Who on earth—?"

At least, she was wide awake now. Antony settled down to tell her about Mrs. Duckett. It wasn't until he replaced the receiver some ten minutes later that he remembered the envelope, and felt again a vague curiosity as to its contents. But when he had ripped it open there was no note inside, only an untidy bundle of newspaper clippings. No need to go further than the headlines . . . JUDGE REBUKES POLICE WITNESS . . . CASE IMPROPERLY PREPARED, SAYS JUDGE . . . ALIBI PROVED . . . HOW WAS IDENTITY PARADE ARRANGED?

Now, who had sent him all this? He didn't need any proof of what Sergeant Duckett had told him about the "other case" involving a Pakistani. He looked again at the envelope, but the address was clear enough: *Antony Maitland, Esq., Q.C., Midland Hotel, Arkenshaw.*

It wasn't until he was getting into bed that it occurred to him to wonder what he'd have thought of the story if he'd come to it fresh . . . if Star hadn't maneuvered her father into the position of telling it himself, however unwillingly.

IV

Other people in Arkenshaw that night were thinking about the case, some few with complacence, but most with consternation. In the white-paneled, chintzy drawing room at Number 19 Badger's Way, Sam Barlow threw down the evening paper and remarked for the twentieth time, "I don't know why they had to start it all again, I don't really."

Sam was a gray little man of fifty with a wispy moustache and a high-pitched, querulous voice—as incongruous in his surroundings as his wife's conception of a boudoir was out of place in a semidetached house in the suburbs. Glenda, a luxuriant blonde draped—inevitably if mistakenly—in pink chiffon, lowered her magazine. She had her feet up on the sofa and was leaning against a pile of downy cushions. Her expression was meant to be languid; an unprejudiced observer—which Sam was not—would merely have thought her bored. Her voice had a bored note too.

"Why worry? It's not as if it was going to do you any harm."

"But, Glenda!" For a moment he seemed to despair of ever making his meaning clear. "They'll keep on at me," he said.

"Everyone knows by now that you can't identify the men," said Mrs. Barlow bracingly.

"Yes, but will they *accept* it? Now they've brought in these two new men . . . strangers," said Sam, aggrieved.

"Don't you think that makes it more fun?" The bored look vanished and her eyes sparkled as she spoke, but for once her husband was too preoccupied to notice the transformation.

He said huffily: "I don't know how you can call it fun. And when I think of you having to get up there before all those people—"

"I shall wear my new black," said Glenda to herself; but she had wisdom enough not to repeat the thought aloud. Instead she remarked casually, "I was reading a piece in the paper about this Mr. Maitland."

"When was this? I didn't see it." Sam seemed to find this an additional source of disquiet.

"Months and months ago. He was at some assizes or other, and there was a dreadful scene in court, and someone shot himself," said Glenda; she couldn't really remember the details, but it made just as good a story this way. "And someone told me he always wins his cases, but I shouldn't think he could win this one, would you?"

"No, I . . . I don't know. You know, Glenda, we thought Beas and Mohamad must have been guilty, even though we couldn't say for sure it was them we had seen, until—"

"Until that cat Emily Garrowby proved it couldn't have been. If it weren't for backing her up, I'd have half a mind to put a spoke in this chap's wheel myself."

"But . . . but, Glenda—"

"I could easily say I'd been thinking it over, and I saw the thieves clearly enough to know they weren't Beas and Mohamad. And I could say I'd been too shocked before to think clearly, and confused by the fact that they were certainly foreigners." She was being deliberately provocative, but Barlow's voice rose almost to a wail.

"But, Glenda, it wouldn't be true!"

"No, of course not, silly. I didn't say I was going to, did I?" She was bored again, inclined to petulance; he always reacted the same way to her teasing. "But you think they'll win, don't you? Beas and the other one."

"They did before. And they have a very eminent counsel."

39

"Oh, yes, everyone's heard of Kevin O'Brien. They say he's charming," said Glenda, but unemphatically enough to please even her husband.

"And you mustn't trouble yourself about it, dear," he told her; "nobody blames us for them being accused in the first place; we only told the truth."

"All the same, it would be a pity if they didn't win," said Glenda. But she wasn't thinking of Maitland, or O'Brien, or the two policemen, or even of Ghulam Beas; the younger one, the one they called Jackie . . .

V

Martin Ward had struggled unenthusiastically with his homework that evening; a waste of time, when he wouldn't be there to hand it in next day. Somewhere at the back of his mind was the knowledge that his father's insistence had been reasonable, he'd miss enough time from class as it was; but he'd no intention of admitting the fact, and slammed out of the house in a temper when he had finished, rather to his parents' relief.

By the time he reached the Marshalls' he had walked himself into a better humor. Jimmy seemed pleased to see him, and led the way down the narrow hall to the kitchen, shutting the sitting-room door as he passed.

"Weren't you watching—?"

"Same old stuff," said Jimmy. The sound of voices and laughter from the television program followed them down the hall. "Thought you'd be along earlier," he added, and opened the larder door and scanned the shelves in a critical way. "Does your mum carry on about Coke?" he asked. "Mine says it rots your guts." But there was a carton in the corner for all that.

Martin ignored the slander on the absent Mrs. Marshall, whom he privately thought a little too consciously genteel. He accepted the bottle that was being held out to him, and tugged at the drawer where he knew the opener was kept.

"Oh, I was reading, and then I just thought I'd come round," he said. He had no intention of admitting to the homework.

Jimmy, who was a year older and four inches taller, a fair, slim boy with already some pretensions to elegance, eyed his friend tolerantly. "Feeling squeamy?" he asked.

"No."

"I could ask Dad for some brandy, if you like. Or Mum for her smelling salts."

"Don't be so daft." Martin was a tough-looking youngster with a square jaw, but now Jimmy laughed again at the ragged note of nervousness in his voice.

"It's a repeat performance," he said. "Nothing to get the wind up about."

"It's all very well for you." Martin scuffed moodily at the rug in front of the open range. "It isn't you they think's telling lies."

"You shouldn't have been so bloody positive, old boy," said Jimmy, in the drawl he assumed when he wished to impress his hearers with all the weight of his seventeen years. Martin's expression grew more mulish.

"But I was . . . I am."

"Come, now! Come, now, which do you mean?"

The mimicry of their English master was accurate enough to draw an unwilling grin from the younger boy. "You *know* what I mean," he protested.

"Yes, but you needn't make such a thing of it. If you're afraid of what people say—"

"I'm not!"

"Aren't you? You could always hedge, you know. Tell them you're not sure."

"But it wouldn't be true."

Jimmy shrugged. "Have it your own way. I'm only trying to help." He raised his bottle of pop, and drank, and lowered it again and gave his friend a searching look. "It wouldn't make any difference to the verdict," he said.

"Perhaps not."

"You know how it will go."

41

"Same as last time, I expect."

"Well, then! Do yourself a bit of good."

Martin had his most stubborn look. "I can't help it if nobody believes me," he said.

"Maybe you're right. Maybe they wouldn't believe you whatever story you told."

"See if I care," said Martin defiantly.

VI

"I don't know what you want with all this legal stuff, I'm sure," said Mrs. Thompson, wife of the landlord of the Sun in Splendor. She folded a towel, and placed it carefully on the growing pile on the kitchen table. Her husband lowered his newspaper, and gave her a reproachful look.

"It isn't a matter of wanting to give evidence," said Adam Thompson. He was a heavily built man, and he spoke portentously; the words fell weightily into the silence. "When you gets one of these here sub peeners—" He broke off and sighed, and for a moment the only sound in the room was the Ingersoll alarm clock, ticking busily on the mantelshelf.

"That's what you said last time," said Mrs. Thompson comfortably. "I never did know rightly what it meant."

"A Latin phrase, sub peener. Meaning, you've got to go, or else. So that's how it'll be when the case comes on, Mother. We'll be in court, me and Maggie, and how you'll manage single-handed in the bar—"

"Same as Maggie's managing now, while you gets your supper," his wife told him. "It won't be the first time, and you'll be back before we open in the evening anyway. Still and all," she added, reverting to her grievance, "I don't like all this swearing."

" 'Tisn't that as bothers me, it's the waiting about," said Adam, and sighed again. "And Maggie'll expect her wages, what's more, whether she's here or not."

"Now, Adam, you wouldn't want to be mean."

"Wouldn't I?" asked Adam, picking up his paper again.

VII

In the bar Maggie Jowett was pouring Scotch for a thin man in a neatly pressed, shabby suit. "Celebrating?" she asked as she pushed the glass toward him. Her tone was both friendly and jeering.

"Fortifying myself," Hugh Lawford corrected her. "Have one with me, Maggie? You may need it before you're through."

"*I* don't need Dutch courage," said Maggie, but she was careful to pour another measure of whisky for herself before letting her eyes stray to the table in the corner where an elderly man in a dark suit was staring sadly into the depths of a double brandy. "Don't know why poor Mr. Saddler's taking on so," she added, half-scornful, half-sympathetic.

"Bad for business," said Lawford. "These sort of cases, whatever you say, there's someone takes you up wrong."

"But it can't matter now. It's all been gone into once."

"Raking things up, you see, reminding people." But Maggie's attention had already wandered from the solitary drinker. She turned her eyes speculatively on the man at the bar.

"Nor I can't see what you've got to be so chuff about."

Lawford laughed; there was no doubt about his sense of well-being. "Does me good to think of old Duckett's face when he has to call for the defense."

"But you were his witness last time, in a manner of speaking. You weren't so pleased about it then."

"Now, that's where you're wrong, my girl. Evidence for the Crown that was . . . this time it's different."

"Well, and if it is, I still don't see—"

"Let it be, Maggie." There was finality in his tone. He took a quick swig of whisky and turned, leaning on his

43

elbow to survey the crowded room. Much as it had been eight months ago, the night the Barlows were robbed. Even to the little group of "foreigners" standing near the fire. (Against their religion, isn't it? thought Lawford contemptuously. So what are they trying to prove?) But these men were strangers, whereas most of the others were regulars, and known to him. Local interest in the case ran high, and there'd been a good deal of talk when he first came in, but now they'd returned to their own affairs again. His eye was caught by the opening of the street door, and he turned again, grinning, to Maggie when he saw Tom Randall pushing his way across to the bar. "Gathering of the clans, eh, lass?"

Randall was a burly young man with brown hair and heavy eyebrows that gave his face a louring look quite at variance with the equability of his temper. He eyed Maggie with respectful admiration (she was a handsome woman, a redhead for the last nine months at least, since she came to the Sun) and asked for the usual.

"Have one with me, Tom. Something stronger tonight. Another Scotch, Maggie."

"But I like beer, Mr. Lawford."

"Yes, but you can't drink confusion to our enemies in draft bitter," said Hugh, who knew the other man's habits.

Tom considered this. "I don't think I have any enemies," he said at last. But when Maggie pushed across the glass of whisky, he accepted it without further demur.

"Manner of speaking," Lawford told him. "Still, wasn't there some business about where the wood came from for that shed you put up for your uncle?"

"Nay, I bought that all fair and square," Tom protested.

"That didn't stop the coppers nosing about, did it? Well, then!" said Lawford, and raised his glass with a satisfied air.

"If you mean about tomorrow, I'm *their* witness. And so are you, and so's Miss Jowett here."

"And all our evidence put together doesn't amount to a row of beans. Does it, Maggie love?"

44

"I don't know what's got into you," Maggie grumbled. "I don't think Sergeant Duckett would frame anybody, nor that poor lad, Ryder, neither. But then," she added, frowning, "I wouldn't believe—what they said—of Jackie; or even of the other one, though he's enough cheek for six."

"You don't have to worry, Miss Jowett," Tom consoled her. "You don't have to make up your mind about anything, you just have to tell the truth."

Three men approached the bar, clamoring for refills, and as Maggie turned to serve them, Adam Thompson came through from the room at the back. He couldn't help wondering what that rather slow lad, Randall, could have said to make Hugh Lawford laugh like a fiend.

VIII

Miss Emily Garrowby's house, at 21 Badger's Way, was a credit to the neighborhood, with its fresh paint, its clean, starched curtains, carefully whitened step, and trim garden. Everyone admitted this, though some of the men had been heard to murmur that she must have a hold over Dick Bloxby to make him use the lawn-mower and shears so regularly and keep the flowerbeds so free of weeds. Most of them called on his assistance from time to time, but never with such effect.

Inside was perhaps a little old-fashioned, a little over-neat, but that was understandable in a maiden lady; besides, old Mrs. Garrowby would never have countenanced change, and now she was gone it wasn't to be expected that her daughter would want things any different. Miss Garrowby talked about traveling when she retired in five years' time, that might brighten her ideas. Meanwhile, as long as the children didn't play too noisily, or the young people come home too late, she was a pleasant enough neighbor, no trouble to anyone.

Glenda Barlow, who lived next door, wouldn't have

agreed with this. She hardly saw the people at number 17, with which number 19 shared a party wall, but every time you went out of the house, there was Miss Garrowby, peeping. And—what was worse—every time anyone came in. The thing was, school holidays were far too long. It was all very well for Sam to say she was harmless, and let her have her fun. He wasn't at home all day; it wasn't at all nice to be so overlooked. Still, if it hadn't been for her . . .

"It really was a blessing," said stout Mrs. Newbould admiringly, "that you happened to be looking out of the window that night." She had dropped in to take a cup of tea with her neighbor, purely out of kindness, because she didn't like to think of her sitting alone, and perhaps worrying about tomorrow. Mr. Newbould had choked over his soup when she said this, and she had added severely that she was really making a sacrifice; because Miss Garrowby used such strong, black tea . . . Mrs. Newbould wouldn't tolerate it herself, even in the kitchen. And then Clive had to add, "*They* wouldn't stand for it," as though she was an inconsiderate employer, which anyone would tell him she wasn't.

He had been right about one thing, though; she didn't really have much in common with Miss Garrowby. That hair style, for instance; Emily went to the hairdresser faithfully every week; why didn't the girl tell her it was twenty years out of date? And her suits, though well cut and of good material, must be specially made for her to manage to be so old-fashioned. Following her train of thought, and unconscious of the rather drastic twist of subject, Mrs. Newbould added abruptly, "What will you wear tomorrow?"

Emily Garrowby gave her a wary look. She had no illusions at all about her neighbor's motive in calling; the whole street was feverish with curiosity, but you could give Mrs. Newbould credit, at least, for doing something about it. "My tweed costume, I suppose," she said. "It's comfort-

46

able, and quite warm." The last words were added defensively; it was only too obvious what the visitor thought of the idea.

With your beige twin set and the Woolworth's pearls you always say your mother left you, thought Mrs. Newbould. Oddly enough, the sudden spurt of anger she felt at what she considered as stupidity was an almost completely generous emotion. She said, "Yes, very nice," in a flat tone that conveyed very well what she meant. "I only thought —" But she let the sentence die; it was really too difficult to explain.

"Besides," said Miss Garrowby with sudden energy, "the hat I bought the last time doesn't match my winter coat." If Mrs. Newbould hadn't known better, she might have thought the smile that accompanied these words was deliberately provocative. "I don't usually wear one," Emily added, making her meaning clear, "but of course I have to in court."

Mrs. Newbould thought this a dreadful admission, and her own smile became rather fixed. She drank some of her tea, hiding a grimace at its bitterness, and went back again to her point of departure. "If it weren't for you I can't think what would have happened to those two young men."

"We don't know, do we? They might have been acquitted."

"With the police swearing they saw them! My dear Miss Garrowby, you know perfectly well—" She broke off there and lowered her voice a little, confidentially. "Why do you think they did it?"

"How could I possibly know a thing like that?"

For a moment the visitor was doubtful whether she should take offense. But the words didn't sound like a snub. In fact, she was beginning to think that Emily, for all her book-learning, was a little dull. "Clive says it's known all over town that Sergeant Duckett dislikes foreigners. Very hard on them, he is, when he gets a chance. There

47

was a case before when the judge was really angry. And I suppose the constable would have to do what he was told, wouldn't he?"

"Oh, no, I don't think so. Not if it was wrong. But I shouldn't be discussing the case, Mrs. Newbould. It isn't at all the thing, when I'm a witness and the matter is still undecided."

"It's been decided once," Mrs. Newbould pointed out.

"Not really. Not whether what the policemen did was wrong."

"How could it be any other way?"

"I'm not on the jury," said Miss Garrowby firmly. "That's for them to say. After all, if the original accusation was made in good faith—"

"They must have seen what happened as clearly as you did."

Perhaps the stubborn note in Mrs. Newbould's voice discouraged further argument. Emily said, "Yes. Yes, of course," and picked up her cup. An intricate pattern, blue, and gold, and green; and the china very delicate. That was important, wasn't it? These things I have loved . . .

"Clive says there's no doubt about it," Mrs. Newbould insisted. "It was a deliberate frame-up." The word sounded so strange, coming from her lips, that Miss Garrowby wanted to laugh. To steady herself she began to paraphrase, as she might have done for her English class.

"You mean, if the two Pakistanis were innocent of the charge against them, it follows that the two policemen are guilty." She paused, and now she did laugh, a little shakily. "A simple exercise in logic," she said. "But I don't like to think it's my evidence—"

"I wouldn't care about that. It's justice, isn't it?"

"Oh, yes," said Emily, and sighed as deeply as, in another part of the town, Adam Thompson had done. One hand went to her throat, tugging at the despised string of pearls.

Mrs. Newbould's rather bulging blue eyes became fixed. "I've never seen that ring before, Miss Garrowby. And on

48

your engagement finger!" She giggled. "Don't tell me—"

"No . . . of course . . . how stupid of me." She was tugging at the ring, a plain gold band set with a single stone that looked like a sapphire. "I must have been dreaming."

"I've never seen it before," repeated her guest. She was thinking that with a flush in her cheeks the other woman looked quite pretty. (And I've nerve enough for most things, she said later to her husband, but not to tell Miss G. she really ought to use a bit of color.) Her hair could have been pretty, too, if she'd only use a rinse to brighten it up a bit and if it weren't tortured into those dreadful, rigid waves. For a moment she'd wondered . . . after all, Badger's Way was a good address, and no doubt old Mrs. Garrowby had left her daughter comfortable . . . no reason why someone shouldn't take a fancy to her, brains and all. But Emily was saying positively: "Aunt Mary left it to me, but I don't really care for jewelry. And Mother never liked to see me wear it, she said it reminded her." She smiled, quite composed again. "I'll just slip it onto my right hand now, so there can't be any mistake."

Absentmindedly Mrs. Newbould passed her cup to her hostess for a refill. Her mind was busy with romantic imaginings. But, after all, Miss Garrowby, who was already talking of her retirement . . .

She wouldn't tell Clive what she had thought. He would only laugh. And somehow—she didn't stop to examine the feeling, or realize its generosity—she didn't want him to laugh about that.

IX

"I am wondering whether we are wise to have done this." Chakwal Mohamad had been standing for several minutes by the window, looking down at the windswept street, but now he turned and fixed his gaze on his friend. "You do not think that this time it might go wrong?"

Ghulam Beas had taken off his jacket and was sprawled

on the bed. He was a short man, very dark of complexion, and with rather heavy features. He had broad shoulders, and looked enormously strong. "Put on some music, my poor Jackie, and relax," he said. He spoke excellent and colloquial English, with only a slight carefulness in the enunciation to betray the fact that it was not his native tongue. Mohamad had much less facility, even though he had been a small child when he left his own country and had only a few words of its speech remaining to him. They spoke English for his convenience, but often the idiom escaped him.

Now he shrugged, and his dark eyes took on a mournful look. "Your music will not be soothing me," he said, and walked across to the armchair near the hearth, where a gas fire was hissing. He was a little taller than his companion, slightly built, and moved with a grace that was quite unselfconscious. A handsome young man by any standards, and neatly, almost foppishly dressed.

The room they were in was Beas's bed-sitting-room, the first-floor front of a big house not too far from the town center, in a road that was still respectable though it had seen better days. It was a big, colorful room with a high ceiling; a crowd of books, battered but still in their dust jackets, spilled over from the shelves onto chairs and table and floor; a pile of records with shabby covers, frequently handled ("noisy, modern stuff," Jackie was apt to complain); curtains and bedcover in a bright, geometrical pattern; a kitchen table with an uncovered typewriter, a pile of paper, and a further clutter of books. It was all too familiar to Chakwal Mohamad for him to notice it now; but Ghulam, to whom it was so much more familiar, was rarely unconscious of his surroundings. He pulled himself a little higher against the pile of cushions, and put his hands behind his head, looking around him with satisfaction. Jackie was nervous; this legal stuff wasn't in his line, that was true, and how best to calm him?

"I am thinking—" Mohamad began again.

50

"How can it 'go wrong,' as you put it, Jackie, when it is already proved that we were falsely accused?"

"Yes, I know this. But still, the police—"

"Their word against ours. And ours was believed." He paused, but Jackie still looked dissatisfied. "They have a new lawyer, is that troubling you?"

"I do not like to answer questions. I am getting confused," Jackie explained.

"But you've only got to stick to the facts."

"Yes, of course," said Jackie, unimpressed.

"And we've got O'Brien, don't forget that."

"No, I do not forget it. Mr. Jones is telling me he is excellent man."

"What more do you want?"

"But still, I am not liking this Mr. Maitland," Mohamad persisted.

"Don't be stupid, Jackie, there's nothing he can do to you."

"He can . . . he can confound me."

"It doesn't matter. It isn't only our word, you know. Miss Garrowby saw what happened."

"So she did," said Jackie. He smiled now, because there had been a note of anger in Ghulam's voice, and it wasn't any use to annoy him. Besides, he would never understand that you could be confident in one way, and still be uncertain of your own strength. "Right is on our side," said Chakwal Mohamad. "I am not troubling myself any further."

TUESDAY, 3RD NOVEMBER

I

Mr. Justice Gilmour was by nature a pessimist, but when his duties led him to the Yorkshire (Arkenshaw) Division, on the North Eastern Circuit, he generally felt almost cheerful, as one whose worst fears have been realized. When it came to damp, and drafts, and ill-placed lights, the courtroom in Arkenshaw was unsurpassed.

On this particular morning, however, the familiar magic seemed to have lost its power. When they had finished with the silly fellow who thought he was clever enough to embezzle from a firm of chartered accountants—and his lordship couldn't believe that the closing speeches would detain them long; the defense had nothing to say, and the prosecution need say nothing—he must inevitably turn to the next item on the list, and he didn't like cases that involved the police. And if anything had been wanting to complete his gloom, the plaintiffs were two gentlemen of color. Whichever way the verdict went, there was likely to be an outcry . . . someone was being unfair . . . someone was being victimized. And who more likely than the judge to be the one person whom everyone would blame?

The embezzler got two years, which was six months longer than he was expecting, and thought his counsel was to blame when in fact his own obviously sanguine disposition had soured the judge's mood still further. The next case was called. Mr. Justice Gilmour eyed all the protagonists with impartial severity, and then turned his attention to counsel. O'Brien, though the better part of his practice was in London, had appeared before him on several occasions; well, he might woo the jury as he would with his soft-spoken ways, Gilmour knew him too well to be taken in. His junior, Martin Roberts, had appeared for the defense—if the judge remembered rightly—when the present plaintiffs were charged. A capable man, perhaps a little dull, but at least he should know the evidence backward. A small, tight smile disturbed his lordship's gravity for a moment as he reflected on the aptness of the phrase, but it disappeared as his eyes moved on to Maitland. He knew him by reputation only, but that was quite enough. Unorthodox, thought Mr. Justice Gilmour grumpily; and besides that, counsel had a humorous look that he mistrusted.

John Bushey was also thinking about his leader, but with rather less ill-humor. He took a detached view of the present proceedings, and had no objections to fireworks as long as no one expected him to set them off. Not that there was much to be done in this case, cut and dried so far as he could see.

Kevin O'Brien was well into his opening now, and Maitland might have been asleep for all the attention he was paying. In fact, he very probably was asleep. Young Conway evidently thought so; he was fidgeting about on the bench behind them. Bushey turned, and gave him an admonitory look . . . what was there to be done at this stage, after all?

Maitland was thinking that O'Brien was as cunning as they came. He wasn't much concerned at this stage with the contents of his opponent's speech; he knew the facts only too well, but the manner of it was exactly right. That more-in-sorrow-than-in-anger approach would impress the jury with the reasonableness of the plaintiffs' contentions, and make even more effective the righteous indignation their counsel was certain to display later on. Meanwhile, O'Brien wasn't pulling any punches; the perfidy of the defendants was to be regretted, but was there in plain terms for anyone to hear.

It would be nice if Chris Conway would relax for a moment, or at least stop breathing down the back of his neck. A nice lad, all the same, and undoubtedly a distinct im-

53

provement on the chap O'Brien was saddled with. The plaintiffs' solicitor was as unlike as could be to the man he had seen at the hotel last night, being tall and thin, with gray hair, a severe eye, and a mouth like a rat trap. Mr. Ashby . . . or perhaps Mr. Jones? Conway had spoken of "a very respectable firm," and this representative of it looked as though he had no human weaknesses at all. Whereas his own instructing solicitor . . . Antony let his mind wander for a moment in speculation as to how serious Conway really was about Star Duckett. What a name to give the poor girl, and perhaps, after all, it had been Grandma's choice, and not the sergeant's. But then he thought how scandalized Chris would be to know that his affairs and not his clients' were occupying counsel, and just as he was turning his attention to O'Brien again he felt John Bushey's movement beside him as he twisted around to glare at Chris, and thought—with renewed distraction— that he was lucky in his junior. Bushey was some years older than his leader, and belied his name by being almost completely bald, as had been evident in the robing room just now. He was solidly built, a detail man, which was helpful, and not altogether without humor. Antony had a nasty feeling that couldn't be said of the judge. Uncle Nick had known Gilmour quite well at one time . . . "a fair man by his own lights" (wasn't that what he'd said of him?) "but not altogether a convivial spirit." Well, that was one way of putting it. Maitland had a feeling he might wish to express himself rather more bluntly before the trial was over.

O'Brien, it was obvious, was reaching his peroration. Antony opened his eyes and pushed himself up into a more upright position and shot a quick glance at the jury. Lapping it up, the lot of them. He wondered how many of them had already made up their minds as to the outcome . . . for that matter, they'd probably reached their verdict before ever they came into court. Not that they wouldn't mean to be impartial.

Anyway, the case had made the headlines in the national press. A change of venue wouldn't really have helped.

"And before I finish, I must remind you," O'Brien was saying, again parading his impartiality, "as his lordship will certainly remind you before he asks you to consider your verdict, that the rights and wrongs of this case were not decided when my clients, Mr. Beas and Mr. Mohamad, were acquitted in that other court. The issues here are different, and I would ask you to follow the evidence as carefully as if you had never heard a word of it before. As if these people were not your neighbors. But when you have done so"—his voice rose confidently—"I shall ask for your verdict in the absolute certainty that each one of you will give it in favor of the plaintiffs."

Maitland caught his eye as he sat down again, and gave him an appreciative grin. Then he picked up his pencil, and began to draw a knight in armor on one of the envelopes he had brought with him. He was just about to go on to the dragon when he realized that the subject was inapposite, and abandoned it. The other envelopes were already scrawled over, so he made do with the back of his brief and drew instead St. Patrick killing snakes. A poor likeness, but at least the miter was easily identifiable. By the time he had finished, the first witness had been sworn in.

"Your name is Ghulam Beas, you are thirty-five years old, and you reside at number thirty Ingleborough Square in this city?" Beas assented to each of these statements in turn. "You are a journalist by profession?"

"I am."

"For how long?"

"Since I came to this country, sir. Ten years."

"All that time in Arkenshaw?"

"Yes."

"Had you any particular reason for making your home here?"

"There are many of my people. There is also prejudice. Perhaps I can help."

55

"You have written, then, with particular reference to the problems of the Pakistani population in this part of the world."

"Yes, sir. I have."

"And met with much opposition?"

"Opposition, yes. And also much kindness."

"But all this time you have supported yourself by your writing, without any great difficulty."

"You will understand, I know, that it is not a steady income. I mean, not regular, so much a week. But, yes, it is a good living. I am content."

Maitland was watching the witness, and a frown had appeared between his eyes. A self-possessed figure, Ghulam Beas, and with a fine command of the language in spite of the rather jerky way he was giving his answers. His pride in his achievement was obvious . . . it was also completely natural. And if all this were true (and it sounded true), why on earth should he have embarked on a perilous enterprise like robbing the Barlows' house?

"And now perhaps you will tell us, Mr. Beas, what happened on the night of the twenty-fourth March of this year."

"I shall be happy to tell you. It is, after all, why I am here." (Maitland grinned to himself; a sort of engaging simplicity of manner . . . was that the true face of Ghulam Beas, or just the one he wished, at this moment, to present?) "I am with my friend, Chakwal Mohamad, who is also called Jackie, and we are in the Sun from—"

"The Sun?" queried the judge, looking over his spectacles at counsel.

"A public house, my lord. The Sun in Splendor."

"Hm. Is that what you meant?" he asked the witness. (O'Brien looked black for a moment at this apparent evidence of distrust, and Maitland's expression was unnaturally solemn.)

"Oh, yes, my lord. The Sun in Splendor in Masham Street. My friend Jackie is a Christian, you see, and I am an agnostic, and so we go to the pub for a drink. It is, besides, a good place for a writer to be finding his material."

"I see," said the judge in a hopeless voice that seemed to convey his utter bewilderment. "But, Mr. Beas, you have told us you are an agnostic."

"That is so."

"Yet you took the oath on a Christian Bible."

"Is not this right, my lord?" In the dark face the flash of his smile was undeniably attractive. "In this country, I think, it is the custom that agnostics shall swear in this way."

"It is open to you to affirm your testimony, Mr. Beas."

"I am corrected then. I had not thought that all who took the Bible in their hand were believers," said the witness humbly. "But there is no disrespect, my lord, for I am telling the truth."

"Hm," said the judge again, and gave a testy nod in counsel's direction. O'Brien took up his questions smoothly.

"You arrived at this public house . . . at what time, Mr. Beas?"

"At nine o'clock. At about nine o'clock, I should say. We were there until closing time, and we spoke to several people, and when we left we did not walk away immediately but stood for a few minutes in the street outside."

"Still talking?"

"Yes. With our friend, Konat Iskander. Whom perhaps I should not call a friend but an acquaintance . . . with your permission, my lord," he added, looking up at Gilmour.

"Why?" asked the judge unhelpfully.

"Because . . . because at that time I do not know him well."

Mr. Justice Gilmour inclined his head. O'Brien said, "Please go on, Mr. Beas," and Maitland turned his head and gave him another grin, this time not altogether devoid of malice.

"Well, then we walked away, along Masham Street, and a little way along Cargate, and turned into Badger's Way."

57

"Was that your regular way home?"

"Oh, yes, sir. For Jackie, and also for me."

"And was Mr. Iskander still with you?"

"No, he went the other way along Masham Street."

"Can you tell us what time that would be?"

"When we left the Sun?"

"The vicinity of the Sun. After you had concluded your conversation."

"Oh . . . five minutes, perhaps, after closing time."

"Mr. O'Brien. I have no wish to be captious," said the judge untruthfully, "but you must ask the witness to be more exact."

"Closing time is ten-thirty here, my lord."

"No doubt you have taken steps to confirm that to your own satisfaction," said the judge in a prudish tone, "but you are not giving evidence."

"At what time, Mr. Beas, did you leave the vicinity of the Sun?" asked O'Brien, speaking very quickly and in a monotone, so that it was perfectly obvious he had lost his temper.

"Ten-thirty-five, sir, as near as I can say."

"And how far from there to Badger's Way?"

"I cannot tell how far, but I have walked the distance since—slowly, as we did that night. It took me eight minutes, and I cannot say, but perhaps it would be longer when I was talking to Jackie."

"Thank you, Mr. Beas. Now, you were walking along the pavement—"

"Yes, on the same side as number nineteen. That is, the left-hand side of the road, coming from Cargate. And we were talking together with great interest, so that I did not notice the two policemen until they were a few yards away. We were opposite the gate of number nineteen when we came up to them, and Sergeant Duckett told us to stop. And we could hear a man calling from the house, but we could not see him because that window is round on the other side."

"What then?"

58

"We stopped, of course, as we were ordered. It is not good to disobey the police. So the sergeant asked us what we were doing there, and where we were going, and as I am telling him a man runs out of the house and says he has been robbed. And he says—"

"We must let Mr. Barlow give his own evidence, Mr. Beas."

"Of course, I am sorry. But I may tell you, I think, that the sergeant says, 'We saw these two men coming down the path from your front door,' and I say very loudly that this is not true . . . how could we have been in the house when we have only just come from Masham Street? But no one listens. So then when it has been found that Mr. Barlow has indeed been robbed we are asked to 'accompany them to the station.' I see then how it will be, and I tell Jackie to say nothing."

It was after the luncheon recess that Maitland rose to cross-examine. Mr. Ghulam Beas, encouraged by his counsel, had had plenty to say, and very neatly indeed had he said it. Once or twice Antony had caught an inquiring look from John Bushey; they could certainly have objected, but with what the *Arkenshaw Telegraph* so originally called the ugly specter of racial prejudice hovering over the courtroom it didn't seem that it would be a popular move. O'Brien obviously knew this, and was taking full advantage of the defense's dilemma, allowing himself a good deal of latitude.

Maitland was thinking that a short course with a bomb-disposal unit would have been good training for dealing with a singularly sticky situation. He had a strong feeling that Beas, if incautiously handled, might blow up in his face. He began carefully.

"Mr. Beas, you have spoken several times of Sergeant Duckett. Were you in fact acquainted with him before the night of your arrest?"

"I knew him by sight, sir. I knew of him, also, as being no friend to my people."

There, you see! said Maitland to himself. "Is Badger's

Way a well-lighted thoroughfare?" he asked with a gentleness that would have aroused immediate comment among those of his colleagues who knew him well.

"Fairly well lighted."

"Yet you did not see the two schoolboys, who must have been walking almost abreast of you on the other side of the road."

"I have said we were talking. Interested in our talk."

"Or the policemen, who were directly ahead of you."

"No. We did not see them."

"There is a street light outside number nineteen, is there not?"

"Between number nineteen and number twenty-one." A pause, almost imperceptible. "Perhaps we were dazzled a little," the witness suggested hopefully.

"The path to the front door is well lighted, however."

"Oh, yes."

"No shadows?"

The witness smiled. "Nothing, sir, I assure you, that could have been mistaken for two men walking from the door to the gate."

"I see. Now, Mr. Beas, you told my friend that you had money in the bank."

"Nearly five hundred pounds."

"We are to infer then that you could have had no motive for—what was your phrase?—this petty thievery."

"That is right, sir."

No doubt where the jury's sympathy lay; for all his short stature Ghulam Beas made a dignified figure. "I wonder now," said Maitland, making up his mind. "My learned friend did not ask you about the state of your account immediately prior to this occurrence."

"My lord?" exclaimed O'Brien, getting up in a hurry. The outraged tone was stock-in-trade, of course, but when Maitland turned to look at him he could see that his opponent was really angry. Conway had been right, then . . . and so had his own first impression of O'Brien as a crusader. That was only to be expected, of course; for a mo-

60

ment he felt a pang almost of envy. If he had a parallel certainty to match against it . . .

"Yes, Mr. O'Brien," sighed the judge.

"I must object to the introduction of this irrelevant matter."

"Your lordship will remember that a moment ago my friend assumed the relevance of the witness's bank balance . . . for his own purposes."

"Well, then, and so it was relevant," said O'Brien, with a fine disdain for logic. The judge shook his head.

"I must confess to a certain curiosity myself, Mr. O'Brien."

"But, my lord, my client is a stranger here—"

"Who, on his own admission, has been making a good living in this country for ten years," said Maitland, apparently addressing the electric light fitting above his lordship's head. Kevin O'Brien laughed suddenly and sat down; but there was no amusement in his eyes, and the two spots of angry color still burned in his cheeks.

"You may continue, Mr. Maitland."

"Thank you, my lord. Mr. Beas—?"

"You asked about my bank account, sir. As you have guessed, it was 'not so hot' at the time we are speaking of." In spite of his fluency, there was—as always—the faint stressing of the colloquial phrases he used. "But there was money owing to me for articles which had appeared in the local paper, and in some magazines. I am not financially embarrassed, sir . . . then, or at any time."

So much for that. "Why *did* you bring this case, Mr. Beas?"

"Not, I assure you, sir, for money."

"Have you suffered any inconvenience as a result of the accusation?"

"But, sir, of course."

"Let me put it to you more clearly. Since your acquittal?"

Again the momentary hesitation. Maitland pressed his point. "Any loss of income? Any assignments canceled?"

61

"Perhaps not. Not to my recollection."

"And on the personal side . . . have your friends avoided you? Have you not been conscious rather of their resentful sympathy?"

"They were resentful, yes, on my behalf."

"And rightly!" snapped O'Brien, but this time he did not get up, and Maitland resisted the temptation to look around at him.

"So that the sole purpose of this prosecution is . . . moral indignation."

"A desire for justice, sir," Beas corrected him mildly.

"You are fortunate in being able to afford to indulge your whims, Mr. Beas." This time it was Maitland who deliberately let the silence lengthen. "Mr. Iskander was perhaps one of these sympathizers."

"I do not quite understand, sir. When he saw that I was persecuted—"

"You will forgive me, Mr. Beas, that is for the jury to decide."

"Well, he was angry and . . . yes, he was sympathetic."

"Though, as you were careful to explain to my friend, up to that time he was merely an acquaintance, someone you did not know very well."

"He is not grinding an ax, sir, I assure you, when he tells you my story is true," said the witness earnestly.

Mr. Justice Gilmour looked reprovingly at counsel. "What does he mean, Mr. O'Brien? What *does* he mean?" he inquired in a plaintive tone.

II

Where Beas had been serene, his friend Mohamad was palpably nervous. His evidence-in-chief gave him no trouble; O'Brien was gentleness itself. He's probably brought the Blarney Stone into court with him, thought Maitland uncharitably; it was an odd feeling, to know himself so definitely and unequivocally in the wrong before he even opened his mouth. He had chanced his arm with Beas, because there were things he wanted to know—and if he didn't ask, who would tell him? On the whole, he thought his present unpopularity was worth it; he couldn't go through the whole case treating the plaintiffs and their witnesses with kid gloves. But Mohamad was a different matter; a handsome youth with an attractive way with him, and the jury probably already ranged behind him to a man. Or a woman . . . that stout, motherly-looking soul, for instance, who looked as if she did her own baking and ate oven-bottom cake and treacle every day for tea. But that wasn't really the point. Jackie looked as though it would be easy to break him down, in which case—paradoxically enough, it would be the defense that suffered. In the doghouse without hope of reprieve, thought Antony, glumly mixing his metaphors, and set himself to court the witness as blatantly as O'Brien had done.

A few innocuous questions, confirming Mohamad's status as a medical student—"Yes, I am in my fourth year, and I am winning a scholarship and also there is the grant from the Arkenshaw Society"—his friendship with Ghulam Beas—"For two years now he is amusing me" (nice way of putting it, that!)—their meeting in the Sun in Splendor. It wasn't until they were actually retracing their steps down Badger's Way that Jackie began to jib . . . he didn't remember seeing the schoolboys . . . he hadn't seen the police either until they came face to face outside the gate of number nineteen . . . he had been surprised when told to stop, because, after all, it wasn't very late. Which was all very fine, if he hadn't sounded not so very far from hysteria. Maitland began to dislike the whole business. To a boy as nervous as this, accusation, arrest, and trial must have been . . . torment. If he had got caught up in some way in the duel between Sergeant Duckett and the foreigners . . .

He had to remind himself that it was, after all, the two policemen who now stood accused.

63

"You didn't actually bump into Sergeant Duckett and Constable Ryder, did you?"

"No. Oh, no."

"You saw them, then, at some little distance."

"I suppose—"

"Try to remember. There was the street lamp, and its light would shine ten—fifteen?—yards along the pavement."

"I am thinking you are right, sir."

"Did you see them in the darkness beyond? No? As they walked into the circle of light then?"

"I do not . . . yes, of course! That is how it is." He smiled at Maitland with an obvious, almost childlike delight at being able to give him the answer he seemed to desire.

"Were they walking toward you purposefully? As if they had seen you and made up their minds to speak to you."

"No, they are walking slowly, as we are."

"Then did they hesitate at all? Consult together?"

"No." This time he sounded more doubtful.

"Just walked straight up to you and told you to stop?"

"Yes. And *then* we hear that Mr. Barlow is crying out."

"Not before?"

"I am positive, sir," said Chakwal Mohamad.

There was no shaking him from that, nor even from his assertion that he had never been inside the Barlows' house, never seen the wallet, or the coin collection, or the ancient gold noble (six and eightpence, a lawyer's fee, but both worth a good deal more than that today) that had been found in his pocket. And do I really want to shake him? thought Maitland. It sounds like the truth.

"Thank you, Mr. Mohamad. I have no more questions." He thought as he sat down that he felt almost as depressed as the judge was looking. And that was saying a lot.

III

Looked at in the right way, it might be considered amusing that the tactics that had aroused O'Brien's anger,

64

and probably alienated the jury as well, should prove to have been equally unpopular with his own team. With Chris Conway, at any rate; Bushey confined his "comment" on the day's hearing to puffing at his pipe and looking down his nose, but Conway—when a comparatively mild criticism produced no noticeable reaction—proceeded to become very plainspoken indeed. Maitland, who was standing near the window in Bushey's chambers, listened without change of expression. He looked, in fact, extremely relaxed as he stood there, his hands in his pockets and one shoulder propped against the paneling that, in so old-fashioned a room, probably concealed the shutters. He seemed to be dividing his attention between his companions and the street, but when Conway stopped at last he left the window and came to sit on the corner of one of the empty desks.

"I shall need a view of the pub," he said, "and of Badger's Way, of course."

It was a long room, rather bare except for the four plain but seemingly well-used desks, and until Bushey got his pipe going there had been the heavy smell of stale smoke. Antony wasn't sure which he preferred, or—more correctly—which he liked least, but if for nothing else they must be grateful that the other occupants had all left for home before the court adjourned. Bushey had seated himself at what was presumably his own desk, but Conway was standing with his back to the grate, apparently oblivious of the fact that the fire had died long since. Now he stared at Maitland for a long moment, and then raised his hands in a gesture obviously intended to express both despair and incredulity.

"Haven't you been listening to *anything* I said?" he asked. He sounded more plaintive now than angry.

"Yes, indeed." Maitland's tone was negligent. John Bushey took his pipe from his mouth and blew out a great cloud of smoke.

"Well then!"

"What do you want me to say? I could remind you, of c-course, that—s-subject to your instructions, my d-dear

Conway—the way I conduct the case in court is my own affair."

Conway's look of surprise was almost ludicrous. There was a moment of dead silence before he managed to say stiffly, "I am aware of that." Antony felt a pang of regret for his own loss of temper. Chris was young, and worried. But, damn it all, he was worried himself.

Bushey looked from one of them to the other. "I think Conway feels that perhaps you don't altogether appreciate the—the delicacy of the situation."

"Well, if I hadn't before"—he broke off and smiled at Conway—"I've had every opportunity of learning."

Chris returned his look stonily for a moment, and then gave an exclamation that was halfway between bewilderment and exasperation. "Have it your own way," he said.

Bushey had the air of giving all this his close and careful attention, without in any way becoming involved in the disagreement. "What did you make of him then?" he asked.

"Of Ghulam Beas? I didn't like him," said Maitland promptly.

"No, but do you think he was telling the truth?"

"I think he has it in for Sergeant Duckett; perhaps for the police in general."

"Then—"

"It isn't as simple as that," said Maitland, without waiting for Bushey to complete his thought. "I think the issue is between those two men, but I can very easily visualize circumstances where the temptation to shop Comrade Beas might be almost irresistible."

"To you, you mean," said Bushey. His laugh was unexpectedly loud and boisterous.

"Precisely. And to save you the trouble of formulating the question, I will add that I used the word 'comrade' loosely, without any *arrière-pensée*." He glanced at Conway and noted with regret that the worried look was back again now that he'd forgotten to be angry. "It makes a situation I don't much care for," he said, "but it's really beside the point what Duckett might have done. We don't *know*."

"We don't really know anything," said Chris dismally.

"Oh, come now! Some people called Barlow were burgled; that isn't under dispute, I believe."

"No, but that's about all we can be sure of. You saw the copies of Beas's articles for the *Telegraph*?"

"I read them in the train. On the whole, they were milder than I expected."

"You might like to talk to Simpson," Conway suggested.

"Simpson?"

"The editor who commissioned them."

"Yes, of course. We're calling him, aren't we?"

"Only to say when the arrangement was made. But I got the impression he'd had to tone down Beas's remarks a good deal, that might tie in with what you were saying just now."

"An unwilling witness?" said Maitland.

"His sympathies are obviously with the other side."

"Then we'll treat him delicately and keep him to his proof," Antony decided. "All the same, it was a good idea. I wonder what he knows." He thought about that for a moment and then asked, "You didn't happen to send me an envelope full of clippings last night, about what Star Duckett called 'the other case'?"

"No, I didn't. Everything was with the brief." Conway frowned over the question for a moment. "I can't think who would have done," he said.

"Never mind. I don't suppose it matters." (But he knew it did . . . someone wanted him to know.)

"Star said I should tell you about that, but honestly . . . what good would it have done?"

"You don't think O'Brien will use it?"

"Why should he? He doesn't need any more than he's got."

"He may before we've finished," said Bushey surprisingly.

Chris looked doubtful. "He may," he conceded. "Anyway, where do we go from here?"

"To the Sun in Splendor," said Bushey, who had a literal mind.

"Yes, but . . . in court, I meant."

"What," said Maitland inconsequently, "is the Arkenshaw Society?"

The other two men exchanged glances. Bushey seemed more resigned than anything else, but Conway was quite simply puzzled. "Oh, that's the Findlaters," he said. Antony's eyes turned on him, patient but unmistakably insistent. "Philanthropists in a big way. Nominally the society is an association of local businessmen; actually, everyone knows it's mainly the Findlater money."

"Mohamad said—"

"Yes, scholarships for deserving students are one of their things. My father told me they used practically to run the local hospitals before National Health. But there are still plenty of people who need help, one way or another."

"Are they mill owners?" said Antony, thinking of the forest of chimneys and the gaunt shape of Comstock's Mill dominating the town.

"Not now. Grandfather was . . . the grandfather of the present man, I mean."

"First he made money from the mill," said Bushey, "and then he cornered something—"

"Tops and noils, most likely," murmured Antony; he had seen a sign on the opposite building during his vigil at the window, and the words had taken his fancy.

"—and really made a pile. And then he sold out at the height of the boom—uniforms and things—in the first war, and the family have been living on his glory ever since."

"Nice for Jackie."

"What did you think of him, anyway?"

Maitland grinned again. "To tell the truth, I was far too frightened of upsetting him to stop to consider his character."

"Were you?" said Bushey. "Were you, indeed?"

"Oh, yes. A pleasant lad, but—for better or worse—under Beas's thumb. And that doesn't mean," he added, as he saw Conway's expression sharpen, "that I think there was a conspiracy between them. Not necessarily."

"No." Chris looked despondent for a moment, but then he cheered a little. "At least," he said, "you can't say that about Constable Ryder. That he was under the sergeant's thumb, I mean."

"Don't you think he would have backed him?"

"Oh, well, yes, I suppose he would. But I didn't mean that exactly."

"I know. There are more ways of killing a cat, however, than choking it with cream."

"What the hell does that mean?"

"I haven't the faintest idea." He met Conway's indignant stare and added gently, "I just feel like being cryptic, I'm afraid. Now, before we get to *their* witness from the pub tomorrow, let's see if I've got what *our* witnesses will say straight."

"All right. The landlord says the clock was three minutes fast—"

"Not enough to make any material difference," Bushey put in.

"—and he only remembers serving two foreigners that night, and didn't notice when they left."

"Beautifully imprecise."

"Yes, and the barmaid confirms what he says about the clock, but that's all she's sure about. She didn't notice how many foreigners there were, or how long they stayed."

"By the way, neither Beas nor Mohamad is a Sikh."

"What of it?"

"I was wondering whether their dress in any way distinguished them from the rest of the Pakistani population."

"But they wear just the same as anyone else," said Conway, obviously finding this unreasonable.

"The same as any citizens of Arkenshaw. But what about the rest of the foreigners? No turbans, no long hair?"

"Oh, I see. A few of them stick to their turbans. A very few. As far as appearance goes, Beas and Mohamad are nothing out of the way."

"And the other two men who will be giving evidence . . . what will they say?"

"Lawford—"

"Who is a burglar himself," said Bushey. "Yes, really," he added, as Maitland's eyes turned on him inquiringly.

"—and Randall, who is a bricklayer," said Chris, ignoring them both, "agree that the foreigners left before closing time, but aren't sure how many of them there were. Randall thinks four or five. It's too damned contradictory for anything," he added discontentedly. "Enough to confuse the jury . . . I hope. But it's the best we can do."

"Well, we'll see what can be done with their Mr. Saddler tomorrow. And I see they'll be proving arrest . . . that won't be very exciting, will it? But I *am* interested in Miss Garrowby. Perhaps if we could just go over her evidence too—"

IV

In the event, Maitland and Conway went alone to the pub. Bushey, after all, knew the district, and his sole contribution to the success of the expedition was to unearth from a cupboard a woolen scarf, hand-knitted in all the colors of the rainbow, which he handed to his leader with the comment that it might come in useful.

Antony received it with gratitude. "In goodly colors gloriously arrayed," he said, eying the repellent object admiringly.

"That's why I leave it here," Bushey assured him, and went away grinning.

It was cold outside, and the wind met them when they reached the corner. By the time they came to the street where the Austin was parked Antony was again regretting the thinness of his raincoat. Chris had fallen silent, and they accomplished the brief journey to Masham Street without conversation. The Sun in Splendor was a long, two-story building, apparently a relic of a bygone age; the street seemed to have grown up around it—dreary little rows of terrace houses, very like the one where Constable Ryder was staying.

Conway parked the car and put out a hand to open the door. "I suppose you want to walk," he said without enthusiasm.

"Yes, but I think we should fortify ourselves first." Maitland stood eying the building doubtfully. "Do you really feel it's well named?" he asked.

"It isn't too bad inside," said Conway, coming up to his side.

"That's good. Which door, do you know? Are we about to enter a maze of social distinctions?"

"All one big happy family," Chris told him. He seemed to know his way, and made for a side door without hesitation. It was warm inside, with only a handful of people near the fire; a pleasant raftered room with no style about it, but an indefinable air of welcome. "Let me," said Conway, and made his way to the bar. Antony strolled across the room and sat down at a table near the window.

" 'Evening, Mr. Conway. Looking us over?" asked the big man behind the counter. His eyes went past Chris and rested reflectively on the stranger.

"That's right," said Conway amiably.

"Ah, well. It'll all be the same in a hundred years," the landlord remarked philosophically. "What will it be?"

"Black Label, please. Two doubles."

Antony smiled as Conway set down the glasses and slipped into the chair opposite him. "The right idea," he remarked with satisfaction. "Do you think Grandma Duckett would approve?"

"She isn't teetotal. Well, not exactly."

"Expound."

"She makes her own."

"Moonshine?" said Antony, raising his eyebrows.

"Oh, no. Parsnips, and blackberries . . . stuff like that. As a matter of fact," Chris admitted, "some of it isn't half-bad, except that the parsnip wine has been known to knock strong men out cold."

"Well, well. Was that the landlord you were talking to?"

"Yes. Adam Thompson."

"What sort of a man is he?"

"Good reputation for straight dealing. Not overgenial. A bit close. Popular enough in the neighborhood."

"Good. Tell me something, Conway"—Maitland picked up his glass and seemed to be admiring the contents—"have you been doing your homework, or do you really know everyone in Arkenshaw?" He raised his eyes again as he finished speaking.

"That's a trick you use in court," said Chris inconsequently.

"What? Oh, never mind." He wasn't really interested. "You didn't answer my question," he pointed out.

"A bit of both, I suppose. We're provincials, you know; with a provincial interest in each other's doings."

"And very nice too. I want the best information, you supply it. I'm grateful," he added formally, and looked across at the bar again when he saw that Chris looked a little taken aback. Maggie Jowett had just come in and was speaking to Thompson. After a moment Adam nodded and went out of the door that led to the living quarters. "I can see now that the name of the pub isn't entirely inappropriate," said Maitland with appreciation.

Conway twisted around to look. "Oh, Maggie!" he said, and turned again, smiling.

"The Miss Jowett who will be giving evidence?"

"Yes. And if you want to know about her, she's very well liked. Generous. Pays her bills, but not always straight away. There's a husband somewhere, Jowett's her maiden name. She came here from Leeds two . . . three years ago."

"Conway's potted biographies. What about old rat trap? Do you suppose he's in conference with Kevin O'Brien somewhere, both of them becoming steadily more irritated as the minutes go by?"

Chris made no pretense of failing to recognize the description. "Well, what about him?"

"The plaintiffs' solicitor. Ashby? Jones? I don't even know his name."

"Jones. The senior partner. Why are you interested in him?"

"Well, I wondered. He might have been instrumental in interesting O'Brien in the first place. They may have a professional respect for each other, I can't imagine they're personally compatible. He might even be the person who persuaded Beas there was a case to be made out . . . if he needed any persuasion."

"But why on earth—?"

"I don't know. Anyway, he looks completely devoid of the milk of human kindness," said Antony in a discontented tone.

"He isn't exactly the companion I'd choose if I wanted a night out," Conway admitted. "But a public-spirited chap, so far as I know."

"I thought as much," said Maitland, in the tone of one whose worst fears are realized.

"I suppose, though . . . I suppose you might have something there," said Conway slowly. "He's a member of the panel who attend on a sort of rota system to give free legal advice. He could have got into it that way, couldn't he, if Ghulam Beas consulted him?" For a moment Chris sounded almost enthusiastic; then he frowned. "I don't see that it really matters, though."

"Neither do I. I'm afraid I was just curious," said Maitland apologetically. "Tell me about Miss Garrowby instead. We've discussed her evidence till I'm sick and tired of it, but what's she like?"

"You won't see her in here," said Chris dryly.

"No, but tell me—"

"She's lived in Arkenshaw all her life. Thirty years ago, when her father died, she and her mother moved to Badger's Way. Mother quite well off, died five years ago . . . all these dates are approximate. Miss G. teaches English at the Modern School; it has a new name now, but that's what everyone calls it. Lives simply, not much entertaining since she was on her own, small circle of friends, reads a lot."

"Now how on earth do you know that?"

"Library," said Chris succinctly.

"And the boy . . . the one whose evidence contradicts hers."

"Martin Ward."

"That's right. I know his father was born under Gemini," he added helpfully.

"I think Sergeant Duckett told you most of it. Father's a solid citizen, treasurer of the Arkenshaw Society, as a matter of fact. Mother's a bit of a do-gooder," said Conway thoughtfully, "but quite a decent type." (Antony smiled and finished his whisky.) "The boy does rather well at school, not brilliant, but a plodder. Someone who was in court last time told me he seemed a sulky little devil. I wouldn't know." He caught sight of Antony's glass, and picked up his own in a hurry. "Oh, I say, ought we to be getting along?"

"Another?"

"No, thank you. I'd rather—" He broke off, looking confused.

"Got a date?"

"I thought if it wasn't too late I'd go and see Star after supper." His tone was a little defensive, and he got up as he spoke; but Maitland thought to himself, "All is forgiven," as he followed Chris to the door. He was beginning to have quite a respect for his young colleague, and had no wish to be at odds with him; though, on reflection, honesty compelled him to add to this admirable sentiment, "so long as he lets me go my own way."

Outside, Antony stopped to look up at the inn's signboard, which was swinging dangerously and complaining as it swung. A conventional sun, repainted not long ago,

74

from the look of it. "Not exactly an inspired illustration," he said, and paused to check his watch before turning left to follow Conway along the pavement. "I've a feeling I ought to know where the name comes from," he added.

"Unless it's something to do with Louis XIV," said Chris. He lengthened his stride as the other man came up with him, and Maitland, who had settled down to an easy pace, said: "Hey! I'm timing us," he explained. "Though I'm sure you've done that already."

"Well, I have, as a matter of fact."

"And was our friend Mr. Beas accurate?"

"Within a second or two," said Chris grudgingly.

"That's bad."

"Yes, I think so. If they really left the Sun after closing time they couldn't possibly have been roaming around the Barlows' house for ten minutes before the police arrived."

"Never mind. The evidence from the pub is vague enough, in all conscience."

"So vague it could be true," said Conway, declining to be comforted. "Once you start believing *them*."

Maitland could think of no comment on that, and left him to his gloom. Anyway, he had to concentrate on keeping his moderate pace; it was so cold, the temptation to step out briskly was a very real one.

Cargate was the main road from the center of the town, the one they had used the previous night, if he wasn't mistaken. It was busy now with homegoing traffic, and they had to wait to get across. Four tram cars in convoy, a double-decker bus marked "Limited Stop," a pack of minicars that gave the impression of yapping excitedly at its heels. "Next on the left," said Conway, gaining the safety of the opposite pavement. They passed a row of shops and turned into Badger's Way.

A wide road lined with semidetached houses of depressing similarity, but solid enough to belie the whimsicality of its name. Even at this hour it was utterly deserted, a strange contrast to the busy highway. The street lamps were rather widely spaced, each with its pool of light, but

75

there were no real pockets of dark between them. "Eight minutes and thirty-five seconds," said Maitland as Conway halted abruptly and indicated a brick gatepost with an ornate figure nineteen. "But I daresay we overdid it rather, and there wouldn't be so much traffic later on." He turned and stood surveying the house. Stucco, and lattice windows, and a pale blue front door with a panel of leaded glass at the top, and iron hinges that might well have graced a medieval monastery. "No garages," he said.

"I think they've built a sort of mews, somewhere around the back. There weren't so many cars when these were put up, but farther along some of them have their own."

"Barlow?"

"He has a Hillman."

"And the house beyond is Miss Garrowby's? Yes, I see. Walk down the road a bit, will you, and then come back. I want to find out how soon you're visible." He retreated himself as Conway obeyed him. "Well, I don't know," he added a minute later, as they met again under the lamp. "I could see you, all right—I mean, I could see *someone* was coming—but then, I was looking for you."

"Does it matter?"

"It might," said Antony. Conway sounded as if he was beginning to feel the cold. "All right, let's get back." He jerked his head toward number nineteen as they passed it. "Tell me about the man from the Prudential," he demanded.

"As a matter of fact, he works for Imperial Insurance."

"What odds? Barlow, if you must be accurate."

"Well, he's an insurance agent . . . you know that. Not a very impressive appearance, but I think," said Chris, warming to his theme, "there must be more to him than meets the eye."

"Tell me."

"It's his wife. The glamorous Glenda." He paused a moment, and then said, "Wow!" as though he could think of no more fitting explanation. Antony burst out laughing.

"Could you find words, do you think?"

"Hardly. She's twenty years younger than he is, for one thing. Well, perhaps not quite that, but she looks it. Blonde. My father says she's the old-fashioned-vamp type," said Conway, "but she looks modern enough to me. And she runs up bills, but he always pays them promptly . . . in fact, I'd say he gives her everything she wants, within his means. He's said to be a good salesman, but—I'm guessing now—he probably has some money of his own. Otherwise, why should she have married him?"

"Miaouw," said Antony. "Not his fatal beauty, then?"

"Wait till you see him."

"I'll take your word for it. If I got on one of those trams," said Antony, quickening his pace, "would it take me back to the hotel?"

"A number four would drop you right outside. But I can easily—"

"If you go now you'll be in time for the second house at the cinema." Conway opened his mouth to protest further; a tram came clattering down the road toward them. "If I can once get across," said Maitland; he halted on the curb, watching his chance. "I have an ambition to ride in one of those things," he added over his shoulder. "I want to prove to myself that I'm not afraid of them."

Conway shrugged as he watched his companion dart into a gap in the traffic; a moment later he followed at a more decorous pace.

V

Somehow, in spite of its reeling motion and the unholy row it made in its passing, the tram didn't jump the rails and the journey was stimulating, but otherwise uneventful. Maitland dined in the mess that night, and surprised those of his colleagues who knew him by being unusually silent. O'Brien, on the other hand, was in one of his most forthcoming moods; for some reason, this evening, he was exerting all the warmth of his personality, his beautiful voice at its most vividly persuasive, fascinating his audience with a deliberation that was obvious only if you kept yourself consciously aloof. And that wasn't easy, thought Antony wryly.

He had finished his dinner and was turning over in his mind an excuse for retiring when the waiter sidled up to him and said quietly, "There's a gentleman here who'd like a word with you, sir." It was with something like relief that he rose to make his apologies, but as he went into the lobby and the talk and laughter broke out again behind him he was aware of a moment's regret that he hadn't been in a more convivial humor.

The visitor turned out to be Constable Ryder. He was standing four-square in the middle of the lobby with a look of dogged determination on his face and his eyes fixed on the door of the room that was given over to the use of the gentlemen of the bar. "Like a cat at a mouse-hole," thought Antony, and repressed a desire to ask whether the constable had expected him to sneak out by the back door. Then as he approached he saw that Ryder was not alone; Star had been hidden for a moment by her companion's bulk, but judging by her expectant look she was also part of the deputation. For some reason her presence struck Antony with a faint sense of injury, as well as with surprise.

"I'm sorry to disturb you," said Constable Ryder, as soon as his quarry was near enough to make speech reasonable, "but she *would* come."

Glancing at Star, Antony decided that if she hadn't been quite so pretty he'd have described her expression as mulish, but when she caught his eye she relaxed a little and smiled at him. "Well, I'm sorry too if we're being a nuisance," she said. "But I do think . . . go on, Jim . . . tell him."

"If you want to talk," said Antony, looking around him, "hadn't we better find somewhere to sit down."

Ryder obviously thought this an insuperable difficulty. He stood where he was, looking helpless, and it was left to

Star to take charge of the party, which she did with her usual composure. "There's a little room behind the lounge. It isn't very comfortable, so there probably won't be anyone there." On inspection, they found that she was right.

The worst thing about the room was its bleakness; or was that merely a reflection, Maitland wondered, of his own depressed spirits? There was a sofa along one wall, and Star seated herself and patted the place beside her encouragingly. Antony appropriated the hard chair near the writing table, sitting sideways with his left arm over the back, so that he could face the others; after a moment Jim Ryder folded himself into an uncomfortable position beside the girl.

There was a silence. Ryder was perspiring gently, though the temperature was by no means excessive. Antony, who had a sudden, unpleasant premonition of what they were going to tell him, said abruptly, "Does Sergeant Duckett know you're here?"

Star gave her head a decisive shake. "No, of course not."

"Don't you think you should . . . consult him?"

"But I know very well what he'd say. He'd say it was all nonsense." She saw his expression change and added quickly, "What do you think we've come for, Mr. Maitland?"

"Never mind about that." His eyes shifted away from hers, and he picked up the steel-nibbed pen from the table beside him and began to gouge a hole in the blotting pad. Star gave him a considering look, and then returned to her original charge.

"You'd better tell him, Jim."

Constable Ryder cleared his throat. "If you think we'd do better to speak to your dad first—"

"I don't think so. Go on!" Her tone was rousing, but— contradicting its hardness—her hand went out to cover his.

"Well, you see, sir, it's along of what Star told me you'd asked t'sergeant. About why they was bringing the case."

79

"Yes?" Maitland was suddenly still, the stabbing motion of his hand arrested, and when he raised his head and looked at Ryder his eyes were intent.

"It isn't what I think," said the constable quickly. "Couldn't make head nor tail of it myself, not unless they was feeling resentful, which would be natural like. But Star got it into her head you thought there was something behind it, and so I said 'appen it was to do with this illegal immigration racket."

"What!"

Ryder seemed to think the sudden urgency in counsel's tone was meant as a reproof. "I didn't mean . . . it was nobbut a joke really," he said.

It occurred to Maitland that the difference between the constable's former self-possession and his present pronounced state of jitters was rather more than could be accounted for by the girl's presence, but he hadn't time to bother about that now. He turned his head until he could look at Star. "You didn't think it was funny yourself, Miss Duckett?"

"Do you?" she said, challenging him, and after a moment he smiled at her.

"If you could tell me a little more—"

"There isn't really much. I mean, everyone knows there've been more foreigners coming in than there should have been. And it was investigated, I suppose, but no one found out anything; and the people concerned, the ones who were found out . . . well, they'd been supplied with work permits—"

"Employment vouchers," said Ryder apologetically.

"—and so on, but it was through someone in Pakistan. Or so they said. And it was the welfare people who were worried about it mostly, because of housing conditions and all of that; and, anyway, no one wanted to see them starve. And, of course, they hadn't really got jobs to come to, so they sometimes went to work for less than our people, and then the unions had a grievance too."

"These employment vouchers . . . were they issued in the name of a real firm?"

"No," said Ryder, obviously taking the question as being addressed to him. "They'd be made-up names, and the addresses mostly in the north—Newcastle, Stockton, places like that."

"How long has this been going on?"

"A year . . . two years."

"Longer nor that. Even before the act was passed—"

"The one that was supposed to make it more difficult," Star put in.

"The Commonwealth Immigration Act of 1962," said Constable Ryder, and paused to admire the explicitness of the statement. "Even before that there was some hanky-panky about money, though I'm not quite sure how it was worked. But it took awhile for the newspapers to catch on."

"And when they did," Star added, "they said it was the fault of our 'unenlightened immigration policy.' Whatever that means."

"All this is common knowledge?"

"Yes. But the bit that isn't is what Jim told me tonight. He said that Dad had a sort of a—a thing about finding out who was getting them their papers; he was sure it was someone here. And I know Dad, Mr. Maitland . . . if he once gets an idea in his head, he'll never give it up. So I thought perhaps . . . perhaps—" For the first time her assurance deserted her. She broke off and looked at him appealingly.

"It's not so daft, at that," said Constable Ryder, suddenly aggressive. "Suppose he was on their track, and they thought they'd fix him."

Maitland was supposing it. "Have you any reason to think—?"

"He did say to me once that there was some as might be in for a surprise. But then after that he seemed discouraged, and I thought he'd 'appen been following a line and

81

it had fizzled out, you see. But it's like Star says . . . he'd never have let up."

"Why didn't you tell me this last night?"

"Nay, then, I thought you'd laugh." (But was that all that had been bothering Ryder?)

Star's eyes were fixed on Maitland's face. "It isn't much," she said, unexpectedly diffident.

"It *could* be the answer to my question," he told her doubtfully.

"But you don't think it is." She got up as she spoke and began pulling on her gloves. If she was disappointed, neither her voice nor her expression betrayed her.

"I haven't had time to think about it yet." He became aware that Star was holding out her hand to him.

"It was good of you to listen," she said formally.

"I'm glad you came. Really I am." Her eyes met his, grave and searching. "No, I mean it. It's just that I—"

"I wonder what you were expecting," she said thoughtfully. And then she smiled. Something, somehow, seemed to have restored her self-possession.

He said, on an impulse: "Miss Duckett, last night—" The smile faded slowly. "What about last night?"

"Why did you want me to know this wasn't the first case involving a Pakistani where there'd been an acquittal?"

"Because I thought you ought to know the worst that could be said, but Chris said it wasn't relevant and it would be silly to bring it up. Besides, if it was just spite on Ghulam Beas's part, it might have helped you to understand."

"You think he might have known about the first case, and been influenced by it."

"Of course he knew. He wrote it up for the paper."

"I see. Did you send me some clippings about it?"

"No, why should I?" She looked faintly surprised, but obviously it seemed to her no very great matter. "There was another thing, Mr. Maitland." The faintest hesitation, and then she added in a rush, "Dad always said it was perjured evidence . . . the witness, I mean . . . the one who gave the accused man an alibi."

"Then why in the name of all that's wonderful didn't he tell me that himself?"

"Because he thought . . . because people didn't believe him," said Star, as if that explained everything. She stood a moment longer, eying him in a considering way, and then began to walk toward the door. "Good night, Mr. Maitland," she said, over her shoulder.

"Good night," echoed Constable Ryder. He took a few steps, following her, and then turned and added in a conspiratorial tone, "Not to worry, sir. I wouldn't have troubled you with all this rigmarole . . . only you see how it is."

Afterward Antony wondered whether he had voiced his agreement aloud. He stood where they had left him, staring at the door, and after a moment he put up his left hand and ran his fingers through his hair.

The thought went through his mind, inconsequently, that Star was in some ways very like her grandmother.

VI

When he reached the hall both his visitors had disappeared, but the door was still rotating, and Kevin O'Brien was standing at the foot of the staircase gazing at the entrance in a thoughtful way. He turned his head as he heard Maitland's step, and when their eyes met Antony was aware again, as he had been earlier in court, of the other man's rancor. Then O'Brien's smile flashed out. "It's a shame, so it is, the amount of overtime a man must put in."

Antony strolled across to join him. He thought, "Faker!" but he said only, negligently, "A deplorable necessity."

"Over and above the call of duty," said O'Brien. "Very

commendable . . . on occasion." He glanced at the door, and though his tone was still friendly his doubt as to the eligibility of the present instance could not have been more clearly expressed. "I'm an idle man myself. When I see a somnolent dog, I prefer to let it sleep."

"You're probably wise," Maitland agreed; and there was the anger in his companion's eyes again. No doubt about it, O'Brien had his client's cause at heart, and was so convinced of its justice that he couldn't conceive of anyone with a similar knowledge of the facts having any doubts at all. There was, it must be admitted, a certain attraction in the proposition that the plaintiffs had been victimized . . . two strangers who had fallen foul of organized authority . . . members of a persecuted minority group. Maitland's own doubts made him vulnerable, and almost envious of O'Brien's certainty.

"I wouldn't expect you'd be agreeing with me," O'Brien was saying. "I like a quiet life myself, but from all I hear, it doesn't suit you so well."

It ought to have been amusing . . . it would certainly have amused Sir Nicholas . . . to see Kevin O'Brien as full of the crusading spirit as ever he had been himself. Antony said, "I'm beginning to wish—" and caught himself up on the admission. "I have to telephone," he added, and put a foot on the bottom step of the stairs. "See you tomorrow." He had encountered O'Brien several times before this, but always when the case was cut and dried, a matter of careful study and presentation, no more than that. And they'd got on well enough, but he was beginning to realize how slight their acquaintance was.

"See you in court," echoed O'Brien. And Maitland said to himself, "Oh, well!" and went on up the stairs.

It was a relief to reach his room and shut the door on the world, if not on its problems. He was still preoccupied when he put through a call to Jenny, so that he was almost startled when he heard her voice. His greeting was so heartfelt that she sounded a little startled herself.

"Is everything all right, darling?"

"Yes, of course. Why shouldn't it be?"

"You sound a bit . . . peculiar," said Jenny, with precision.

In those surroundings the choice of phrase was, perhaps, inevitable. "I feel fair moidered, if you want to know."

"Murdered?"

"Moidered . . . confused . . . disconcerted . . . *bouleversé.*"

"Oh, dear," said Jenny. "Uncle Nick has been prophesying doom."

"About the case? How right he is."

"He said he didn't like to think *what* might happen when you were let loose among a lot of policemen." She paused, and as though he could see her, he could imagine her doubtful look. "What has happened, anyway?"

"Nothing much. I changed my mind once . . . well, nearly. And now I'm wondering whether my first idea was the right one, after all."

There was another small silence. "From here, you know, that doesn't make much sense," Jenny told him.

"I don't suppose it does. You see, love, I wasn't going to admit it to Uncle Nick, but when I came here . . . well, I wasn't prejudiced *against* the plaintiffs—that was true enough—but I think perhaps I was prejudiced in favor of my clients."

"I suppose there's a difference," said Jenny consideringly.

"Of course there is." The suggestion was just what was needed to clarify his thoughts. "I forget what percentage of the complaints of police misconduct that are officially investigated prove to have *some* foundation, but it isn't very large. And—"

"You don't have to convince me, you know. Anyway, you aren't always so complimentary about the police yourself."

"I told you—"

"Don't start on the percentages again, darling. We've admitted you were prejudiced; the rest is just rationalizing. In any case, that isn't what's worrying you."

"No," said Antony. He sat for a moment, staring rather vacantly across the room. "I had a theory," he went on, interrupting Jenny's protest at the sudden silence, "a preconceived notion, if you like that better. And when I arrived here I was all set to try to do something about it, but then I began to get doubtful."

"I knew you were, last night."

"So I thought I'd better not try to dig too deep. But then tonight Constable Ryder came to see me. I tried to head him off, I thought he'd come to confess; which was a silly idea, I suppose, because he had the girl with him—"

"Star?"

"Yes, Star."

"Do you think she was called that because of the astrology?" asked Jenny irrelevantly.

"Not if Conway's right . . . he knows everything, that lad." Antony was momentarily diverted. "He says Star's mother died when she was born, so her name was the sergeant's choice; and old Mrs. Duckett was living in Huddersfield then."

"But you didn't tell me what Constable Ryder had to say." Unfairly, Jenny's voice was reproachful.

"He gave me a possible answer to a question that's been nagging at me . . . what was behind the prosecution, I mean."

"If anything."

"Yes, of course . . . if anything. I came here thinking it was a simple matter, just between the two parties, but then I began to see that if Beas had it in for Sergeant Duckett, and perhaps for the police in general, equally the sergeant had it in for the foreigners, and perhaps for Ghulam Beas in particular. Then this cropped up."

"What?" asked Jenny, not unreasonably.

"The suggestion that the sergeant might have been

86

framed—that's what it amounts to—because of certain investigations he had in hand."

"But that's dreadful, darling."

"It's bad enough," Antony admitted. "The trouble is, at the same time Constable Ryder showed me an additional reason why he might have backed his sergeant up in making a false charge. He's in love with the girl."

"How do you know?"

Antony thought about that. "It was obvious," he said after a while, "to the meanest intelligence."

"What about Star?"

"I don't know. She was holding his hand."

"I hope she isn't playing fast and loose with your nice Mr. Conway," said Jenny primly. "But what are you going to do?"

"Have another talk with Sergeant Duckett, I suppose." He did not sound as if he found the prospect particularly enthralling.

"Will *he* tell you the truth?"

"I don't know that I want him to."

"Don't be silly," said Jenny severely, "of course he must."

"Of course," said Antony, who had no intention of involving himself in further explanation. But for the first time that evening he felt almost lighthearted.

They talked for some time after that, and the sense of comfort persisted even after he had put down the telephone. But he didn't sleep well that night, and he found himself wondering, in one of his moments of wakefulness, why he hadn't told Jenny about the oblique and unsatisfactory conversation he'd had with Kevin O'Brien.

I

Chris Conway was inclined to be grumpy next morning. Maitland told him about Ryder's visit, but neither of them found it necessary to mention Star. "I don't think much of that," said Conway bluntly when the story was finished. "Or . . . do you?"

"I don't know what I think," said Antony crossly. His mind was occupied—not hopefully—with the next move. "I'd like to talk to Sergeant Duckett during the luncheon recess."

The morning was occupied with proof of arrest . . . the station sergeant, and the C.I.D. man who had been on duty. It was odd, Maitland thought, to have listened so many times to almost precisely the same evidence, and now the whole thing was being turned upside down. He wondered if the judge might have been struck by the same idea, but when he looked up at the bench there was nothing to be learned from Gilmour's melancholy countenance. Bushey had undoubtedly thought of it . . . but Bushey was too cheerful this morning to suit his leader's mood; he preferred Chris's bad temper, or even his lordship's determined gloom.

There was a momentary stir of interest when the finding of the gold noble was reached. O'Brien's junior, Roberts, seemed to be making rather heavy weather of his examination . . . the identification of the coin, the witnesses' assurance that it had been taken from Chakwal Mohamad's pocket. Well, if you had unpalatable facts to disclose, better to do so openly; and there was the further point, which had no doubt occurred to O'Brien, that if once the jury could be brought to accept the plaintiffs' innocence, the finding of the coin automatically damned the defendants . . . it must have been a plant. As Maitland listened to his junior, who had the thankless task of repeating the questions, the frown was back between his eyes.

After that there was Konat Iskander, a compatriot of the plaintiffs, who also had acquired an excellent command of English in spite of the fact that he had only been in the country "a little less than three years," he said. And, "Yes, I am meeting with them at the Sun that night—"

"The twenty-fourth March?"

"Other nights, too, perhaps, since then. But that is the night we are speaking of, I think." This was obviously intended as a plain affirmative, and even the judge did not ask for further clarification.

"Please tell us how long you were with Mr. Beas and Mr. Mohamad," O'Brien went on.

"At the pub, since about nine-thirty of the clock. Perhaps a little later when I get there, I am not remembering very well. And then they are calling for the closing, and so we must go out . . ."

An excellent witness, Maitland thought, and sounded sure enough of his facts. Too sure? But that was hardly a fair observation. Iskander was taller than either of the plaintiffs, a well-set-up man of thirty—thirty-five?—with a cheerful, friendly manner. He had given his occupation as a conductor with the Arkenshaw Public Transport, and it was easy to imagine him in this capacity. Antony himself had purchased his ticket on the tram last night from a chap who might easily have been the witness's brother, and who had greeted each successive passenger with such apparent delight as to make them feel their advent had been the one thing needed to make his day. Altogether, you had to admit Iskander made a good impression, as Beas and Mohamad had done. Beas, now, had no pretensions to good looks, only a certain dignity . . . which, come to think of it, characterized all three of them.

But suppose, just suppose for a moment, there was

something in this wild idea that Constable Ryder had laid before him so unwillingly yesterday evening. If one could smile and smile and be a villain, that ought to bring Konat Iskander well within the classification. But there were degrees of villainy, after all; it was practically impossible to imagine him in a leading role.

O'Brien had tidied up his witness's evidence now, and left him to John Bushey's tender mercies. "How long have you known Chakwal Mohamad, Mr. Iskander?"

"I am meeting him for the first time that night. March twenty-fourth," added the witness, with a smile of pleasure.

"And Ghulam Beas?"

"Perhaps in six months I am seeing him once . . . twice."

"Six months before the night in question."

"Oh, yes."

"And did you meet him that night by chance?"

"No, not really. Mr. Beas is collecting some figures . . . how many Pakistani are employed by the tramways . . . how many as conductors, in the offices, as cleaners . . . and so he is telling me he would like to know something—something personal. How we are feeling about our work; how we are being paid; how the others, the white people, are liking us."

"And the meeting was arranged so that you could give him this information."

"He is telling me he will be there, and so I am going to help him."

"On the basis of one or two previous conversations?"

"I am sorry—"

"You had met only twice before?"

"Yes, I think."

"Where?"

"At the house of a friend. Mr. Thomas Harvey."

Bushey repeated the name, which had suffered some mangling. "And at this Mr. Harvey's house Mr. Beas said to you that he would be at the Sun on the evening of the

90

twenty-fourth March, and would like some information from you for the article he was writing."

"I am feeling sure you are right."

"Because that was the only place you had ever met him."

"Yes."

"You are a member of the social club attached to All Saints' Church, are you not?"

"Since first I come here." But the question was unexpected, and for the first time he showed some hesitation.

"Three years?"

"Nearly three years."

"Do you attend there regularly?"

"I am not going there often." He wasn't smiling now.

"Thank you, Mr. Iskander, that is all."

No reexamination. No way for O'Brien to tell what the defense was getting at. Maitland glanced at his opponent as Bushey sat down again, and saw with a quite reprehensible touch of malice that he was puzzled. That was a bit more of Chris Conway's "homework" . . . the curate of All Saints' would say that Iskander attended the club every week; and that during the previous winter Ghulam Beas had been a guest member, because he was gathering material for the series in the local newspaper about the living and social conditions of the immigrant population.

The first of his articles had appeared in the *Arkenshaw Telegraph* on the twenty-third March, as the reluctant Mr. Simpson, the features editor, would testify.

The reason for the lie was obvious enough when you read the report of the previous trial, and realized how violently Iskander's evidence had been challenged on that occasion. But it was too small a matter to carry much weight with the jury, Maitland thought ruefully; it didn't even carry any weight with him. For all that, Conway had done an excellent job, and deserved better of fate than to have two clients who were probably guilty, or that he should have instructed counsel who couldn't make up his mind . . .

The witness who was now being sworn was a thin, bald, middle-aged man with a dyspeptic expression. Arthur Saddler, grocer, with a shop in Cargate that served a good class of customer, and a comfortable home and a comfortable wife upstairs. Or so said Conway, whom Antony was rapidly coming to regard as omniscient.

Mr. Saddler did not seem happy, but his evidence was clear enough. He had been at the Sun in Splendor on the evening of twenty-fourth March and had seen and recognized Ghulam Beas, whom he already knew by sight. Mr. Beas had two companions, of—of his own nationality, said Mr. Saddler, triumphing over a difficult linguistic problem. And they had stayed until closing time, and he had noticed the three of them afterwards, standing talking on the pavement outside.

" 'God made the wicked grocer for a mystery and a sign,' " said Maitland to himself, as he listened with half his mind to O'Brien's skillful guidance of the witness; the quotation gave him the first gleam of pleasure he had felt that morning. If Star Duckett was right, there ought to be a villain in this business somewhere . . . a fine, upstanding, moustache-twirling villain machinating away behind the scenes and pulling the strings to set his puppets dancing. But you couldn't fit Arthur Saddler into that part, not by any stretch of the imagination. And, anyway, didn't everything he had learned confirm his own original theory that the whole thing was a duel between Sergeant Duckett and Ghulam Beas that had somehow got out of hand?

He was aware of a sudden surge of impatience . . . impatience with himself most of all for having thought he could do any good by coming here. If he had been confident of the defendants' innocence there were questions that could be asked, lines of inquiry that might—just possibly—turn the tables. As it was, there was nothing to be done that Bushey couldn't perform very competently. O'Brien had finished his examination now—an exhaustive one, he wasn't leaving anything to chance—and Bushey was on his feet dealing gently with Mr. Saddler . . . con-

92

fusing him, to put it bluntly, but the man was a natural confusee. The trouble was, his doubts didn't really sound any more convincing than his previous certainty, and O'Brien could certainly put Humpty Dumpty together again on reexamination. . . .

On an impulse, Maitland scribbled a note, and pushed it along the table under his junior's nose. Bushey glanced down, paused only briefly, and asked as smoothly as before: "Where were you sitting when you were in the public house?"

"By the window."

"So that you had a good view of the street outside."

"Yes."

"And of the people who left by the front door."

"Yes," said Arthur Saddler, still more doubtfully.

"Mr. Saddler, I should like you to think again of that evening. You recall seeing Mr. Beas standing talking with his friend outside the public house—"

"With his friends," repeated the witness, nodding.

"That picture is quite clear in your mind?"

"Very clear indeed."

"But are you so certain *when* you saw them?"

"When I went out—" But the assurance trailed off in obvious doubt.

"Might it not rather have been . . . I am putting the suggestion to you, Mr. Saddler, that you saw them through the window while you were still in the bar, some time before it closed."

"Well, I . . . it might, I suppose . . . I don't think that was how it was," added the witness in a hurry. Kevin O'Brien was already on his feet to reexamine when Bushey sat down. Bushey glanced questioningly at his leader, and received in return a reassuring nod.

To anyone more than a few yards away it would have seemed that the defendants' counsel was most carefully occupied with his brief. And so he was; by the time the recess was reached, he had a fine crop of sketches. "What's the devil doing there?" asked Conway, looking down idly

93

while he waited for Maitland to find the one envelope he simply must have when he talked to Sergeant Duckett.

"The 'hell-instructed grocer,' " said Antony, not quite as vague as he sounded; and grinned to himself when he saw that his words meant nothing at all to the other man. It was reassuring to know there were some limits to Chris's general knowledge.

Bushey had a conference. "Next week's bread and butter," he explained, departing in some haste and ignoring altogether Maitland's attempt to return the multicolored scarf which he had brought into court among his papers. As Antony followed more slowly out of the courtroom, Conway caught his arm.

"You were asking about the Arkenshaw Society," he said. "That's Frank Findlater over there, talking to your friend Jones."

"The—er—the reigning Findlater?" asked Antony, looking across with interest to the other side of the hall, where two men stood in earnest consultation. Old rat trap looked as severe as ever; his companion was a big man of about fifty with a cheerful air and a ruddy complexion, certainly overweight but with no suggestion of flabbiness about him. And that was one minor mystery solved, at least—he was the same man who had been dining with Kevin O'Brien on Monday night.

"One of them," Conway was saying. "There's a brother, too, Victor, who's a year or two younger." They were moving toward the front door now, and Jones acknowledged Chris's greeting, but his companion turned and said, "Hold on a minute, Chris, I want a word with you," and added with a smile at Maitland, "I won't keep him long."

It was natural for Antony to move out of earshot with the lugubrious Mr. Jones. They stood near the main entrance, looking through the glass doors at the gray prospect of a windswept street, and inevitably the solicitor asked him, "How do you like Arkenshaw?" and he replied, as he had done to O'Brien: "Cold. But I suppose the wind drops sometimes."

The corners of Mr. Jones's mouth twitched slightly, presumably in acknowledgment of the lightness of Maitland's tone. "We pride ourselves on our hardihood," he said. And then, with a return to his normal gloom, "When the wind drops it will rain." There was a pause, and perhaps he realized the deadening effect of a remark not calculated to promote conversation, for he added with a determined air, "It's a pity the assizes aren't held at a more pleasant time of year."

Antony was aware of a deliberate attempt at friendliness, which surprised him because it seemed so pointless; another kind of man . . . but Jones didn't seem the sort to indulge himself, or others, in small talk. He was also conscious, as their exchange of ideas continued on the same rather stilted lines, that there was something in "old rat trap" that he found repellent. He considered the word, and decided it was by no means an exaggeration; and was relieved when he heard Chris's voice behind him and turned to hear a muttered introduction and to find his hand engulfed in Findlater's and shaken with the same energy that seemed to characterize the big man's every move.

Findlater's eyes were on a level with his own. "We've heard of you, Mr. Maitland." (Was he speaking for the town, or merely for his own family?) "A great pleasure to make your acquaintance, though I wish"—the hearty voice was lowered a little—"the occasion had been more pleasant."

Antony murmured something; both Conway and Jones were looking nervous, as though fearful of being swept into some extrajudicial indiscretion on the tide of Findlater's goodwill. "All in the day's work for you, I expect," he went on. "That's what Johnny tells me." He broke off to clap the unappreciative Mr. Jones on the shoulder.

"I consider the day ill-spent," said Maitland gravely, "when I don't sup full of horror."

"Eh? Oh . . . very funny." His laugh rang out, causing a passing civic dignitary to pause and look at the group with dislike; and then, seeing perhaps of whom it consisted, to

95

smile in rather a sickly way. But Findlater's laughter was infectious; even old rat trap was betrayed into a polite titter, and it was easy to see him as the mainspring of the town's charitable activities. The phrase "overwhelmingly generous" occurred to Antony as being in this case completely apt; indeed, Findlater probably overwhelmed everyone with whom he came into contact. He was talking now about the possibility of a future meeting . . . mustn't miss the opportunity . . . get in touch. And Chris was beginning to get restive, and his own mind was being teased by the impression that there was something here that was important . . . the interrelation of the two men's characters, perhaps; he was beginning to be very interested indeed in Mr. Jones. Or perhaps it was just the effect that a man like Frank Findlater must have on his fellow citizens. Only he couldn't quite see . . .

Conway had succeeded in maneuvering the party nearer the doors now, and was holding one open invitingly. The sweep of cold air was too powerful a hint to be ignored. They trooped out after a brief skirmishing for the last place. "Can we drop you somewhere?" asked Findlater.

At the bottom of the broad flight of steps stood an opulent-looking Cadillac, in what was clearly marked as a no-parking area. The colored chauffeur, well wrapped up against the wind, had scrambled out of the driving seat and come around to open the car door. His turban was a bright splash of color against the gloomy background. Something about him reminded Maitland of Chakwal Mohamad . . . perhaps it was the way he moved, perhaps the flashing smile. Chris was saying, "Thank you, but we're only going as far as the office." (In Arkenshaw, of course, everyone would know exactly where that was.) Jones was already climbing into the car.

"All right, Tom, you can take us to Brinkley Crescent," said Findlater, and raised his hand in farewell. "We shall meet again," he assured Maitland, winding down the window especially to do so.

II

Chris had arranged for sandwiches and coffee in his office, and Sergeant Duckett was waiting when they got there. He seemed moody and disinclined for speech, which Antony didn't think surprising. No use trying to get anything out of him until they had settled down to their meal.

"Sorry about this," said Conway, waving a disparaging hand as he ushered them into the room. "I only know one place where we could eat and talk freely, and that's because the food's so frightful nobody ever goes there."

It seemed to Maitland that there was little enough need for apology. Conway might be the junior partner, but his room was comfortably old-fashioned, somebody had made up the fire against their coming, there were plenty of sandwiches, and the coffeepot sat warmly in the hearth. Sergeant Duckett sat himself down in one of the armchairs, with the air of one disclaiming all responsibility for the proceedings; Chris fussed gently over his visitors' comfort and then retreated to his own chair behind the desk; Antony parked cup and plate on a handy table and took his own favorite position, with one shoulder propped against the corner of the mantel. But he made no immediate attempt to break the silence.

"Well, now, then," said the sergeant after a moment, "you'd best tell me what this is all about." Over the rim of his cup he looked up angrily at his counsel, but it was Conway who spoke first.

"I met Mr. Findlater as I left the court," he said awkwardly.

"Aye, I saw him."

"He gave me a message for Star. He said he'd had a word with Mr. Greenhalgh, and she wasn't to worry about her job."

"About losing it, you mean, if those two win their case. Kind of him!" said Duckett with heavy irony.

Chris seemed to have little relish for the role of envoy. "I thought you might like to know."

"As things are going so badly. Is that what you got me here to tell me?"

"No, it was Mr. Maitland—" Duckett's eyes followed Conway's gesture until they rested meditatively on Antony's face. Antony's own gaze was fixed on a point somewhere over the sergeant's head.

"Why don't you like foreigners?" he asked idly.

"Because they mean trouble, that's why."

"So I gather. This illegal immigration, now—"

"What about it?"

"That's what I'm hoping you'll tell me."

"It doesn't seem to me that it's owt to do with . . . all this."

"No. But do you think it could have?"

"Now, look here—" The cup went down with a clatter. "I don't know who's been stuffing you up with fairy tales—"

"You were investigating the matter, weren't you?"

"Yes, I was." Duckett bit into a ham sandwich, and chomped in silence for a while. His eyes were fixed on Maitland's face, and at last, when no further questions were forthcoming, he burst out, "If you want to know what happened, I'll tell you. After those two were acquitted, they told me I'd best drop the inquiries. Inspector would deal with it himself, they said. *My* work on the case might be 'open to misconstruction.' " His tone was bitterly resentful.

"They?"

"Superintendent Morrison."

"And the inspector in question?"

"Townsend. Seems there'd been some talk," he added grudgingly, "like our Star was saying."

Antony bent to pick up his cup. "Where were your inquiries leading you?" he asked.

"They gave me no time."

"Well, let's see. How many people had come in illegally?"

"More than we ever knew of. Sithee, it isn't easy. Papers

seem in order, so long as they behave themselves why should we check up on them? It's obvious enough when we do, but nobody thinks of it unless there's trouble, or a question of deportation, summat like that."

"Is that how the first case came to light?"

"It is. Chap stabbed another. Not fatal, but . . . there you are. And when we had a look at his employment voucher the firm he was supposed to be going to didn't even exist. In Northallerton, it was supposed to be. And the ministry said they'd never even heard of him."

"The Ministry of Labor?"

"That's right. There'd never been an application at all."

"And since then you've uncovered a good many instances?"

Duckett turned to favor Chris Conway with a long, hard stare. "Since you know so much about it—" he said.

Chris choked over his coffee, and Antony said hastily: "You're the expert."

"Well then, once we knew there was something to look for, it was obvious what had been happening. But you can't check on everyone. I don't know as you'd want to, even with *them*."

"What sort of people?"

"All sorts." Duckett sounded exasperated. "They move in with their relations—that's one of the things that make it so difficult—and there's overcrowding right off. I tell you, there's some decent parts of town that's a fair disgrace. And then they can't find work, and the climate doesn't suit them so they're on the National Health. Anyone'll tell you it's a reet mess, and Arkenshaw isn't the only place it's happening either."

"Somehow or other I got the impression that the employment problem had more or less solved itself by now." He glanced at Conway as he spoke, and Chris gave a quick nod of confirmation.

Sergeant Duckett said sourly, "That's all you know. There's some of them that feckless—"

"These investigations of yours, were you solely concerned to find out who had entered illegally?"

"Nay, I thought I told you. It was who was behind it I wanted to know."

"Someone in Pakistan?"

"Why should I worry about that end of it? The print job was done in England, at least that's what the experts thought . . . paper, and ink, and that. And if you ask Bill Sykes he'll tell you—"

"Is his name really Bill?" interrupted Antony, who knew the chief inspector well and was unable to resist the digression.

"Well, no." For the first time the sergeant relaxed a little, though he did not go so far as to smile. "It's Marmaduke . . . don't let on I told you. But, of course, we called him Bill."

"Of course. What will he tell me?"

"That the chap at the other end is a bookseller. Well, he gets parcels from all sorts of places, we don't know which is the cover and I don't know as we've much chance of finding out. The authorities *there* will talk about cooperation until they fair sicken you, but they don't really want to put a stop to the business, you see."

"So the main organization is here. But not necessarily local." He was watching the sergeant as he spoke, and saw him open his mouth and then shut it again with a snap. "You think it is here . . . in Arkenshaw?" he prompted.

"I don't know."

"I'm not asking for proof."

"Which is just as well . . . you'd get none. But I'll tell you this, it's a moocky business. Someone's making a packet out of the poor sods—"

"How much?"

"They most of them play dumb, you know," said Duckett scornfully. "Hardly let on they know a word of English, let alone how they got here. But there was one that talked to me, said he'd paid a hundred pounds for his papers."

"That's the hell of a lot of money," said Maitland.

Perhaps pleased with the impression he had made the sergeant leaned forward and said eagerly: "If you ask me, it doesn't end there. When they get here they're scared stiff . . . and I don't mean of me," he added, with a return of truculence. "It's my belief they're still paying."

"Forged documents supplied on the installment plan?" He sounded angry and incredulous, and Duckett went on quickly, almost as though he thought the other man might consider him in some way to blame.

"That's what I *think*."

"Why?"

"Well, it's like you said, there's jobs to be got . . . now. There's some as go as servants, and the trams employ a lot, and then there are the mills. They may be living in over-crowded conditions, but the money's good. Then there'll be trouble . . . stealing . . . sometimes just food, and you've no choice but to believe them when they say they're hungry. Go back home with them, no furniture in the house. One place the neighbors told us they'd been buying stuff on the hire purchase . . . leastways, there'd been a young chap around each week collecting. Stuff had been repossessed said *our* chap (who'd been caught pinching food off the stalls in the market); funny thing, though, no one had seen it go, and he didn't know where he'd bought it, said he couldn't remember. Another of them told us he was hard up because he'd been betting, but *he* couldn't give us any details either. And the same young fellow— same description, anyway—had been seen calling at his house, but there was hardly a stick of furniture, nothing they could have been paying for on the never-never."

"Did he explain—?"

"I told you. Ask a question they don't want to answer, they just don't understand you."

"It isn't a pretty picture," said Maitland, and glanced at Conway again. To exploit the defenseless, wasn't that the height of cruelty? "This 'young chap' you speak of—?"

"A foreigner." He seemed to be going to leave it there, but then he added grudgingly, "Good-looking, they said. Well dressed, well spoken."

"And elusive."

"Seemingly," said Duckett, and scowled at his interrogator.

"Anything distinctive about him?"

"Nowt."

"Well, I can see why you want to find the person responsible."

"It isn't only that," the sergeant told him, as though the imputation of a sympathetic motive was somehow offensive. "There's the town to think of, and lately there's been that much graft."

"In what way?"

"False evidence, for one thing."

"That bag-snatching case you mentioned to me . . . who was the witness, the one who provided an unexpected alibi?"

"Another of these here foreigners."

"An illegal immigrant?"

"No. But I think he'd been got at."

"Bribed?"

"I've got no proof of that," said Duckett sourly.

"Violence?"

"Nor of that neither."

"And the man who was accused of bag-snatching?"

"The girl was positive enough when she identified him," said the sergeant resentfully.

"Yes, I'm sure. But who was he?"

"Ahmad Khan."

"Had he a job?"

"Aye, a well-paid one in the printing trade. As a matter of fact, he came to the newspaper first on, though he moved after a bit."

"You said . . . well paid."

"There was no mystery what he'd been doing with his money."

"A girl?"

"A local lass who did ought to have known better."

"Had he any connection with Beas, or Mohamad?"

"Not as I knows on."

Maitland's attention was concentrated on the sergeant, and rather to Conway's surprise he showed no sign of irritation. "Well, is this . . . this graft you talked about confined to the foreign population?"

"It's since they came," Duckett insisted.

"You say you've no proof of bribery. Did anyone ever try to bribe you?"

"They did not."

"Or use threats?"

"Not to me." He hesitated, and then added as though he were ashamed of the thought, "About the foreigners, it could be blackmail."

"Someone who knows who the illegal immigrants are, you mean."

"That's just it. No one believes me."

"But the witness you mentioned—"

"There's others."

"Have you had a case where an information was laid?"

"Well, only one. It was a family matter, a quarrel. That's what it seemed."

"I see. And when Inspector Townsend took over, did you tell him your suspicions?"

"Oh, him!" said Duckett scornfully. "He says leave well alone . . . stop the gaps. Immigration can do that at the port of entry now they know what to look for . . . let the rest go."

"So no one is getting in now without the proper papers."

"I didn't say that."

"Can't you give me a few more details?"

"Nay, I can't. Why should I, any road?" He was belligerent again.

"Then tell me one thing. Have you any reason to think that Ghulam Beas is in any way implicated?"

Very deliberately the sergeant piled cup and plate together, and pushed himself up out of the easy chair. "'Appen tha' means well," he said, his speech suddenly broadened almost out of recognition, "and 'appen tha's joost making a song and dance. It's nowt to me now . . . all this. And nowt to thee, either, think on." He stood a moment, glowering, and then turned to Chris and said brusquely, "I'd best be getting back." A moment later the door closed behind him.

"So that's what you think," said Conway.

Maitland had remained motionless through all this. Now he picked up his coffee and strolled across to take the chair Duckett had vacated, helping himself to another sandwich on the way. "What?" he said unhelpfully.

"That Ghulam Beas . . . well, I suppose, that he had some personal reason, not just spite, for bringing this action."

"The possibility has crossed my mind."

"But if that's the case—"

Maitland smiled suddenly. "What then?" he asked.

"If . . . if we could prove it—" He broke off, and slapped his hand down on the desk. "Why—good lord!— the theft might have been deliberately engineered."

"There are difficulties about that, you know."

"Well, but . . . if we could show malice—"

"It isn't as easy as that."

"I thought this was the kind of thing you were good at." Conway sounded aggrieved. "I mean, surely you can suggest something."

"A dozen things." Maitland was scowling into the depths of his cup. "If only I knew," he added slowly, "whether our client wants us to pursue the matter."

"He would if he understood the connection."

"Do you think so? He wasn't exactly cooperative, do you think?"

"If you'd asked him straight out—"

"I might not have liked his answer. He's mad to get to the bottom of this racket, and I don't blame him. But what if he thought Beas . . . oh, well." He looked up and added soberly, "I'll tell you one thing, he's wrong about the blackmail."

"How do you mean?"

"Well, if anyone's going to arrange for a spot of perjury, an illegal immigrant is the last person he'd use. Too vulnerable. That case he mentioned—the family quarrel—was probably just that."

"In any case," said Chris, "it isn't only the foreigners."

"This tale of bribery and corruption isn't just a figment of Sergeant Duckett's imagination then?"

"No, I wouldn't say that." Conway made the admission reluctantly and hesitated before he went on. "It's difficult to explain about Arkenshaw, sometimes I think it's as if there were two towns, one for the elect, you know, and the other for the rest of us. Only the dividing line isn't always very clear."

He paused, and looked at Maitland as though willing him to understand, and Antony said slowly: "You mentioned a solicitor called Walters . . . was that the name?"

"The one who acted for Beas and Mohamad in the summer? That's right."

"Is he a member of the establishment?"

"I don't quite . . . well, if you put it like that, I suppose he isn't."

He looked puzzled, and Maitland said vaguely: "I just wondered. But to go back—"

"I find it as difficult as Sergeant Duckett did to put a finger on what's wrong, but sometimes a case just feels that way," said Conway.

"Why didn't you tell me?"

"But this is different, don't you see? Iskander might have been got at . . . I know nothing to suggest it, mind. But Miss Garrowby . . . wait till you see her."

"Very well." He got up to refill his cup, and carried the coffeepot over to the desk. "There have been a number of charges of this kind of thing lately, up and down the country, but none in the Arkenshaw Division, so far as I recall."

Chris was uneasy again, and not merely because his cup had been filled almost to the brim. "It may be just talk," he said, and frowned reprovingly when Maitland stopped pouring and gave him an unbelieving grin. "Oh, well, anyway, there isn't any proof." The phone rang, and he picked up the receiver with an air of relief that quickly changed to reluctance. "You'd better . . . no, ask him to come in," he said after a moment.

Antony replaced the coffeepot on the hearth, and started across the room toward the door. "I'll see you in court," he said.

"No, don't go. It's about the case."

"Oh?"

"At least . . . it's Oliver Ward. Martin's father."

"Our star witness," said Maitland, with a private grimace as he thought how ineffectual the boy's testimony had proved before.

"That's right. What do you suppose he wants?"

"Don't worry, we'll know soon enough."

Oliver Ward was a man very much of Sergeant Duckett's build, but a little shorter and more definitely committed to stoutness. He had a faintly petulant expression, as though at some chronic grievance; but more than anything else at the moment he was a worried man. He hardly waited for Conway's introduction and the renewal of Maitland's offer to withdraw before saying vigorously, "No, no. No need of that. It's about that boy of mine."

"Is Martin ill?"

"No, not that. He's attending at the court, of course, waiting to give his evidence. But the thing is, Mr. Conway, it doesn't seem to me . . . well, what I'm trying to say is, need you call him?"

"Why, yes. I'm afraid we must."

"What good will it do, that's what I want to know? What good will it do?"

"He's our chief witness. You know that, Mr. Ward. I'm sure you followed the original trial."

"Of course I did. And that's why I say it's no good your calling him. You'll agree with me," he appealed to Maitland, who had retreated to his place by the fire. "His evidence wasn't believed before, why should there be any difference now?"

"Does Martin want to change his story?"

"No." He looked at Conway, and then back at Maitland again. "I can speak freely," he asserted. "The boy made a mistake, we know that; but he's stubborn about it, won't admit—"

"Aren't you prejudging the issue, Mr. Ward?"

"Hasn't it been judged already?"

"Far from it."

Ward's lips tightened. Antony thought, here we go! and waited for a tirade; it was a surprise to hear the other man saying mildly, "It's a strain, you know, for a lad that age."

"Martin's sixteen." That was Chris, feeling perhaps that he had been out of the conversation long enough. "Hardly a child."

"You young people!" Ward smiled indulgently, which quite revolted Maitland, and went on in a very understanding way. "I wouldn't expect you to feel as I do, Mr. Conway. But there's been talk, you know, people say he's lying, and we've got to think of his future, Mrs. Ward and I."

"You don't seem to have much faith in him yourself," said Chris bluntly.

"He believes what he says. In all the circumstances, I think he must be wrong." He looked at Maitland again, and added, "You won't mind my speaking frankly. It can't make any difference to your case . . . it's hopeless already." He paused, and then added earnestly, "Don't you agree?"

"Who lives may learn," said Maitland lightly. He unhitched his shoulder from the mantel, and strolled across the room to stand near the desk, looking down at Ward. "Since you ask me," he went on, and now his tone was se-

107

rious, "I don't agree with you at all. If Martin is an honest boy, and it seems he must be, you'll be doing him no favor by asking him to hold his tongue."

"Are you implying, sir, that *I* am dishonest," inquired Ward, bouncing up as he spoke. Even so he had to tilt his head to meet Maitland's eye, and this increased his annoyance.

"As it happens . . . no. Merely that I think you have allowed your—your paternal feelings to outweigh your discretion," said Antony in a honeyed tone. "But I'm sure Mr. Conway will forgive you," he added kindly.

Ward's color deepened alarmingly. "I take it, then, that you don't mean to listen to reason."

"It isn't really my decision. Will you listen to reason, Conway?"

"I would, with the greatest of pleasure. But I'm afraid, Mr. Ward, there's nothing I can do about Martin. We need his evidence."

"As you wish." The petulance was very marked now; he turned his shoulder to Maitland and addressed Chris directly across the desk. "You may regret this, you know," he said stiffly, and marched out of the room without any further words of farewell.

Conway sank back in his chair and expelled his breath in a long sigh. "Did you have to do that?" he asked.

"Believe me, it was quite irresistible." Antony's eyes rested for a moment thoughtfully on the door through which Oliver Ward had departed. "I'm wondering if, perhaps, it wasn't also informative," he said.

"What d'you mean?"

"I wish I knew." He stood a moment longer, and then moved away restlessly, across to the window and back again. "We were talking about corruption. Is he a case in point, or was it just coincidence?"

"You do ask the damnedest questions," Conway complained. "I don't know, but I think he's honest."

"Something in a bank, you said."

"Chief cashier at the district branch of the Northumbrian and Wessex."

"Still, if he *had* been got at, he could have gone about suppressing the boy's evidence some other way. Brought some pressure to bear—"

"There are two things against that," said Conway slowly. "After the publicity about the first trial, a complete reversal might not sound so good. And you don't know Martin, I doubt from what I've heard if he'd be susceptible to coercion."

"I see. All of which leaves us exactly where we started." Maitland took another turn across the room. "That free legal advice you spoke of," he said, coming back to the desk, "is that another arrangement of the Arkenshaw Society?"

"Yes, of course."

"There's no 'of course' about it. Or is there?" he wondered. "Is Findlater paying for this prosecution, do you suppose?"

"I shouldn't be surprised. If Beas consulted Jones, and Jones was sympathetic and talked to Findlater . . . it's a sort of logical progression, isn't it?"

Antony smiled at him. "So that's explained," he said. "Does the explanation content you?"

"What do you mean?"

"It still leaves one question, to my mind: which came first, the hen or the egg?"

His tone was frivolous enough, but something about his expression made Chris uneasy again. "There's been a lot of feeling," he said. "Victimization, that sort of thing. I can quite understand—"

"Righteous indignation," agreed Maitland, with a look of distaste.

"Why not?"

Maitland made no attempt to answer this. He went back to the window again. "A private charity of Findlater's," he said, looking out. "Not one of the society's benevolent schemes?"

"Of course not!" Conway sounded shocked. He waited until Antony turned around to look at him, and then added, "All this is guesswork, you know."

"I wondered how long it would be before you remembered that." He grinned again, seeing that Chris was inclined to be both puzzled and indignant. "About Miss Duckett," he said. "The question is, why *should* she have lost her job?"

"Local feeling." Seeing Antony about to speak, he added quickly, "She's been expecting it, anyway. I thought it was pretty decent of Mr. Findlater myself, but I wish now I'd waited and told Star tonight. If I hadn't felt Sergeant Duckett would be pleased . . . after all, even if they move, it's easier to find work if you've got a job already."

"Is that what they're going to do?" He sounded startled, and Chris eyed him curiously.

"What do you think?" he asked.

"I suppose . . . yes, I suppose it's the only thing they could do." He started to move back across the room, then paused and gestured in the direction of the window where the firm's name could be seen, printed backward. "Conway, Bates and Conway," he remarked. "Is the first Conway your father?"

"My great-uncle. He's dead." Chris was getting past surprise at the repeated changes of subject, but he did add, "Why?"

"You mentioned your father once or twice. Have you ever discussed this talk of corruption with him?"

"Not really. He's a G.P. and hasn't much time for such things. Though he does carry on sometimes," said Conway carefully, "about the general lowering of standards . . . everywhere, I mean, not just here."

"Spontaneous combustion?" Antony sounded interested. "That's an uncomfortable theory, you know. On the whole I prefer Constable Ryder's villain . . . the one who might have decided to 'get' the sergeant," he explained.

"Yes, but which do you think is most likely?" asked

110

Chris morosely. He glanced at his watch, and got up in a hurry. "I say, you know, we're going to be late."

Nothing more was said until they were going up the steps of the town hall between the twin lions . . . an intimidating pair of beasts, perhaps because of the suggestion that, though temporarily couchant, they might at any time turn rampant and pounce on the unwary. Antony was thinking that he knew now how the early-Christian martyrs must have felt when Conway interrupted his meditation, saying abruptly, "What are you going to do?"

Maitland turned his head. He sounded solemn enough, but his eyes were amused. "I'm going to take the first opportunity of talking to Grandma Duckett," he said.

This was too much for Chris. "Why on earth—?" he began explosively.

"To get my horoscope read, of course." He paused a moment before crossing the hall to observe Conway's reaction, and then pushed open the door that led to the courtroom and was immediately engulfed by a clamor in many ways reminiscent of the parrot house at the zoo.

Conway entered on his heels, and they reached their places just thirty seconds before the usher called for silence.

III

Maitland's first sight of Miss Emily Garrowby surprised him. He watched her covertly while she took the oath. But what had he been expecting, anyway? A typical old maid? If it came to that, she was typical enough: a tall woman, rather too thin; the tweeds hung like a sack, and the hat was, undeniably, a disaster. But there was something about her . . . a humorous look? It was odd he should think that, because obviously she didn't relish her present position in the witness box at all. Perhaps all he meant was that she was a human being, not a lay figure any longer.

111

He listened while O'Brien took her through her evidence-in-chief, which she gave in almost the same words as the transcript he had read of the previous trial. And his dismay grew as he heard her: a careful woman, an exact woman . . . no wonder the jury had given her credence. The charitable could think that Martin Ward had been mistaken, but nobody could imagine Miss Garrowby in error over so important a matter. And the trouble was—the conviction was forced on him as he listened—she was unquestionably sincere.

Understandably, O'Brien was rubbing her story well into the jury, taking no chances that they might forget what she said, or misunderstand its import. Maitland interrupted twice, when he felt she was being led too blatantly; and again when the mixture of O'Brien's conclusions and her own became too much for him to bear in silence. But he was in no doubt at all that his objections were unpopular, the feeling in the court was solidly behind the plaintiffs. Only the judge remained impartial, treating each point sadly on its merits as it arose, and interpolating his own questions from time to time in a despairing tone on matters he found obscure. Even Bushey . . . who knew what Bushey was thinking? And if Chris Conway was "for" his own clients, it was a somewhat shamefaced adherence.

O'Brien was finished at last. The witness was thoroughly calm now, her story firmly fixed, no doubt, in the collective mind of the jury. Maitland got up in his leisurely way, and watched her as she moved a little to face him. A sensitive woman, he thought, who had once been quite pretty. . . .

"Miss Garrowby, on the evening of twenty-fourth March you were looking out of your bedroom window?"

"Yes." She was nervous now, not at ease as she had been with O'Brien.

"This was at a little after ten-thirty."

"I am not sure of the exact time."

"But you had retired for the night. Perhaps you noticed the time when you went upstairs."

"It was ten-thirty-five when I turned out the sitting-room light. I looked round before I did so, standing in the doorway, to see if all was tidy, and I noticed the clock then."

"And after that?"

"I don't understand you, I'm afraid."

"Did you go straight upstairs?"

"No, I checked the front door and the back, and poured myself a glass of milk in the kitchen."

O'Brien was sitting back in his place, well content that the defense should be digging its own grave. Beyond his absorption with the witness Maitland was vaguely aware of this, but he hadn't time to worry about it now. He kept his eyes fixed on Miss Garrowby's face and prompted gently, "Did you drink the milk there and then?"

"I took it upstairs with me; *and* my book; *and* my reading glasses."

"Do you usually read in bed?"

"Always."

"These domestic details, Mr. Maitland—" said the judge on a note of protest.

"If your lordship pleases, I am interested in the time element."

"Yes, yes . . . but your interest should be confined to essentials."

"Assuredly, my lord."

"Very well, then. Very well."

Maitland bowed. It was perhaps as well Gilmour had no idea how little of his attention had been given to this exchange. "So by ten-forty . . . I think you said it was at ten-forty you looked out of the window."

"No, it was the police who said that."

O'Brien growled something under his breath.

Maitland said quickly: "By ten-forty your preparations for retiring could not have progressed very far."

"No," said the witness noncommittally.

"Your bedroom has a bow window, has it not? So that when you looked out you would have a good view of the street."

"Yes, a very good view."

"And Badger's Way is well lit. There is, in fact, a street lamp outside number nineteen."

"Between my house and number nineteen. I could see quite well."

"Tell us, then, what you saw."

There was a little pause, and the faintest quiver of impatience in her voice as she replied, "As I have said—"

"As you have already told us a dozen times," said Maitland, gravely sympathetic.

"Yes." She gave him a darting, suspicious look, so that he remembered her occupation and thought that perhaps she might be too perceptive for her pupils' comfort. "Sergeant Duckett and Constable Ryder were walking past my front gate. I know the constable to speak to, and the sergeant by sight. Farther away, passing number seventeen, were Mr. Beas and Mr. Mohamad."

"The two couples converging?"

"That is right. Then I heard—"

"One moment, madam. Am I right in supposing that you had also some acquaintance with the two men who are the plaintiffs in this action?"

"No, I had never seen them before. I should have made it clear—I believe I did make it clear in my evidence—that no one else was in sight."

"You did not see the two schoolboys at the other side of the road?"

"No, I did not."

"Your attention, in fact, was held by the policemen, and the two men who were approaching them."

"I could see the path of number nineteen quite plainly."

"You could have seen the other side of the road equally well, could you not? I believe my friend will admit that

114

two boys were walking there"—O'Brien, thus appealed to, gave a grim nod—"and yet you did not see them."

"I couldn't look everywhere at once."

"There could have been somebody on the path then, whom you did not notice because you were looking at the people on the pavement."

"No. I saw the path quite clearly; it was empty. Besides, I saw them meet and speak together, Mr. Beas and Mr. Mohamad—"

"Whom you did not recognize."

"—and the two policemen." The point of his interruption dawned on her, and she added, "There was no one else."

"Well, then, you saw the two couples approach each other. Was there any hesitation on the part of the policemen? Did they stop and consult together?"

"No." She frowned over the question, not understanding it. "They just walked straight on, and met the others at the gate of number nineteen. Outside the gate. But before that—"

"What, madam?"

"I heard Mr. Barlow calling out."

"Could you see him?"

"No. I learned later that he was calling from the bathroom window. The bathroom is at the side of the house."

"But you could hear him clearly."

"Quite clearly. He was shouting. He said, 'Help, help, murder.' "

"Yet all this time you kept your eyes fixed on the people in the street."

"I suppose I looked away for a moment. No more than that."

"And *then* the police and the plaintiffs met."

"Yes, they spoke together."

"For how long?"

"It seemed quite a long time. Perhaps two minutes. Then Mr. Barlow came out of his front door and ran down the path to join them. They all seemed to be arguing, and after that they went into the house. All except the constable, who stayed outside."

"And you went back to bed."

"I hadn't been to bed." Her tone reproved his inaccuracy. "And of course I wondered what was happening, so I didn't retire straight away."

"Of course not. Did you really think Mr. Barlow was being murdered?"

"My lord!" said O'Brien. He sounded as scandalized as though the suggestion was in some way grossly improper.

Mr. Justice Gilmour considered. "I can see no harm in the question, Mr. O'Brien," he sighed.

"My learned friend," said O'Brien, with apparent dislike, "is trying to confuse the witness."

"*Are* you, Mr. Maitland?" asked the judge, turning a melancholy eye on the defendants' counsel.

"Why, yes, my lord." He sounded cheerful, but inwardly he was cursing. Trust O'Brien to sense when he was circling before the attack; the impetus was lost now . . . and he had so few weapons, after all.

His lordship seemed a little taken aback by this frankness. "Well . . . well . . . perhaps—"

"I will withdraw the question," said Maitland hastily. They might be here all day while the old boy made up his mind. He started again, more cautiously this time, going over the questions he had already asked—because surely even O'Brien could find nothing to object to in that—and finished up as impressively as he could with the suggestion that the shouts from next door must have distracted her attention from what was going on in the street. O'Brien was looking like the cat who had swallowed the cream. "Badger's Way is a quiet road, I imagine," said Maitland, casual again.

"Very quiet." Miss Garrowby relaxed a little. She had been nervous at first, people said these lawyers could make you say anything, and this tall man who was questioning her might have a gentle, almost deferential manner, but she was quite intelligent enough to recognize the hint of cynicism behind the suavity. So far, however, it had been all plain sailing, and this was just another way of reaching the same climax. . . .

"Especially in the late evening, I suppose," counsel was saying.

"Yes, indeed."

"Not much reason to look out of the window in the ordinary way."

"I happened to glance out—"

"Your curtains were drawn back then. Were you undressing in the dark?"

"No. No, of course not."

"Tell us then what you did."

"I looked out—"

"You were preparing for bed, you told us that."

"I slipped into my dressing gown."

Maitland smiled. She wondered now how she had ever thought him casual; he had a sardonic look, she thought. "And the light was on in the room, and the curtains were tight drawn across the window. Isn't that so?"

Kevin O'Brien was on his feet. The judge said, "No, Mr. O'Brien," almost before his protest was uttered.

"Isn't that so?" Maitland insisted.

"I think . . . yes. Yes, that is correct."

"So before you could look out . . . did you switch off the light, Miss Garrowby? You couldn't have seen much of what was going on outside if you didn't do that."

"I turned it off."

"And you drew back the curtain. Why?"

"To look out."

"But why *then?* If you'd glanced out when you were ready for bed, when you opened the window perhaps . . . but a night like that, with the temperature in the twenties, you wouldn't want it open until the last minute."

"I always sleep with my window open," said Miss Garrowby, clutching at the only safe point in all this surmise.

"Yes, I daresay. But you weren't ready for bed, you told us that."

"I don't think—"

"You couldn't have completed your preparations in the two—three?—minutes since you came upstairs."

"No."

"Yet you turned out the light and pulled back the curtain, just to look out of the window on a quiet street with very little traffic and very few pedestrians. Have you some special interest in your neighbors' affairs?"

"No interest at all."

"And, anyway, they were safely at home, weren't they? The Barlows."

"I don't know. I don't remember."

"Then why did you look out? Something you heard?"

"Perhaps."

"What then, what did you hear?"

He was pressing his questions now, and she looked at him helplessly. "I don't know."

"I think I can tell you, Miss Garrowby. You heard your neighbor, Mr. Barlow, shouting from his bathroom window, and it was perfectly natural for you to want to know what it was all about. But by the time you got to the window—by the time you had slipped into your dressing gown, and turned out the light, and drawn back the curtain—Ghulam Beas and Chakwal Mohamad must already have been talking to the two police officers by the gate of number nineteen." He paused a moment, and then added deliberately, "I suggest to you, madam, that that is what you saw. You couldn't possibly have seen them walking along the pavement."

And, incredibly, he saw that the shot had gone home. The words of protest were there, "No . . . that isn't right . . . I *did* see them." But she was shaken, only too clearly shaken; it showed in her face, and in the desperation with which she spoke. When she had finished, she stood staring at him, tugging at her pearls.

118

Maitland, waiting for the inevitable furor of O'Brien's objections to subside, hardly heard what the plaintiffs' counsel was saying. Bushey looked up and grinned at him; he didn't notice that either; he had reached the point he wanted, but there was still one thing more.

O'Brien sat down again, obviously dissatisfied. Presumably Gilmour hadn't taken kindly to the interruption. "You may proceed, Mr. Maitland," said the judge; he sounded as though the prospect depressed him. Maitland raised his eyes and looked across at the witness again.

"There is just one more question I wish to ask you, Miss Garrowby, and I want you to consider it carefully. Do you understand . . . fully . . . the implications of the evidence you have given in this court?"

The woman in the witness box stared back at him. She had a sudden, insane feeling that this couldn't be happening . . . that she, Emily Garrowby, in her old tweeds and the felt hat she had worn only once before, at the "other" trial, should be standing here swearing two lives away. That was what it amounted to, wasn't it? . . . or nearly. Because Constable Ryder might be young enough to make a fresh start, but Sergeant Duckett wasn't. Defending two innocent men had been one thing . . . a duty . . . inescapable. This was different. She didn't like the idea, she wasn't a vindictive woman . . . only now she felt almost vindictive toward counsel, who was bringing her face to face with the difference, making her regard it. It wasn't fair, just as his cross-examination hadn't been fair . . . leading her on . . . deceiving her. And how was she to blame? It is the truth that will destroy them, she told herself, stiffening her resolution; the truth, not I.

A long moment of silence. "I understand quite well," said Miss Garrowby, speaking very slowly and clearly. "But I have only borne witness to the truth."

IV

After that, as was to be expected, O'Brien's reexamination was not conducted in any haste. It was growing dark outside the long windows, and the lights in the court had been switched on for some time, when the prosecution's case was closed and Maitland—with a hopeful look at the judge in case he was ready to adjourn—got up to open for the defense. He stood a moment, shuffling his notes, as though they weren't completely illegible, even to himself; it required a conscious effort to bring the right note of easy confidence into his voice.

Bushey, beside him, thought, "He's pleased with the way things went this afternoon, I just hope he's not making too much of it." Conway, who couldn't see counsel's face, but who thought he was coming to know him very well indeed, was aware of something amiss; he couldn't understand it. Maitland should have been encouraged at least . . . the length of O'Brien's reexamination of Miss Garrowby was in itself a triumph. Kevin O'Brien, who knew his opponent fairly well and didn't trust him an inch, watched him with open bewilderment for a moment before retreating into the refuge of his own thoughts. Maitland was tired, that was it; he was holding himself more stiffly than usual, which was always a sign, but he had enough sense to hide his weariness from the jury. He was talking about his clients, about the story they would have to tell. . . .

". . . and as it was a cold night they were walking down the road together, rather than stand talking on the corner. My learned friend has given his version of what happened next, but I think you may feel that everything went too easily, too smoothly, that—according to his story—they seem to have worked together as a well-rehearsed team . . . when, after all, they could have had no previous knowledge of the situation into which they would fall. Are we to believe that they had agreed together on some previous occasion, 'If ever we get a chance we will frame a charge against two of the foreigners who have made their homes in Arkenshaw'? What would have been the point of such a plan? Had they some special cause of malice toward the plaintiffs, or would any of their fellow countrymen have done as well? And even supposing the latter to be true, why should they have supposed that such an opportunity would ever present itself? The witnesses are agreed, even Mr. Beas and Mr. Mohamad agree, that there was no consultation between my clients in the moments immediately preceding the arrest. Then we must consider—"

Listening, O'Brien was generous enough to admit it was effective, but there was a slow-burning anger in him too; for himself, he wouldn't have defended those two bastards for a pension. They'd get what was coming to them, he'd see to that, but he didn't like Maitland's part in the business. It was Kevin O'Brien's simple belief that he had given up all his illusions long ago, so what he felt was disappointment merely, nothing to do with surprise.

Maitland, trying to hear his own words objectively, recognized his speech for what it was: a piece of special pleading, with no conviction behind it. He thought, still objectively, that the jury were not unimpressed; O'Brien was simmering gently; Mr. Justice Gilmour looked sadder than ever. He'd adjourn, for a certainty, as soon as this was over. Best not be too long about it anyway; the jury might begin to realize how skeletal a structure he was building. And when he had finished, when the judge had decided he could bear no more and dismissed them all for the day, there'd still be Conway's questions to face, because probably he was inexperienced enough to think . . .

He began to wonder, idly, whether Chris felt he was getting his money's worth. He might have preferred some high-flown talk of *nisi prius* actions, joint tort-feasors, and injuries *ex delicto*. But would an Arkenshaw jury have stood for that kind of thing? O'Brien hadn't risked it either.

"But I don't understand," said Chris Conway, forty minutes later. The court had emptied itself with alacrity; only O'Brien and his satellites were left, conferring in low tones near the doorway, and Maitland, who had sat down in his place again after the judge had gone and was now

121

piling his books and papers together with all the deliberation of a man erecting a house of cards. "I don't understand," repeated Chris, facing him across the table. "I thought it was pretty good . . . Miss Garrowby, I mean. I know she didn't admit anything—"

"It had to be done." Maitland looked up at John Bushey, who was standing beside him poised for instant flight. "It wasn't all gain," he said. "*You* know."

Bushey, who had been completely deceived in his leader's mood, found himself reassuring where he had expected to have to depress overconfidence. "It gives us a chance," he said. "They may listen to the Ward boy now."

"But—" said Conway.

"You said yourself she didn't admit anything. Her—her consternation," said Maitland carefully, "doesn't prove a thing."

"It's the impression on the jury that matters."

"She has the air of a martyr," said Maitland, absorbed in his own thoughts and disregarding this obvious truth.

"Do you think so?"

"Well, at least, of someone utterly sure of her cause. As for the jury, what do you suppose they'll think by the time O'Brien's through with our witnesses. He'll be out for blood, make no mistake about that. And by the time he's finished with racial prejudice, and the persecution of innocent strangers, and my badgering of a defenseless maiden lady . . . you want to be off, Bushey. Don't let me keep you."

"Well—" said John.

"There's no more to be said tonight. We're coming now." But he watched his junior cross the court and disappear into the lobby, and still made no attempt to move. Chris bent down and started bundling the documents unceremoniously into Maitland's briefcase.

"I don't care, you ought to be pleased about it," he said stubbornly. "So what's the matter?"

Antony smiled at him, a little wryly. "I'm wondering if O'Brien's right . . . what he's thinking," he explained.

122

"You can't know—"

"Oh, yes, I can." He paused, watching Chris's hands tugging at the straps of the briefcase. " 'For your legal cause or civil you fight well and get your fee,' " he said, and raised his head to meet Conway's bewildered look. "I'm sorry, you don't read Chesterton, do you? I seem to have him on the brain, but this is so very apt."

"I don't understand."

"Of course you don't.

> For your legal cause or civil
> You fight well and get your fee;
> For your God or dream or devil
> You will answer, not to me.

Though I wouldn't be at all sure O'Brien's feeling as reasonable as all that," he added reflectively, and came at last to his feet.

Conway tucked the briefcase firmly under his arm. "I'll get the car and run you back to the hotel," he said, and this time there was some humor in Maitland's grin. "What then?" Chris demanded abruptly as they went toward the door.

"I shall ask for an early dinner, and then—remember?— I want to see Mrs. Duckett. What are the chances of my finding her alone?"

"Wednesday evening . . . Sergeant Duckett usually goes to the Slubbers' Arms to play darts."

"What on earth is a slubber?" Antony demanded.

"Chap who prepares the wool for spinning," said Chris, in an any-fool-knows-that tone of voice.

"Just think how much fun Gilmour could have with that one." Maitland sounded regretful.

"I daresay. But as for Sergeant Duckett, with all that's happened—" said Conway doubtfully.

"He'll go. Now of all times."

"I suppose . . . yes, I think you're right. And Star will be out," he added positively. "You can rely on that."

"Good."

"So you can have a nice, peaceful talk. But I think you might tell me," said Chris, pushing open the swing door, "what you want to see Grandma for."

"I did tell you." He glanced sidelong at his companion and added, annoyingly, "I can't help it, can I, if you don't believe me?" And then he saw that Kevin O'Brien, with his instructing solicitor in attendance, was still lingering on the pavement outside.

Jones was turning away as they reached the bottom of the steps, and paused only briefly to greet them; but O'Brien stayed where he was and favored them with his most amiable smile. "Are you coming back to the hotel, Maitland?"

"I'll get the car," Chris offered. "There's plenty of room."

"Sure, and we'll not be troubling you," said O'Brien briskly. "Good night to you, now." He turned away, and Antony glanced ruefully at Chris before he followed, turning up the collar of his raincoat. "It's a fine night for a walk," added O'Brien inaccurately, as they fell into step together.

The weather had turned muggy, and a fine drizzle was falling. "Let's just say we need the exercise," Maitland suggested. They crossed the street and started down the hill between tall blocks of office buildings, soot encrusted.

"I was talking to Jones when you came out," said Kevin, ignoring the correction.

"So I saw."

"You've upset him," said O'Brien humorously, making no mention of his own feelings.

Meeting his eye, Antony was not deceived. He began to wonder what the other man wanted, and said challengingly: "Should I apologize?" It was an odd thing that O'Brien seemed to have the knack of making him feel at a disadvantage.

"What would you be doing that for, now?" The lilt—al-

124

most wholly spurious—was back in his voice again. Antony found it annoying, and his own tone was grim.

"You tell me."

O'Brien laughed. "When I think of Arkenshaw, it's always of a night like this," he said irrelevantly, and lifted his face to the rain.

"Nostalgic," said Maitland dryly.

"It is so. Always at dusk, with the lights coming on and their reflection in the wet pavement . . . we go along here," he added, grabbing his companion's arm and steering him into a narrow side road. It was darker here, with old-fashioned street lamps and cobbles underfoot. On the left was the high wall of a warehouse, with a row of what had once no doubt been advertised as gentlemen's residences on the other side.

"I thought—" Antony began, and stopped because he could see O'Brien was grinning.

"We could both do with a drink, and I'm still a member of the club. And if anything was wanting to complete my nostalgia," said Kevin, gesticulating toward the tall gable that loomed against the darkening sky beyond the warehouse, "that would be it."

"The chapel?" said Maitland, seeing the dim gilt lettering of the notice board, with only the words "Primitive Methodist" clearly visible at the top. But even as he spoke he heard the singing. "Oh . . . *Messiah*," he said, enlightened.

"It's the wrong time of year, of course," O'Brien told him.

"Surely . . . for Christmas?"

"In Arkenshaw we do *Messiah* in Lent," said Kevin firmly. (*"All we like sheep have go-o-one astray,"* thundered the unseen choir, with the usual Handelian economy of words, giving him the lie.) "Good heavens, man, it's the only amusement we allow ourselves." He caught Maitland's sleeve again, pulling him across the cobbles from one narrow pavement to the other. Their objective was obviously one of the larger houses, with a worn but highly polished brass plate over the bellpull that proclaimed the Arkenshaw Club. "Here we are," announced O'Brien with satisfaction. "Right opposite the chapel; you can't say that's not well thought of. If you need reviving after choir practice, or are in need of a little uplift after a lively evening—" He broke off as he pushed the door open, and grinned appreciatively when he saw the gloomy comfort of the hall and its unmistakable air of rectitude. "Well, perhaps not lively," he said. "But at least they'll give us a drink, which is more than we'd get across the way."

"I didn't know there were any Primitive Methodists now," said Maitland as he removed his coat. The point had been worrying him ever since they passed the chapel.

"There aren't." O'Brien was still unaccountably cheerful. "Not since nineteen-thirty-something. But you can't expect Arkenshaw to change anything so quickly, especially as the sign's still legible."

The bar was paneled, and no more cheerful than the hall had been. The steward, who greeted O'Brien by name, looked at least ninety and received their order in a depressed way as though his worst fears had been confirmed. "Later in the evening," murmured Antony, following his host to a table strategically placed near the radiator, "I've no doubt the revelries commence."

"The attendance will go up," said Kevin. This wouldn't be difficult; at present they were alone in the room. "To tell you the truth," he added, looking around, "it doesn't change much."

"I don't suppose it does," said Antony. The steward reappeared with the drinks, and departed sighing.

"Cheers." O'Brien raised his glass, and sipped, and set it down again with a quick nod of approval. "When I was a boy," he said, "I used to imagine the Bacchanalian orgies that went on behind this respectable facade."

"The reality must have come as a shock to you."

"That's part of growing up, isn't it . . . the disillusionment." Maitland glanced at him, but the remark, it

126

seemed, was to be taken at face value. "I used to think, too, that *Messiah* was the most splendid thing I'd ever heard, and wish it wasn't always 'the others' who did it."

The room was warm and the chairs unexpectedly comfortable, and the Scotch—a blend unfamiliar to Maitland —went down extremely well. Perhaps a reminiscent vein was only to be expected; perhaps there was something to be said for the Arkenshaw Club, after all. Antony abandoned himself to his companion's mood, grunted encouragingly, and disposed himself to listen.

"There was a woman at our church," Kevin was saying, "who sang twice as loudly as anyone else—"

"There always is."

"—and half a beat ahead, too. The choir got discouraged, and just faded away. Musically, we had to be content with church concerts . . . have you ever been to a church concert, Maitland?"

"No."

"Where *were* you brought up?" asked O'Brien, raising his glass and squinting at the contents in a most distracting way.

"In Sussex, but I usually went abroad in the school holidays. My father was foreign correspondent for *The Courier,* so I joined him if he wasn't too far away." He paused, but O'Brien seemed to be waiting for him to continue and after a moment he went on. "Dad expected a fair degree of independence, and by the time I was thirteen—which is when he died—I could find my way over most of Europe without any fuss."

"And after that?"

"I was in London with my uncle."

"No more dashing about the Continent?"

"Oh, well, sometimes, in the long vacation. Uncle Nick was quite shocked the first time, I remember, because *I* wanted to organize *him.* After that, I emulated Br'er Fox."

"Sir Nicholas Harding," said Kevin, drawing out the words so that they became almost a question. "You're still associated with him, aren't you?"

127

"Yes, of course." (Surely O'Brien knew this part of his history at least.) "I've been in his chambers ever since I left Whitehead in 1950."

"I didn't know you were with Joe Whitehead."

"He was a nice old boy; I rather think I was a trial to him."

"No!"

"And to bring you up to date," said Maitland, with a touch of malice in his tone, "the house—my uncle's house in Kempenfeldt Square—was divided years ago to give us our own quarters."

"Convenient." O'Brien showed no signs of being abashed.

"And sometimes exasperating."

"I can imagine that," said Kevin encouragingly.

The conversation seemed to have got off the rails somewhere. "Talking of church concerts, they're a provincial phenomenon, aren't they?" said Antony, wrenching it back again with more determination than tact.

"Yes, I suppose they are." O'Brien showed no unwillingness to return to their point of departure. "There was always a little man who fancied himself as a comedian, who used to sing, 'I met her in the garden where the praties grow'; and a large stout, sentimental man in a brown suit . . . *he* used to sing 'The Rose of Tralee.'"

"It must have been a riot," said Antony, awed by this glimpse of debauchery, Arkenshaw style. "I can see I missed something."

"Half your education," O'Brien told him. "I used to think it would be worth going over to chapel, just to hear *Messiah* right through."

"Do you still think so?"

"My horizons have broadened." He sounded half-apologetic. "I'm more interested in people now . . . what makes them tick."

Antony thought, "So I'd noticed." Aloud he said, "I met a Mr. Findlater today."

"Frank Findlater? Did you, now?"

"Is he an old friend of yours?" (After all, if it came to being inquisitive, why should O'Brien have it all his own way?)

"No," said Kevin. And then, relenting, "Of course I knew *of* him. He seems a friendly soul."

"He was with your Mr. Jones."

"I've known Johnny Jones for years . . . well, ten at least, since the first time he briefed me." He paused, and when he went on it was to twist the subject as drastically as Maitland had done a moment before. "Do you know, one of my happiest memories is hearing Mrs. Maitland explaining the plot of *Rigoletto* to someone at a party."

"Jenny's explanations are notoriously involved." Antony found O'Brien's eyes fixed on him speculatively and thought with surprise: "It's almost as if he wanted to know what sort of terms we were on . . . which is nonsense, I must be imagining things. Or else the whisky is more potent than I thought."

As though to contradict this idea, Kevin picked up his glass and drained it. "Another?" he asked.

"Thanks, but I want to get back." He was uneasy suddenly, as he had been the evening before; and with as much, or as little, reason. "It was good of you—"

They walked back to the hotel in an almost unbroken silence.

V

Having proved his valor once on the tramway system, Antony had no qualms about taking a cab out to Old Peel Farm, particularly as it was now raining steadily. He had forgotten to ask Conway for Duckett's address, but luckily found it among his papers.

There was a light over the front door, perhaps because Star was out; the flagged path looked smooth and slippery under the rain. He rang the bell, and for a long time nothing happened. He was trying to remember whether Chris

129

had rung or knocked when the door opened without warn
ing and he saw Mrs. Duckett's dumpy figure silhouette
against the light from the hall. She peered at him for an in
stant and then said, "Mr. Maitland," and opened the doo
more widely. He thought she sounded relieved, but whe
he could see her clearly her face showed no sign of emc
tion. At her direction he took off his damp raincoat an
hung it on one of the pegs at the back of the hall. When h
turned back to her again he found her eyes fixed on hir
somberly, and perhaps he looked inquiring, because sh
said abruptly, "I didn't know who it might be."

This seemed rather an obvious statement, and sh
wasn't a nervous woman. "Have people been botherin
you?" he asked.

"It's Mischief Night, you know." But he thought sh
was being deliberately evasive. She pushed open the doc
to the kitchen, saying as she did so, "Switch off the light a
you come through." When he had obeyed and followe
her, she took her usual chair, and motioned him to one a
the other side of the hearth with one of her regal gesture

"I'd rather have this—this hassock thing," he told he
and sat down on it, hugging his knees. "Have people bee
bothering you?" he asked again.

"You might say so."

"Has anyone been here?"

"Not yet." She acknowledged his interest with one o
her grim smiles. "There were some letters for Fred, nast
things. I put them on the fire. And all day the phone wa
ringing—"

"Something can be done about that," he told her.

"That's what Fred said. "There'll be no more of that, h
said. So I thought perhaps, when they found they couldn'
get through . . . but, there now, people will be rud
enough on the telephone, when they wouldn't say 'boo' t
your face."

It would take a brave man, he thought, not looking a
her now. The fire was bright, and the kettle on the hob wa

just beginning to sing. Grandma wouldn't appreciate a show of concern, an indomitable old lady . . .

"Fred's not at home," she said, into the silence.

"It was you I wanted to see."

She pondered that for a moment, watching him. A nice-looking young man, she thought, though he'd do with a bit of feeding up, and perhaps was too given to levity; but he wasn't amused now; he was staring into the fire and he looked tired and anxious. She said with a roughness that should have hidden her tension, "You're troubled in your mind?"

"Yes. I suppose you could say, that's why I came."

"Not for your horoscope?" (So Chris had told her to expect him.)

"No." It was a full ten seconds before it occurred to him that the monosyllable alone was rather less than polite, and he looked up at her with a quick smile of apology. He found her eyes fixed on his face, gravely, but apparently without offense.

"How can I help you then?" she asked.

"It's a little difficult to explain."

"Yes," she agreed. She didn't sound sympathetic. Antony looked into the fire again.

"I wonder if you understand that in a civil action like this my duty to my clients isn't precisely the same as in a criminal case," he said. "I mean, if they persisted in saying they were innocent and I was personally satisfied of their guilt, I'd be under no compulsion to act. I wouldn't have to be *sure*."

"Don't beat about the bush, young man," she ordered sharply. "What are you trying to tell me?"

"I'm sorry. I was trying to explain. The problem is, you see, whether I should treat the case like any other . . . do the best I can in court, listen to the verdict, and forget it."

"That was clever, Fred said, what you did today," she told him in a grudging tone. "What more could anyone expect of you, I'd like to know?"

131

"If there's more behind it . . . if the case is being fought out of malice, or for some other reason . . . I could at least try to find out."

"And it isn't what 'anyone' expects of you, it's what you expect of yourself," commented Grandma.

"I suppose that's true." He shifted uneasily under the fixity of her gaze. "But if I do start asking questions—"

"You may find out Fred's guilty . . . is that it?"

He did not answer that directly. "I couldn't withdraw from the case now without prejudicing their chances. And I couldn't act on my present instructions once I knew—"

"There's the other way you said, treat the case like any other, don't probe to far."

"But is that fair to them?"

"You'd best ask Fred about that."

"That's just what I'm trying to avoid. For one thing, he doesn't like questions; and if he told me not to proceed . . . right or wrong, it'd put ideas into my head. If *you* tell me, it's still only opinion." He paused, meeting her eyes steadily. "I know I've no right to ask."

She said slowly, "You want me to tell you whether think our Fred—" She broke off, shaking her head at him.

He got up and stood looking down at her. "I'm sorry," he said again. "Don't get up. I can see myself out."

"Sit down and don't be a fool." This was very much in her former peremptory manner. "Do as you're bid," she added, as he hesitated. "Now then, what makes you think I'd give you a straight answer?"

He answered readily enough, but he kept a wary eye on her. "Because you've faced the truth—haven't you?—even if it is unpleasant."

"Do you think any woman's strong-minded enough for that?"

If he said, "I think you are," he'd only anger her again Even "Yes" might be dangerous, but he risked that much

"And if I tell you to . . . to —"

"To stick to my brief."

"Yes. If I tell you that, you'll do it?"

132

"I shall take your opinion without prejudice, and do the best I can for my clients on the information at my disposal," said Antony precisely.

"That's all very fine, but what will you be thinking?"

"It doesn't matter, as long as I don't *know.*"

"Lawyers!" she said, but her voice had lost its sharpness; this was merely routine grumbling. "If that's the way you all behave—"

"Don't be too hard on us," he pleaded, encouraged by what he took to be a sign of relenting; and added, recklessly, "Is that what you want me to do . . . stop?"

"Don't go so fast, young man," she snapped back at him. And sat glaring at him in silence until he began to fidget. "If you're gormless enough to go ahead with these inquiries you're talking about, I can't stop you, can I?"

"No," said Antony. He was conscious of a surge of relief, almost of exhilaration, because now his mind had been made up for him; so that for the moment he didn't even consider the difficulties that lay ahead. The problem of Emily Garrowby, for instance . . . "Grandma," he told her buoyantly, "you're a jewel!" And then, with belated caution, "I'm sorry . . . Mrs. Duckett."

" 'Grandma' will do, Mr. Maitland," she told him; not snubbing him, but keeping him in his place. Antony said, "Thank you," with unaccustomed meekness, and the old lady smiled at him, he hoped with approval, but it was hard to tell.

"We'll both feel better for a cup of tea," she said.

The teapot was warming on top of the range; the kettle had been boiling unregarded for so long that it was now spitting with futile rage. "Let me do it," said Antony, getting up.

But the heavy iron kettle was a problem; he had to turn his back on her to take it, clumsily, in his left hand. "We're a pair, aren't we?" she said, when the teapot was standing safely at the side of the range, convenient to her hand. "Me with my hands and you with your arm. Was that the war?"

Antony put the kettle down on the hob, and went back to his hassock. "In a way," he said.

"Come now! You must know that," she admonished him, and was surprised to see him flush.

"Well then, yes, it was." His tone was reluctant; he didn't want to talk about it, and the vagueness was in some way a protection. He was surprised to find himself adding, "It's my shoulder, as a matter of fact," in a voice that he hoped was as indifferent as her own.

"Hm," said Grandma, obviously finding the explanation inadequate. "Here's your tea, lad. Drink it while it's hot."

The shelf below the oven made a convenient place for the cup. "May I ask you another question?" he said.

"If you want to, no doubt you will."

"If the verdict is unfavorable . . . what will you do?"

"Sell up and go. What else?"

"I don't know. Would that be so easy?"

"I'm an old woman," she said, as though that answered his question. "But for Fred . . . no, it wouldn't be easy. Nor for Star, neither."

"No, I don't suppose . . . when you're twenty," said Antony seriously, "Everything seems to matter so much. But what I meant really—"

"We've had one offer for the house already. Kind!" said Grandma, not meaning it. "But it might be the best thing at that."

This was so obviously true that it left him without words. He drank some of the tea, and said after a while, "Beas and Mohamad. Sergeant Duckett thought they'd brought the case out of spite. Do you think I may be right . . . that there's something more behind it than that?"

"I've always thought so." She added, almost defensively as she met his eye, "You never asked me."

"That wouldn't have stopped you, if you'd wanted to tell me," said Antony, with truth.

She nodded. This time he was quite sure it was with approval. " 'Appen I thought you wouldn't believe me."

"Would that have mattered?"

134

"It's bad for me, you know, being thwarted." Her amusement was open now. "You wouldn't have said anything, but I'd have seen you thinking, 'She's his mother, that's just the sort of thing she would say.' Besides, I never thought you'd be willing to take it up . . . you, or anyone else."

"It may not do any good," he warned her, and drank some more tea; scalding hot it didn't taste quite so bitter as when it got cold. "Did Star tell you she came to see me last night, with Constable Ryder?"

"She told me." A certain satisfaction in her tone seemed to suggest that the confidence might not have been willingly made.

"Is there anything you could add to that?"

"No." But she seemed to be considering, and he sat quietly, watching her. "What do you think of Arkenshaw?" she said at last.

"It terrifies me," he told her candidly.

"Well, don't believe Fred when he tells you all the trouble is due to foreigners."

"He did tell me that," Antony admitted. "He also implied they were being victimized in some way."

"Human nature, isn't it? If someone's weaker than you."

"Yes, but—"

"If someone's bringing them in illegal—which is what Jim Ryder told you, I suppose—don't you think he'd go on using them, if it suited his book?"

"He could threaten to denounce them to the authorities, but he wouldn't dare."

"Do you think *they*'d know that? Think a minute, what it would be like." She paused, eyeing him, and then said, as though she were angry, "Aye, you've caught on; no need to say any more. Too much imagination, that's what's wrong with you."

Maitland said slowly, "A strange land, a strange tongue, and unfamiliar customs. And always the fear of being found out." He was thinking, too, of the "good-looking young chap" who went around collecting, ostensibly for

furniture bought on the installment plan. But if the ser
geant hadn't thought fit to mention that aspect of the affair
to his family, who was he to do so?

"That's right," said Grandma approvingly; he smiled
then, deprecating his own emotion. "They—they compli
cate things, I'm not denying that," she went on. "But Fred
says you were talking about graft . . . dishonesty . . ."
—the words seemed strange in her mouth, and she stopped
to savor them—"and that's been going on a long time."

"Yes, but is there any proof of that?"

"By their fruits you shall know them," said Grandma se
verely. And added, when she saw he was about to protest
"There's more ways of bribing a man than just giving him
brass."

"I'd thought of that," he told her. He sounded depressed
again. "It makes it difficult, being a stranger."

"Wheresoever the carcass is," said Mrs. Duckett oracu
larly, "there shall the eagles be gathered together."

"Yes, I suppose . . . yes, I see what you mean," said
Antony. He passed his cup for a refill, and went on think
ing about what she had said. But when she gave him the
tea he shook himself out of his abstraction. "You must
have had something in mind . . . or perhaps I should say
someone."

"I never did hold with scurrilous talk," she told him
flatly.

"This wouldn't be—"

"It would unless I could prove it."

One look at her face told him it was no use pressing his
questions, but he didn't want to leave too early. There was
always the possibility, unlikely as it seemed, that some of
the anonymous voices on the telephone might take sub
stance and come a-calling in person. Fred would be in
soon after closing time, but meanwhile . . . "How's Ura
nus?" he asked, and smiled at her.

"He is transiting in .Gemini," said Grandma so
promptly that he was immediately convinced she had
made it up.

136

"Is that good?"

"It might be a warning to some people," she grumbled, "if they had sense to take it."

"What sort of a warning?"

"To take care. But, of course, you don't believe me," she told him challengingly.

"Well—" said Antony. "I was wondering what sign Constable Ryder was born under," he added in a hurry, when she gave him one of her fiery looks.

"Sagittarius." She shook her head slowly over the information. "It's all very odd," she said. "But I only know his sun sign . . . the day he was born."

"Isn't that enough?"

She gave him a pitying look. "You haven't the faintest idea, have you? It's complicated . . . reet complicated."

"Is it, though?" said Antony incautiously.

"Do you know anything about logarithms?"

"Well, it's a long time—"

"Nor yet spherical trigonometry, I suppose," said Grandma relentlessly. He felt she had interpreted his hesitation fairly enough.

"I'm sorry," he told her apologetically. (And if this didn't teach him not to ask idle questions, nothing ever would.)

"Oh, well," she said, taking pity on his ignorance, "I don't myself, for that matter. There's tables, you see, where you can look these things up."

"I see." He was quite sure now she was teasing him, but while she remained serious it probably wasn't safe to venture the most feeble smile.

"You don't happen to know the exact time you were born?" she asked hopefully.

"I'm afraid not."

"Well, it can't be helped, I suppose. Nor yet if Scorpio was in the ascendant?" Her tone was almost wistful. "That would explain a lot of things, that would."

Antony mastered the temptation to ask, "What sort of things?" He had a strong feeling that he was probably happier in his ignorance. "We were talking about Constable Ryder," he reminded her.

"Yes, Jim Ryder." She paused. "Star's sorry for him."

"Is she, though?" said Maitland, a little out of his depth. From what he had observed, Star's sympathy was of a decidedly bracing nature.

"It's all along of this daft idea she's got that her dad's responsible. No, I didn't say she thought he'd done . . . what they're saying," she went on, seeing his startled look. "Only that it's because of him—"

"Yes, I see." His own idea, more or less, but to a young girl, perhaps, Ryder's plight might seem romantic. He considered the word doubtfully, and decided it might as well stand. Grandma, meanwhile, had returned to the heavens, and he listened dutifully. "It's the sidereal time that matters, you see; then if Neptune and Mars are in conjunction, say, with Venus in trine—" But she was an intelligent old lady, in spite of all this nonsense, and if she was right about the eagles . . .

She allowed him to call a taxi when he left, though not until she had assured him several times how easy (and of course economical) the journey would be by tram. She then told him crossly that if he'd a grain of sense he'd wait for "that Chris" where he was; "he's got to bring our Star home, hasn't he?" But Antony had no intention of having his talk with Conway under Grandma's eye (she might condemn it as "scurrilous"), and at last she showed him the telephone "in Fred's den"—a bitterly cold little room at the back of the house, with a roll-top desk and a hard chair; nothing whatever, in fact, to distract its owner from the discharge of his sergeantly duties . . . except, perhaps, the chance of freezing to death.

The Conways' house was only ten minutes away by car, a solid place in one of the residential suburbs. It was a little surprising to find half a dozen dust-bin lids reared carefully against the front door, where they would be bound to fall as soon as it was opened. He was stacking them on one side out of the way, not without a certain amount of clattering, when a little gray woman appeared in the doorway; the last lid fell with a clang, and she said angrily, "Now, if I have to come out to you once more—" She broke off when she got a better look at Maitland, added unemotionally—and perhaps by way of apology—"Those dratted boys," and then told him, "Surgery's over," with all the benevolent tyranny of a trained nurse.

She had a cold eye, but it was a relief to find that he wasn't being blamed for the booby trap. "As a matter of fact, it's Mr. Conway I want to see."

"He's out."

"Yes, I know. I thought perhaps I could wait for him."

She gave him a piercing look, as though she still doubted his respectability. Perhaps it was as well that Dr. Conway came out into the hall at that moment. Antony heard someone say, "What is it, Mrs. Foster?" and then the door opened more widely and he saw a sandy-haired man in a baggy tweed suit in a deplorable shade of cinnamon brown.

"My name's Maitland. I know Chris is out, but—"

"Come in, come in. That's quite all right, Mrs. Foster."

"It may be all right, Doctor, and it may not," she said; but she allowed Antony to pass. "We shall have half the neighborhood traipsing in and out tomorrow looking for what's theirs. But at least," she added incomprehensibly, before whisking herself out of sight, "they haven't taken the garage doors this year."

Dr. Conway led the way to a comfortable, untidily masculine room, and did not speak until the door was safely shut. "I have to keep an eye on her, you know. Keeping you standing in the rain. Take that wet coat off, Mr. Maitland. No, we won't go out into the hall again; just hang it over the back of that chair." As far as Antony could gather, he seemed to regard the room they were in as sanctuary, and perhaps not without cause.

"You'll have to tell me," he said, "why should they have taken the garage doors."

"Well, they did last year, you see. Mrs. Foster was very

upset. And I'm afraid . . . I'm very much afraid they
burned them. On the bonfire, you know. Sometimes I
think they're carrying things too far, but then again, if it
isn't one thing it's another, and really the degree of ingenuity required—" At this point he seemed to realize that
his visitor was on the point of going mad. "Mischief Night.
Mr. Maitland. And the police can't be everywhere at once;
I do see that. Now, you want to wait for Chris?"

"I'm really very sorry—"

"Nonsense! He has been talking about you, you know,
and you must allow me my fair share of human curiosity."
He twinkled happily at Antony and waved him to a chair
near the fire. "What can I get you to drink?"

Dr. Conway was very much what his son would probably be in another thirty years, his face more deeply lined
and with a general air of comfortable shagginess. Maitland
leaned back in his chair and stretched out his legs. "I've
been drinking sergeant major's tea with Mrs. Duckett.
What would you prescribe to take the taste away?"

"A Scotch, perhaps. There is gin if you would prefer it
. . . no? . . . quite right, I am always telling Chris—" He
broke off there and came across the room with the whisky
already poured. "By the way, do you know where Chris
is?"

"No," said Antony, and hesitated. The doctor regarded
the fire, poked it ruthlessly, added three lumps of coal, and
flung himself down in the chair at the other side of the
hearth.

"Is he with Star Duckett?"

"So far as I know." He wasn't quite sure whether this
was the right thing to say, but the doctor did not pursue
the subject, except to remark: "Then he'll be in at ten past
eleven precisely." He glanced at the clock. "Twenty-five
minutes. You know, Mr. Maitland, Chris doesn't talk to
me about his cases, naturally, any more than I tell him
about my patients; but I can tell he's worried about this
one of yours."

"I think we both are." He paused a moment, tempted to

140

let the conversation drift, to forget for a moment . . .
"You could help me," he said, "if you would."

"In what way?"

"I don't really mean gossip," said Antony, thinking as he spoke of Grandma Duckett's disapproval and sounding, perhaps, more apologetic than he intended. "But I'm a stranger here, and Chris is young . . . there are things he doesn't remember. Will you answer some questions for me, and not ask me why I'm asking them?"

"Provided I can do so with propriety. And provided, too," he added, less seriously, "that I shall not be putting myself in the clutches of some member of your profession."

"By getting sued for slander? Not a chance of it. Just for my own information." Seeing the doctor nod, Antony gulped some of his whisky, choked over it, and leaned forward eagerly. "More than anything else I want to know about a man called Jones. John Jones—he's the senior partner in Jones and Ashby."

"I've known him all my life . . . well, since we were boys."

"He isn't a patient of yours?" asked Maitland with sudden anxiety.

"No." The doctor gave him a long look. "Perhaps it's just as well you made me promise not to ask any questions of my own," he observed. "He's Ghulam Beas's solicitor, isn't he?"

"He is."

"Well, let's see. I don't remember his school, but I do remember we considered him rather a swot. He was articled with the firm he's head of now—Ashby, Ashby, and Parkinson it was then—and as soon as he got his finals he became engaged to Dorothy Thorpe." He paused, and then added dryly, "The Thorpes had money."

"Did the marriage prosper?"

"It lasted," said Dr. Conway. There was a little doubt in his voice. "They have two boys and a girl. The eldest boy's in the south somewhere—"

"Shooting big game?"

"Eh? Now, what do you mean by that?"

"You made it sound like 'darkest Africa,' " Antony apologized.

"Oh, I see." The twinkle was back in the doctor's eye again. "He's a research chemist, as a matter of fact. And the younger son has just started his articles with Johnny' firm; and the daughter married one of the latest crop of Findlaters—Tom, I think—last year."

"Frank Findlater's son?"

"His nephew. Frank has a brother, Victor . . . have we finished with Johnny?"

"You haven't told me whether his practice flourished."

"Of course it did. With the Thorpe money and influence . . . besides, I told you he's a clever chap. If he draws up your will, or a trust deed, or whatever it may be, you can bet your bottom dollar nobody's going to have grounds for disputing it."

"Nice for his clients."

"What do you think of him, Mr. Maitland?"

Antony thought about that for a moment. " 'I'm a genuine philanthropist, all other kinds are sham,' " he said, and looked at the doctor with one eyebrow raised inquiringly

"You can't catch me out on Gilbert and Sullivan. Besides, I once played King Gama at school. 'And everybody says I'm such a disagreeable man,' " he added thoughtfully. "Well, well, poor Johnny."

"Am I wrong then?"

"Let's say, not altogether right," said Dr. Conway with caution.

"Is he a philanthropist . . . the real kind?"

"He belongs to the Arkenshaw Society, if that's what you mean; we all do." He paused a moment before he went on, more cheerfully, "Now, there's a racket for you As much as your professional life's worth not to become a member. But, of course, it does a great deal of good."

"Mr. Jones," said Maitland, bringing him back firmly to the point.

"Oh, yes, well, he's one of the 'free-legal-advice' panel. Apparently 'legal aid' isn't as all-embracing as the National Health. And he's on the Scholarship Committee—"

"What do they do?"

"Decide who they're going to help through university, of course."

"How many members?"

"Five."

"Do you know who they are?"

"Only Johnny. And I think Victor Findlater. . . . They all serve five years, so one member changes every year. Retiring by rotation, I think they call it. But there's nothing to stop them being reelected, there aren't too many people with the time, or the inclination, to serve on a committee like that."

"Do you really think Jones is as affluent as ever?"

"He certainly shows no signs of penury," said the doctor. "These days, we're all feeling the pinch."

"Even the Findlaters?"

"Well, no, I shouldn't think so."

"Tell me about Oliver Ward, then."

"He's the father of one of your witnesses," Dr. Conway asserted.

"You promised—" said Antony, and drank the last of his whisky.

"So I did. I wonder what chance there is of my finding out from Chris."

"If you want to get me into trouble . . . I'm not sure he altogether approves of me," Maitland explained.

"That wasn't my impression. However . . . Oliver Ward is the treasurer of the Arkenshaw Society."

"Is he on this committee?"

"No. He's usually in attendance at the meetings, to see they don't get carried away by their generosity, I suppose; but he doesn't vote."

"That's the end of the story. How does it start?"

"I really can't help you there; he's only been in Arkenshaw for ten years or so. I've seen him in the bank, he seems happy enough in his job. Perhaps he hasn't the ambition to go farther than chief cashier."

Antony thought of the man he had met that day. "Perhaps not," he said doubtfully. "Is Martin an only child?"

"Yes, he is." When Maitland did not speak, he got up and took his empty glass. "Nothing very libelous," he said. "I can't imagine how it can help you."

Antony was wondering that himself. "All the same, I'm grateful." He hesitated. "Do you know Miss Garrowby?"

"Emily?" The doctor was busy with the decanter. "I remember her well as a girl. Used to see her at all the dances."

"What was she like then?"

"Very fair. Quite pretty. A bit too clever for some fellows' taste." He came back to the fire and stood a moment eying his visitor gravely. "I suppose you'd say serious minded."

"She's a schoolteacher," said Antony; not that he thought it followed.

"So she is. I haven't seen her for years, or thought of her either, till all this business came up. If you're wondering . . . I'd say her integrity was unquestionable."

"People change."

But in this case he didn't believe it, and he wasn't surprised when the doctor replied positively: "Not so much as that."

"Did you know Kevin O'Brien came from Arkenshaw?"

"I remember the family, of course. Quite a crowd of them, rather noisy, but at the same time self-contained. The boys all left home as they grew up, though."

"Yes, well . . . back to business." He couldn't quite understand his own reluctance. "The foreigners—"

"What about them?"

"I thought . . . have you any among your patients?"

"A great many. I have no acquaintance, though, with either Beas or Mohamad."

"No, this is a general sort of question. I just wondered how they live."

144

"As anyone else. Quite well, some of them."

"And the others? I've a reason for asking you that, really I have," he added quickly.

Dr. Conway relaxed slightly, his natural geniality reasserting itself, but his tone was troubled. "There should be some sort of safeguard for these people, before they're allowed to come."

"That is not, I gather, always the fault of the authorities."

"No."

"Have you some particular person in mind?"

"A girl, very young . . . sixteen . . . seventeen. . . . But I expect Sergeant Duckett has told you, if it concerns you in any way. I admit I don't see—"

"I'd like to hear the story from you," said Antony, with complete truth, if not complete candor. (It hadn't occurred to him that Dr. Conway might know the Ducketts, and now he wondered why.)

"She killed her baby . . . illegitimate, of course, but that wasn't the reason. She was half-starved herself, didn't know what she was doing; and she said it cried because it was hungry."

"But surely that needn't have happened."

"That's half the tragedy, isn't it? It turned out she'd come into the country with forged papers, and so she was afraid to ask for help."

"What happened to her?"

"She went into service; a good place, I made sure of that."

"But how?" The story had shaken him, perhaps all the more because of his previous excitement. It didn't seem quite enough to say there'd been a happy ending.

As if he sensed that his companion was disturbed, Dr. Conway spoke more cheerfully. "A benevolent conspiracy," he said. "I could testify that she wasn't responsible . . . and that was quite true. The sergeant was able to—to fix things with the immigration people; I wouldn't know anything about that." He paused before he added, too revealingly for Antony's comfort, "She lives in a warm house now, and she has enough to eat."

"Are there many like her?"

"There are many cases of hardship, certainly, particularly among those who have no legal right to be here. When they need help they're afraid to ask for it." He seemed to be assessing his visitor's reaction to the tale, and added, after a moment, "Sergeant Duckett hadn't mentioned her to you, had he?"

"No," Antony admitted, but he attempted no excuse.

"The immigrants as a whole cannot be concerned in your case." Dr. Conway was carefully keeping his bargain, but certainly he was curious.

"I'm not so sure about that." Outside a car slowed and turned into the drive.

"That should be Chris," said the doctor, and beamed with satisfaction when he glanced at the clock and saw that his prediction had been exactly right.

"Then I haven't time to explain," said Antony, relieved.

"Finish your drink, it will do you good; I shall take mine with me for a nightcap. I'm not expecting any babies tonight, and all my patients are too busy having flu to have time for anything more serious, so it's a chance for a good night's rest." He talked himself out of the room, and after a few minutes Chris came in.

He showed no sign of surprise when he saw Maitland, other than a quick frown. "I see Dad looked after you. Just wait till I get something for myself." He came back presently and took the chair the doctor had vacated. "What did O'Brien want?" he asked.

"To buy me a drink."

Chris looked as though he suspected the reply of being unduly facetious. "Odd," he said repressively.

"Very odd. We went to the Arkenshaw Club; do you know it?"

"Yes, of course, it's by way of being an institution—"

"It looks like one."

"That wasn't . . . no, but I see what you mean. The Arkenshaw Society has its meetings there."

"Part of the 'two-towns' setup?"

"I suppose it is. My father's a member, but he hasn't been inside for twenty years. With his kind of practice, that doesn't matter." Conway paused, and added awkwardly, "Being a doctor is a vocation with him." Antony, whose spirits were already reviving, gave him an encouraging grin.

"You haven't asked me how I got on with Grandma," he prompted.

"Well . . . how did you?"

"Pretty well. It was touch and go at one point whether she'd box my ears, but it all passed over."

"Oh, I say." For a moment Conway looked scandalized, but then he laughed. "I told you she was a tartar," he said.

"So you did. I'm sorry to lie in wait for you at this time of night, Conway—"

"That's all right."

"—but there are inquiries we should get set in motion before we go into court tomorrow."

"I thought—"

"I know. I've been dithering long enough. Have you a notebook?"

Chris pulled out his diary and a propelling pencil. "You're very decisive all of a sudden," he complained.

"Let's say Grandma has galvanized me. We'll start with Miss Garrowby."

"What about her? You said—"

"Heaven and earth!" said Antony with a sudden reversal of mood. "Whenever I think I'm sure of anything, I come up against that woman."

"It might help if you told me what you thought you were sure of."

"Sergeant Duckett. Disregard Mohamad and Ryder"— he dismissed them with a wave of his hand—"it's the other two who are important. And I've always had the queerest feeling that a man who christened his daughter Star—"

147

"But it's a *ghastly* name," said Chris, taking up, Maitland was pleased to note, the point of least relevance.

"Yes, but . . . oh, skip it. It isn't important."

"I'm not so sure about that."

"The man that has no music in his soul," said Antony vaguely. "I mean, I suppose it is music, to him."

This time Conway had obviously completed the quotation for himself. "That's all very well, but nobody ever said the opposite." He waved his pencil by way of emphasis, and added with an earnestness that deserved a more serious cause, "If you were tone deaf it wouldn't necessarily mean you were fit for treasons, stratagems, and—and whatever the third thing was."

"Don't let's bring logic into this," Maitland pleaded. "We've decided the good sergeant is innocent—"

"Have we?" said Chris, blinking.

"—therefore Miss Garrowby . . . well, that's what we've got to find out."

Conway restrained himself with an effort. "How?" he asked, flattening the diary on his knee.

"Well, first . . . I say, how do you manage to make one of those things work?" asked Maitland, his eyes on the silver pencil. "I never had one that lasted more than three days."

"I treat it," said Chris, with something like a snarl, "with care and consideration. *Are* you coming to the point?"

"Yes, if you'll stop distracting me. One, find out if Miss Garrowby has any cause for animosity against the police."

"Just like that!"

"I don't think it's very likely, but it will have to be considered." Antony disregarded the interruption. "It could be something quite simple, even something that happened when she was a child. Two—this might be more hopeful—who are her friends now, and is there one who might have influenced her in some way? Three, could she be being blackmailed? Again, the reason could be 'way back. Was she ever crossed in love, anything like that?"

"I suppose she was young once," said Chris in a tone hat belied the statement. "I can't imagine it, though."

"You don't need to. Any other information, of course, vill be gratefully received."

"Hell!" said Chris, still scribbling. "How do you sup- ose—?"

"You must know somebody."

"Of course I do."

"Well, if you're worried about costs, there's always the special' fee. Let's use that first, and then worry about the est."

"I can't do that," said Conway, horrified by the notion.

"You can with my goodwill, if you swear not to tell a oul what we're up to. I never feel it's quite fair, and I lon't suppose for a moment your legal-aid certificate—"

"What about your clerk?"

"Particularly not Mallory. I shall tell him I lost it, bet- ing . . . on the dogs," he added, thinking of Sir Nicholas ınd wondering, for an irrelevant moment, if he was still vorried about the tote.

"All right, then. But if you think we can put a full-scale nvestigation in hand in Arkenshaw without raising a dust, ou must be mad."

"Well, your father didn't really know anything about ıer."

"Dad!"

"Why not? He told me quite a lot about old rat trap, for nstance, though he didn't know much about Ward."

"I'd have thought he'd bite your head off if you started ısking questions out of turn," said Chris candidly.

"Perhaps he felt an instinctive admiration for my purity f soul," Maitland suggested. Conway showed his teeth ınd muttered something that sounded more like "Grrr" han anything else. "Then I want a list of the charitable ac- ivities of the Arkenshaw Society for the last three—no, et's say five to be on the safe side—for the last five years."

"That's easy. They publish an annual report. But why?"

149

asked Chris, his relief at receiving one simple reques
quickly overborne by his sense of grievance.

"Because there's more ways of bribing a man than joos
giving him brass," said Antony, absentmindedly mimick
ing the local pronounciation with wicked accuracy.

"That sounds like another quotation," said Chris resent
fully.

"It is. Besides the advice I went for, Grandma gave m
three very useful pieces of information."

"If that's a sample—"

"Don't be so captious. The others were 'by their fruit
ye shall know them,' and—this is the punch line, really—
'wheresoever the carcass is, there shall the eagles be gath
ered together.' "

Conway raised a hand dramatically to his brow
"You're sure you wouldn't like to consult Mother Shipto
too?"

"Not tonight, anyway."

"Anything else?"

"Yes, I've just had another idea. That chap Simpson—i
that right?—the features editor of the *Arkenshaw Tel*
graph," said Maitland with a smile that Conway, who wa
rapidly becoming overwrought, thought positively wolfish

"This is the end," said Chris. "What possible connec
tion—?"

"*I* don't know. He's had some dealings with Ghular
Beas. Write it down," Antony told him.

The pencil point snapped as Chris bent his head agai
over his notebook. "I don't understand what you're u
to," he said, screwing up a fresh piece of lead, "and I don
know why you're so damned pleased with yourself."

"Who was urging me, only today, to do something?
asked Maitland, declining to be ruffled.

"I suppose you wouldn't like me to put a shadow on M
Jones," said Conway sarcastically.

"It might be an idea. No, but you'll put him on your lis
won't you? And Ward, of course."

"Why on earth—?"

"Unless you know what he meant when he said you might regret your decision to call Martin as a witness."

"He was angry. People say things like that when they're annoyed."

"So I've noticed. And sometimes they mean them, too."

"Let's hope he doesn't come after me with a blackjack," said Chris, still skeptical.

"Stranger things have happened. You'd better put down the Findlaters, too."

"Don't be so daft," said Conway. And then, catching Maitland's eye and wavering slightly in his forthright condemnation, "Why?"

"Because . . . oh, because he's a friend of Johnny Jones, and sometimes one thing leads to another," said Antony vaguely. "And if you mean: 'Why any of them?' it's because we haven't a hope in hell of finding anything out about the illegal-immigration racket, but we may be able to uncover something through the local scandals."

"We'll uncover a hornets' nest, I should think. Anyway, why should the two things be connected?"

"Because Sergeant Duckett thinks so. He's got a fixed idea about the foreigners, and blames them for everything . . . which isn't reasonable. But leaving that aside he's no fool."

"No," said Conway, and shut the diary with a snap. "And if you recall, he also thinks the racket is still going on, in spite of the new precautions."

"Yes, that's a good point," said Maitland, with an enthusiasm that ignored his companion's obvious annoyance at being taken seriously. "Now . . . how is that being done?"

"Well, how?" echoed Chris, after a pause long enough to convince him that a reply was expected.

"Someone on the inside? I don't know exactly what's involved, of course, but if you could fake the application documents—the application for the employment voucher, that is—and had the right rubber stamps—or whatever—

151

to signify their acceptance, it would be quite easy, wouldn't it, to insert them in the files?"

"So that when inquiries were made . . . yes, I see that. But supposing an application had already been refused?"

"You're not trying," Antony complained. "Take it out . . . throw it away . . . that's easy."

"Yes, but this would mean someone at the Ministry of Labor, wouldn't it? I don't suppose applications are considered regionally."

"Find out! If our friend Mr. Ward, for instance, has a second-cousin-once-removed who works at the ministry, that would be suggestive. Don't you think?"

"I suppose—" said Chris, unwillingly. Maitland smiled at him.

"It wouldn't do to encourage me, would it? That's what I like about you people . . . so enthusiastic."

"All right! I'll find out," said Conway, as though he was uttering a threat. "But what else . . . I mean, all these people . . . what do you want to know about them?"

"Their connection with Beas and Mohamad . . . if any. Their connection with the people concerned in those other cases you were so cagey about, the ones that ought to have been bothering Arkenshaw's conscience for the last few years. Their connection with Ahmad Khan . . . was that the name of the chap who was accused of bag-snatching? Or with the surprise witness who gave him an alibi." He became aware that Chris had stopped writing, and was looking more unhappy than ever. "That rings a bell," he said.

"The—the other cases," Chris admitted. "I can give you one connection right away. A youth accused of indecent assault."

"Another Pakistani?"

"No. A lad called Thorpe. He's a cousin of Jones's wife."

"We always come back to Jones, don't we?"

"I don't know how we got to him in the first place," said Conway with irritation.

152

"Who was better placed to take advantage of the situation that arose when Beas and Mohamad were acquitted? If Beas asked his advice—"

"If . . . if . . . if!" said Chris, reminding Antony again, irresistibly, of his uncle.

"Was Thorpe acquitted?" he asked pacifically.

"Yes. The girl's father got up in court and swore it wasn't the first time. Always after the lads, he said. Well, of course, after that—"

"Unusual, certainly. He might have been in good faith."

"He might," Chris agreed, obviously not believing it. And added, "Crocodile tears!" after a moment's reflection.

"Very likely. And there's that chap Bushey said was a burglar—Lawford, was it?—I think someone ought to take a look at him. Not in the same connection, of course, but if anyone's worried about the way things went in court today there might be an attempt to tamper with his evidence. He'd be the best prospect, wouldn't he, if anyone wanted to?"

"I don't see how," said Conway, but he was writing as he spoke.

"I can think of ways. Oh, yes, and you'll work from the other end, won't you . . . put Ghulam Beas down, too?"

"I already have," said Chris sulkily. "Are you sure you wouldn't like me to add the vicar of All Saints' as well?"

"It's an idea. No, don't worry," he added, seeing Conway about to protest, and thinking he had probably suffered enough for one evening. "I think that's the lot, except that the financial position of the men on your list is also important."

"*Your* list," said Chris, looking down at it with loathing. "Do you really think that the person behind the illegal immigration is in Arkenshaw?"

"Sergeant Duckett does."

"And that this prosecution is a deliberate frame-up?"

"We've got to start somewhere," said Maitland reasonably. "And, taking Grandma's advice, we shall concentrate

153

our search on people who have in some way connected themselves with this trial."

"I think you're mad," said Chris for the second time that evening, but now with even more conviction.

"Then you'd better humor me, hadn't you?"

"But you said you didn't think the burglary was a put-up job," Conway protested.

"Not in that sense, certainly. But Barlow may have something to tell us about the real reason . . . no, I don't think either Beas or Mohamad was desperate enough to care about the contents of his wallet, or a few gold coins whose value they couldn't possibly know."

"Oh, for heaven's sake!"

Antony got up. "Bear with me," he said, and then, sympathetically, "You haven't really much choice, have you? Can I phone for a cab?"

"I'll take you."

"No, really!"

"I might as well," said Chris ungraciously. "Do you think I'm likely to sleep after all this?"

He didn't speak again until he brought the Austin to a halt outside the hotel. "Look here, Maitland, do you really think we can do anything?"

"I don't know." The exhilaration had worn off now. He felt tired, and cold, and horribly wide awake. "Tomorrow," he said, "and Friday, and the weekend. It isn't long."

"You said," Chris reminded him, with apparent inconsequence, "that if you stopped caring about . . . things . . . you might as well be dead."

Antony pushed the car door open and swung his feet to the ground. "I hold by that," he said. And added, as he turned to shut the door, "I never said it would be comfortable."

VI

Back in his room he turned his back resolutely on the telephone; it was far too late to call home. But then, as he was getting into bed, it rang in his ear, and a moment later there was Jenny's voice, not at all sleepy tonight.

"Did I wake you, darling?"

"I only just got in. I've been working," he added virtuously.

"How are things going? You don't," said Jenny, not waiting for an answer, "sound worried anymore."

"Well I am and I'm not." Any more explanations would be too much, even to Jenny; but, thank goodness, she'd never ask for any. "What have you been doing with yourself, love?"

"Nothing much," said Jenny, very offhand. "The daily round—"

"I know all that." He had asked the question idly, but now he was aware of a sudden sense of foreboding, not unmixed with amusement. "What else?"

"But, Antony, you know you told me . . . you strictly forbade me," said Jenny, obviously relishing the phrase, "to do anything at all."

"Don't keep me in suspense. What are you up to?"

"Only remodeling the bathroom," she told him, diminuendo.

"What!"

"Don't yelp at me, darling, you nearly broke my eardrum. You know we've said for ages . . . it's not that I mind a pink washbasin with blue cabbage-things all over it," said Jenny, obviously trying to be fair, "but it does tie your hands when it comes to decorating, and all those pipes and things—"

"You aren't . . . you aren't doing it single-handed, are you?" The hollow note was still in Antony's voice, but his eyes were alight with amusement. After all, he might have known . . .

"Of course not, I'm not a plumber," said Jenny. And added, inaccurately, "I know my limitations. There's a very nice man called Pat who does most of the work, and another called Mike who hands him things—"

"You're making it up."

155

"I'm not."

"They couldn't be called Pat and Mike," Antony insisted.

"Well, Claude and Cecil, if you'd rather. Don't spoil my story. You see, I thought it was such a good opportunity to do it without upsetting you—"

"The only thing you're upsetting is our bank balance, love."

"But we're not paying for it." Jenny sounded shocked. "That's the landlord's job."

"Does Uncle Nick know that?"

"Of course he does."

"What did he say?"

"He said, 'Thank God,' but I think," said Jenny honestly, "he was referring to the cabbages. And I know we were glad enough to get them when they pulled down number twenty after the bombing, but it will be nice to have something plain. Anyway, the worst should be over by the time you come home."

Antony wasn't quite sure how to take that. "Will it be safe by the weekend?" he inquired cautiously.

"Will you be finished by then? That's wonderful." It did not escape his notice that she carefully avoided a direct reply.

"Almost certainly not, but I want to talk to Sykes."

"Oh?" said Jenny blankly. Then, picking her words with care, "It's quite straightforward, isn't it, darling? Nothing that—that Uncle Nick might get annoyed about."

Antony grinned at the phone. "Quite straightforward, love. Nothing to worry you."

"I don't worry . . . ever."

"Of course not," said Antony, accepting the lie, and remembering, rather guiltily, the last time he had gone out of town to attend an assize. "As for Uncle Nick—"

"He's gone to the dogs," said Jenny dramatically.

"Come off it."

"I mean, really! With Derek. At least, he may be home by now."

"Well, tell him not to make a habit of it. At least," said Antony, yawning suddenly, cavernously, to his own great surprise, "not until he's paid off Pat and Mike."

THURSDAY, 5TH NOVEMBER

I

As was to be expected, each of the defendants in turn was detained for a long time in the witness box next morning. Their evidence was simple enough, but Sergeant Duckett sounded sulky, and the unfortunate Constable Ryder was obviously frightened to death. O'Brien's attack was in each case inevitable and damnably effective.

Nor was there much to be done to place matters in a better light. The only thing was to sweat it out (an inappropriate phrase in that bleak courtroom), and hope that the sergeant's sudden loss of temper when asked to repeat his story a fifth time, and Ryder's incoherence when the judge put a question of his own, would pass with the jury as innocent and natural. Maitland was quite sure they wouldn't, but hope—as Grandma had reminded him—was cheap.

It was over at last. The defendants' story of the evening of twenty-fourth March—that was so like and so unlike the plaintiffs' account—had been reiterated until even O'Brien must have realized there could be no further benefit in asking for it again. Unavoidably, there had been some stumbling, some hesitation. A question to Sergeant Duckett concerning the case of Ahmad Khan had been wrangled over and finally admitted. And the denials were over too, the look-counsel-in-the-eye-and-just-answer-what-he-asks-you-don't-try-to-add-anything-of-your-own denials that had to be demanded on reexamination because everyone expected them; but surely, thought Maitland, looking the jury over with a hostile eye, only the most trusting nature would give them credence, and if ever he saw a bunch of skeptics . . .

They gathered in a cluster in the emptying room as soon as Gilmour adjourned for the luncheon recess, the two policemen and the lawyers who represented them. Bushey said bracingly, "Well, that didn't go so badly!" but Maitland was preoccupied, and said nothing until the sergeant asked him directly, "Well, then, what are our chances?"

"You'd better ask me that again when we've heard the rest of the witnesses."

"That means you don't think much of them," said Duckett gruffly. And added hastily, before Maitland could say anything else, "Nay then, I don't myself." He then took Constable Ryder in tow—"You'll be better for summat to eat, lad"—and left his representatives to their own thoughts.

Maitland said after a moment, "Were you able to set things in motion, Conway? I'm afraid I rather sprang things on you last night." He was aware, as he spoke, of John Bushey's amusement. Bushey had been brought up to date that morning, but there was no knowing what he thought; he seemed to be something of a philosopher, and wouldn't be likely to make any protest unless he thought it would be heeded.

"I managed," said Chris. For some reason he glanced over his shoulder, rather as though he were fearful of being overheard, but the court was empty now. "And I got you these," he added. "Mr. Bates had them in his files."

"What? Oh, the Arkenshaw Society reports." He took a pile of booklets that Conway was holding out to him. "Very chaste," he went on, holding them at arm's length the better to admire the top copy. "Coat of arms, and lots of gold lettering . . . symbolic, I suppose, of their financial position."

"Symbolic be damned," said Chris, who seemed to be still out of temper.

"*Greenhalgh and Blackburn, Printers, Fellgate, Arkenshaw.* I've heard that name before."

"Star works there; she's Mr. Greenhalgh's secretary."

"I remember. Mr. Findlater talked to Mr. Greenhalgh, and . . . where do they hang out?"

"You'd pass their place last night in Fellgate, if you went to the club."

"Next to the chapel?"

"Yes."

"Well, they do a nice job. Stiff covers and all; do they do their own binding?"

"Oh, yes, they put out a lot of local stuff. Guide books, and poetry, stuff like that."

"Do they write poetry in Arkenshaw?" But he began to leaf through the pages of the most recent of the reports without waiting for a reply. "Annual Meeting . . . Balance Sheet . . . subscriptions . . . donations received . . . expenses (the printers aren't overpaid anyway) . . . Scholarship Committee (here we are). Our friend Chakwal Mohamad, tuition fees *and* a grant . . . Spencer . . . Arkwright . . . Bell . . . Townsend . . ." He looked up, frowning "That wouldn't be Inspector Townsend's son, would it?"

"I don't . . . what's the boy's name, anyway?"

"Alan."

"Then it is. What of it?"

"He's been granted the Thorpe Memorial Scholarship for the last"—he paused, turning the pages of the previous year's reports—"for the last three years."

"Well, that's reasonable, isn't it? No good starting what you don't finish."

"No good at all," said Maitland in an odd voice.

Conway said urgently, "What are you thinking?" and Bushey gave unexpectedly his noisy laugh.

"That perhaps I'm beginning to see how the milk got into the coconut," said Maitland slowly, and with complete seriousness. "Never mind. Let's see who these generous benefactors are."

"If you mean the committee, the money isn't theirs, you know."

"They only decide . . . Victor J. Findlater . . . John Cadwallader Jones (*nom d'un nom*) . . . Mrs. Martha

160

Hardcastle . . . the Reverend Paul Sinclair . . . Arthur Thomas. That's this year's list. Mr. Thomas took office last year, and Mr. Findlater, the year before, replacing his brother."

"Mr. Sinclair," said Chris, in an expressionless voice, "is the vicar of All Saints'."

"Is he now?" Maitland sounded delighted; it was only fair that Conway should get a little of his own back, after last night. "A very proper nomination," he added, catching Bushey's eye. "Can I hang on to these, Conway? I'd like to look at them more thoroughly."

"I suppose so." Chris sounded genuinely gloomy again. "You'll let me know, won't you, who else you want me to set the bloodhounds on?"

"That goes without saying." He glanced at his watch. "We've just got an hour," he said. "Shall we go back to the hotel for lunch?"

II

The curate of All Saints' Church (the man who was most concerned, as is the unenviable lot of curates, with the running of the social club) came up to proof. . . . "There is always a social evening on Thursdays . . . yes, I know Mr. Iskander well, he attends regularly, perhaps not every week . . . I had many interesting talks with Mr. Beas last year about his work." And so did Mr. Simpson, the features editor of the *Arkenshaw Telegraph*, whose task was merely to identify the copy of the newspaper dated the twenty-third March which was put into evidence by the defense, and to add under Bushey's prompting that the article he was shown was the first of a series by Ghulam Beas which had been commissioned early in the New Year. O'Brien had a scornful look, Maitland thought, glancing up from the strictly libelous portrait of the judge with which he was further embellishing the back of his brief; neither he, nor his junior, troubled to

161

cross-examine. For the first time, Antony felt that in his opponent's place he'd have played it differently.

Samuel Barlow took the oath nervously, with a wary eye on counsel, and his consternation when Maitland got up to start his examination was so obvious as to be almost laughable. Either this was natural (in which case he was hardly fit to be let out alone in this cruel world) or someone had been incredibly clumsy when Beas and Mohamad were being tried. Gently then . . . the little man could hardly object to giving his name . . . his address . . . his occupation . . .

"Will you be so kind as to tell us in your own words, Mr. Barlow, what happened on the evening of the twenty-fourth March last."

"We went up to bed at ten o'clock," said Sam, and stopped short as though he had come up against a brick wall. Maitland did not speak, but kept his air of courteous attention, and presently the witness went on again, saying very quickly, "We always go to bed then, unless we're out, of course, or unless we're entertaining. I *like* going to bed early," he added, and gave counsel a defiant look. Maitland, remembering Conway's description of the glamorous Mrs. Barlow, sternly suppressed a temptation to ribald comment and remained decorously sympathetic.

"But before you went upstairs—"

"I locked up, of course. The back door and the front. Well, they were locked already, I just wanted to make sure. There wasn't any need with the windows, I mean that weather, and I turned off the lights as I went, and the hall light last of all from the upstairs landing."

"And when you finally retired—"

"That would be at about twenty past. I'm not swearing that, mind, but it must have been about then."

"Thank you, Mr. Barlow. Were any lights left burning?"

"Certainly not," said the witness, as though there were some special virtue in darkness.

"Not even in the bedroom?"

"We're not great readers, Mrs. Barlow and me."

"I take it, Mr. Maitland," said the judge, grieving over the vagueness of this remark, "the witness means the bedroom light was out."

"That is so, is it not, Mr. Barlow?"

"Oh, yes. Yes, indeed."

"Your lordship is quite correct in your surmise."

"Thank you, Mr. Maitland. I think you should see that the witness is more explicit."

Counsel bowed. (If your bloody lordship hasn't given him the jitters. . . .) "And then, Mr. Barlow?"

"We heard a noise." He glanced nervously at the judge and added, slurring his words together in his haste to comply with the request for detail, "Well, it was Mrs. Barlow heard it first, and she said, 'Sam, there's someone downstairs,' and I said, 'There can't be,' I said, 'you're imagining it.' And then I heard it too."

Maitland allowed himself one reproachful glance at the judge. "What exactly did you hear? Footsteps? A door closing?"

Barlow gestured helplessly. "Just as if someone was moving about."

God send that was explicit enough. "What time was this?"

"I don't know."

"An hour . . . half an hour after you turned the light out?"

"Not as long as that. Not as much as a quarter of an hour, I shouldn't think."

"Did you take any action in respect to these sounds you heard?"

"I got up, and opened the bedroom door very carefully, and went out onto the landing."

"Carefully, Mr. Maitland?" Mr. Justice Gilmour seemed to be in an exigent mood.

"Taking care to make no noise, my lord. Isn't that right, Mr. Barlow?"

"Yes."

"And for the same reason . . . because you did not wish

to alarm the intruders," added counsel with a distinctly mutinous look in the judge's direction, ". . . for that reason you did not turn on any of the lights."

"Well, of course I didn't," said the witness, taking heart. "But once I got the door open, I could see my way quite well, because the light in the downstairs cloakroom was on, and when I looked over the banisters I could see—"

"The cloakroom light illuminated the hall?"

"Yes, dimly. I mean, with everything else dark it looked quite bright, and I could see that there were two men in the hall, but I couldn't make out their features or anything else about them. Not at first."

"But later you saw them more clearly?"

"If Mr. O'Brien has no objection to your leading the witness, Mr. Maitland," said Mr. Justice Gilmour reprovingly, "I daresay you will think I shouldn't mind."

"To save time, my lord, and in matters about which there is no dispute," said Counsel, nobly repressing the desire to express his simple agreement.

And O'Brien, half-rising, remarked magnanimously, "I have no wish to embarrass my learned friend," and sank back, well satisfied, when Maitland turned and gave him a furious look.

"I am g-grateful to my f-friend," he said; only O'Brien recognized the slight stammer for what it was, a danger signal. "With your lordship's permission—"

"Pray continue, Mr. Maitland."

"Please tell us, Mr. Barlow, whether you were at any time able to see the intruders clearly, and, if so, how this came about."

Gilmour looked almost approving, but it took the witness a few moments to unravel this complicated demand. He said at last, doubtfully, "I saw the men move across the hall toward the drawing room, and then the door opened and one of them must have switched on the light. And he turned and beckoned to the other, as if—as if he was impatient; and then I could see both of them, quite plainly."

"Could you identify either of the men?"

"No, I'm sorry. Only to say that they were foreigners."

"Foreigners?" said the judge, as if he had never heard the word before.

"In this district, my lord, I believe the word is generally taken to mean people from Pakistan."

"Is that what you meant?" asked Gilmour, looking straight at the witness, who wilted visibly.

"Yes . . . my lord."

"I don't see how you can be certain of that," said the judge discontentedly. "Indian . . . West Indian . . . Negro—"

"Not Negroes, my lord," said the witness unexpectedly. "I only meant to imply that they were colored, and there's that many here from Pakistan . . . well, naturally, that's what I thought."

"I'm afraid, Mr. Maitland," said Gilmour pettishly, "that in this court I demand a higher degree of accuracy—"

"I will do my best to clarify the matter, my lord," said Maitland meekly, and turned again to the witness. But this last, judicial snub had demoralized Sam Barlow completely; it took the best part of ten minutes to elicit the simple statement that he was sure the intruders were gentlemen of color, he couldn't—no, he couldn't!—identify them, but there was nothing in the appearance of either of the plaintiffs that made him think they weren't the two men concerned.

"But, of course, I only saw them like that for a moment, and then they went into the drawing room and shut the door."

"What did you do then?"

"I took Mrs. Barlow by the arm and I pulled her into the bathroom. It's the only room in the house that has a key."

"You locked yourselves in, then." He felt, rather than saw, that the judge's eye was on him, and added smoothly, "Why did you do that?"

"The—er—the telephone was downstairs."

165

"Yes?"

"I wasn't afraid for myself, of course," said the witness, almost gabbling now in his nervousness, "but Mrs. Barlow . . . I didn't like to think what might happen." He glanced rather wildly around and then added, audibly, but with an odd effect of making a confidence, "They weren't *white* men, you see."

"You were afraid for your wife's safety. That is very understandable, whoever the intruders might have been." He heard Mr. Justice Gilmour clear his throat and hurried on. "How long did you spend in the bathroom, do you think?"

"I hadn't my watch on, you know, but I should think it was quite ten minutes."

"Did you hear anything more from downstairs?"

"Not a sound. So after a little while I opened the window a crack. But I didn't see anybody about until Sergeant Duckett came along with the constable."

"Were they walking in silence?"

"No, I heard their voices first, and then I saw them."

"Did you take any action?"

"Well, of course I did. I pushed the window wide and called out to them, and they stopped and looked up, and then hurried along towards the front gate, out of my sight. So then in a few moments I thought I'd see if it was safe to come out, but I told Mrs. Barlow to lock the door again instantly if there was any need."

"Thank you, Mr. Barlow, that's very clear." (Heaven send his lordship thought so!) "Er—was it safe?"

"Oh, yes, all was quiet downstairs." Even this short freedom from the judge's heckling had restored the witness's confidence to some degree. "I went down—cautiously, you know—and there was no one there, so I put on my overcoat and went out of the front door."

"Was it locked, as you had left it?"

"No, the latch had been fixed back, and the bolt had been drawn."

"You said, did you not, that you had *locked* the doors?" Mr. Justice Gilmour complained.

"A—a manner of speaking, my lord. It's a Yale lock, so all you have to do—" The sentence trailed away nervously.

The judge turned an eloquent eye on Maitland, but made no further comment. Counsel said carefully, "You found the front door unsecured, and went out. What happened then?"

"I could see the four men talking by the gate."

"Duckett . . . Ryder . . . Beas . . . Mohamad," said Maitland with an inquiring look.

"That's right."

"How were they standing?"

"Outside the gate. Nothing to show whether Mr. Beas and Mr. Mohamad had come down the path or along the pavement," added Barlow helpfully; giving Maitland yet another proof—if he had needed it—of the disadvantage at which the previous hearing placed the defense. Of course, all the witnesses knew what questions to expect, but the effect was of a voluntary statement, something that had impressed them so strongly they simply had to mention it.

"Was the gate open or shut?"

"It was open."

"The four men were talking together?"

"Yes. I went to join them, and I'm afraid at that time I thought—"

"But after a little more conversation you all went back to the house," Maitland put in quickly.

"Yes, and that was when I saw my wallet. I said, 'That's mine,' and I was going to pick it up when the sergeant caught my arm. He said, 'Let's see,' and then, 'There's something else here, under the bush.' It just looked like a handkerchief, rolled up, but later I was shown my coin collection and asked to identify it—"

"All in the handkerchief?" inquired the judge.

"Forty-three coins, my lord. When they're not in their cases, you'd be surprised how little room they take up."

"No doubt I should," said Gilmour austerely.

"But at that time, you went straight into the house," Maitland suggested.

"I . . . yes, that's right. The constable stayed outside, 'until someone can get here from the station,' Sergeant Duckett said. So he phoned, and then he asked me if I could tell what was missing. I had a look around, he warned me about fingerprints—"

"In case one bit you?" asked Mr. Justice Gilmour with a sad smile.

"I don't—" Sam Barlow looked at counsel a little wildly, and then smiled in his turn, but in a sickly way.

"You might have obliterated them," Maitland told him.

"Yes, of course." Barlow was eager to please, but obviously rattled. "Well, I knew my wallet had been taken, because there it was, outside. And when I checked my coin collection, that was gone, too."

"What was its value?"

"It's insured for a thousand pounds. You see, some of the coins aren't worth anything, except for the interest, but one or two are old, and really valuable."

"There was a gold noble, was there not, that you were asked to identify separately?"

"Yes."

"That was part of your collection?"

"Oh, yes."

"My lord, I am putting this notebook into evidence. Will you look at it, Mr. Barlow? Do you recognize it as your property?"

"Yes, it's my record of the coins, my own writing."

"Will you turn to the place where the noble is described? Thank you. Now, if your lordship will be kind enough to read the entry on the left-hand page, you will find it describes exactly the coin which was previously introduced into evidence."

There was a pause. "I do not understand numismatics, Mr. Maitland," said the judge, looking up.

"The date, my lord—"

"Yes, I can see it is the same," snapped Gilmour, hand-ing the coin and book back to the usher, who carried them over to the jury box.

"Where were these things kept, Mr. Barlow?"

"In the bureau in the sitting room. The coins were in cases in the top drawer, and the wallet was in the top section. There is a flap that comes down for writing, and when I got home at night I just open that and slip my wallet inside, with my office keys, before I go upstairs to change."

"What else did your search reveal?"

"The cloakroom window was open. At least, it was shut, but the catch had been slipped back. It could have been done with a penknife from outside, Sergeant Duckett said."

"My lord!" said Kevin O'Brien, not at all averse from adding to his learned friend's discomfiture.

"You seem to have very little control over your witness, Mr. Maitland," said the judge, more in sorrow than in anger. Perhaps it was fortunate that at this point Maitland began to see some humor in the situation.

"It's very regrettable, my lord. Er—what would your lordship wish me to do about it?" His tone suggested nothing but the most abject contrition.

"You may proceed, Mr. Maitland," said Gilmour severely.

"Was there any evidence that the intruders had been upstairs at any time?"

"None at all. In fact, I'm sure I should have heard them, I was listening."

"And on the ground floor—?"

"Well, they might have been into the dining room, but there wasn't anything to show it. It almost seemed as if they knew about the coin collection."

"Had it ever been mentioned . . . in the local press, for instance?"

"Why, yes." Barlow sounded surprised. "There was a piece about it in the *Telegraph* once."

"The *Arkenshaw Telegraph*?"

"Yes."

"How long ago?"

"A year . . . eighteen months. I have the clipping at home."

"Would you be kind enough to bring it to court tomorrow? Then, if his lordship will permit—"

His lordship nodded glumly. He seemed to regard the entering of fresh items in evidence with resignation rather than enthusiasm. Maitland, not without some qualms, proceeded to play his luck a little further. "Were those the only items that were missing, Mr. Barlow; the wallet and the coins?"

"Yes, that's all." Having answered the question, he paused, but apparently his sense of grievance overcame him. "They had pulled all the papers out of the pigeonholes in the bureau; I noticed that, because I like to keep things tidy, and they'd even looked through my attaché case, but there wasn't anything there to steal."

"What sort of papers had been disturbed?" He was too absorbed to notice that O'Brien looked up and frowned as he spoke.

"Well, in the bureau there's just notepaper, receipted bills, that sort of thing. A few private letters."

"But nothing had been taken."

"No."

"And in the attaché case?"

"Those would be business things."

"Work you'd brought home from the office?"

"Not exactly. There'd be the pamphlets that describe the various policies we offer. And then, if I'd called on someone during the day, there might be a proposal form filled in, and the documents."

"Birth certificate . . . that sort of thing?"

"Yes."

"No money?"

"Oh, no."

"And there was nothing missing from the attaché case either?"

170

"There was nothing there worth stealing," said Sam Bar-ow uncertainly.

Something in his tone caught Maitland's attention. 'Perhaps not. But was there anything missing?" he asked, with a gentleness that made O'Brien frown again.

"I'd mislaid some papers . . . well, lost them, if you ike." Obviously the witness did not relish having to make he admission. "But they had no value."

"A proposal form?"

"That's right. An immigrant lady."

"Did you mention it to the police?"

"Of course not. No one would have taken such a thing. I hought it would turn up."

"And did it?"

"Well . . . no. But it was a queer thing—" He broke off, and was silent for so long that Maitland thought it as well o prompt him.

"No harm done," he said encouragingly. "An easy mat-er to get the particulars again."

"I couldn't, as a matter of fact."

"My lord, if we are to listen to so much irrelevant mat-er—" said O'Brien, getting up suddenly. But the judge's curiosity had been aroused, and he waved a hand rather estily, silencing the objection.

"Couldn't you ask your client . . . the person who vanted to be insured?" he asked the witness. Maitland was perverse enough to feel irritated by the renewed interrup-ion, though the question was precisely the one he had vanted to ask.

"Well, in the ordinary way, of course, my lord." Barlow vas becoming flustered again. "I looked everywhere first, because of the certificates she had given me, you see . . . he might have been annoyed. But a few days later I went o see her again."

"I must say I'm not surprised if she'd changed her nind," said Gilmour tartly.

"Oh, I wouldn't have expected her to do that," said Bar-

low, his professional pride momentarily overcoming hi
awe of the judge. "Not after I'd talked to her."

"But you said—" He turned to counsel and added de
spairingly, "Perhaps you can enlighten me, Mr. Maitland
What does the witness mean?"

"Mr. Barlow, why couldn't you get the particulars to fil
in the proposal form again?"

Sam Barlow glanced at the judge, and then back a
Maitland again, apparently in despair of making either o
them understand. After a moment he made a strange ges
ture, raising both his hands as though disclaiming respon
sibility for what he was about to say. "Because she'd dis
appeared . . . that's why," he said. "I went back to th
house, and they said they'd never heard of her." He me
the judge's eye, and his indignation faltered. "At least . . .
at least, I'm sure it was the same house," he added weakly
"Anyway, I didn't worry, I thought she'd get in touch wit
me. Only she never did."

This time Mr. Justice Gilmour—his lips compressed an
his expression disbelieving—listened with patience t
O'Brien's objection.

III

In spite of her more personable appearance, Glend
Barlow's evidence came as something of an anticlima
O'Brien had cross-examined Sam at length, though witl
out referring again to matters which he had already stig
matized as "being outside the cognizance of this court,
and when Maitland attempted to reintroduce the subje
of the missing papers when Mrs. Barlow was in the witnes
box, the judge didn't even wait for an objection before di
missing the matter in a summary way. Glenda's modest a
and demurely downcast eyes might have been matter fc
amusement if there hadn't been so much else to worr
about . . . there had obviously never been a witness mo

172

ppreciative of O'Brien's blandishments. But . . . "A nice, at red herring," said Bushey in his leader's ear as she tepped down after corroborating her husband's evidence. What do you expect to gain from it?"

"Nothing that will interest *them*," Maitland told him, asting a look of unwarranted dislike at the jury. He was vatching Jimmy Marshall, who was being sworn, and Bushey shrugged and did not press the question.

There was something in the air of languid grace with vhich the boy conducted himself that aroused Maitland's ympathy. Jimmy was playing to the gallery, emphasizing is sophistication, his status as an adult. His evidence was egligible, of course, but perhaps after all it would have een a shame not to allow him his moment of glory. Bushey had insisted that they stick to the order of witnesses who had given evidence for the prosecution at the riginal trial, and it hadn't seemed worthwhile arguing. He as taking Marshall through his story now, which consted of no more than corroboration of Martin Ward's account (still to come) of how they had walked down Badger's Way on the evening of twenty-fourth March, how Martin had said to him, "Something's up," and he had looked across the road and seen four men talking near the ate of a house, he hadn't known then it was number nineteen, but it was quite easy to identify it later because of the treet lamp nearby. He thought two of the men were colred, the others were certainly uniformed policemen. No, e hadn't noticed anything else at the time . . . yes, Marn had certainly seen the men before he did, might well ave been watching them for a few moments as they alked along.

Something had taken O'Brien's attention. Maitland saw im shake his head at his junior and get up himself. Not at it mattered; if Jimmy Marshall's evidence couldn't do e defense any good, it couldn't harm them either.

But there was O'Brien, gentling the witness along the ath he had already taken, as though there might be some

173

admission to be won. Maitland's hand lay slack on th
table in front of him, but his eyes were suddenly intent.
there was something he'd missed . . .

"You 'glanced' across the road, you didn't stand starin,
just walked straight on."

"Yes, sir. You see, it was past ten-thirty, and Martin wa
supposed to be home."

"You didn't think whatever was happening interestin
enough to risk being late."

"I didn't want to get him in trouble, sir."

"Very commendable." O'Brien had his shark smile, bi
Maitland raised his head and looked at the witness wit
open interest now. "You said, Mr. Marshall," O'Brie
went on, "that was all you noticed *at the time.*"

"That's true, sir."

"*At the time,* Mr. Marshall."

"Yes, sir. That was all . . . except for what the constab.
picked up."

Maitland's hand clenched suddenly, and slowly relaxe
again. Behind him he heard Chris Conway catch h
breath and expel it in a long sigh.

O'Brien said, raising his voice a little: "You went back

"I was interested, sir. Wouldn't you have been?"

O'Brien could afford to ignore the impertinence. "Pleas
tell us, Mr. Marshall—" Maitland half got to his feet, ei
countered a particularly stony look from the judge, an
subsided again. Perhaps, after all, it was better to hear th
worst. (But that was making a virtue of necessity; he kne
quite well if he'd objected he'd have been overruled.)

"Martin lives just round the corner from Badger's Wa
so it wasn't very long before I was opposite number nin
teen again. A few minutes, five perhaps. There was onl
the constable left; I stood watching, he didn't notice me

"Could you see him clearly enough to recognize him?

"It was Constable Ryder. I'd known him for some tim
by sight, but I didn't know his name until later."

"Well, what was he doing?"

"Just standing, about halfway down the path."

"Come now, my boy, you made a statement a few moments ago."

For the first time the witness seemed to hesitate. "I didn't think it was anything important. I mean, nobody ever asked me about that." (Maitland listened to him now without any sympathy at all.) "I don't want to get anyone in trouble," added Jimmy Marshall, with a doubtful look in the judge's direction.

"We are not interested in your sentiments, only in justice." That was O'Brien, getting on his high horse. "Or perhaps you subscribe to the belief that 'justice' can only be preserved by upholding the authorities . . . in this case the police."

"N-no, sir."

"Then tell us, please, who you saw."

"He turned to face the house—the constable did—and bent down . . . well, he was crouched, sort of. I couldn't see what he was doing, it took a few moments, he seemed to be feeling under a bush. Then he stood up, and I saw him looking at something he held in his hand, and then he put . . . whatever it was . . . into his pocket."

"I see." O'Brien was scowling now. "Did you go away then?"

"The police car came. I wanted to see what happened." He paused, and then said with a valiant air, as though facing a disagreeable necessity, "I waited until they took the two men away. And when they were getting into the car . . . I mean, one of them was getting in and the other—the taller one—was standing on the pavement waiting . . . I saw the constable take his hand out of his own trousers pocket and slip it into the pocket of the second man's jacket. Of course," he went on, "I don't *know* what he was doing."

Kevin O'Brien allowed himself one brief, triumphant glance in his opponent's direction. "I have no more questions," he said, and sat down with an air of finality that needed no explanation. But Maitland was looking past him to the thin, conventionally clad figure of the plaintiffs'

175

solicitor, whose solemnity was broken for one illuminating moment by a triumphant grin. It almost looked as if old rat trap had been expecting something to happen. . . .

IV

"I'd say," said John Bushey dispassionately, "it was al over, bar the shouting." He glanced at his leader, who had just broken his pencil point over some notes he was making on the back of an old envelope. "Nothing could really help after that," he added, rubbing it in. Maitland compressed his lips, but did not answer.

They were in Conway's office, and Chris was on his knees trying to coax the fire into some sign of life. He turned now, and said in a worried way, "It's something should have known. And just when you'd made up you mind—"

"I haven't changed it." Maitland reread what he had written, crumpled the envelope with an impatient gesture and tossed it in the general direction of the grate. H looked at Chris, and then at Bushey. "Ryder denies it," he said, and his tone was challenging.

"Well, of course," said Chris, picking up the envelop and consigning it to the flames.

Bushey remarked dryly, "Did you expect anythin else?"

"No, I didn't." He was staring into the fire, and his ton was quiet, unemphatic. "You see, I happen to believ him."

"But that's crazy," Conway protested. Bushey clampe his teeth round the stem of his pipe and said nothing, bu his eyes were on Maitland's face. Antony grinned and the said quickly, as though in self-condemnation: "It isn funny."

"No," said Conway. He spoke slowly, as though d spairing of making the other man understand. "Wha

176

Jimmy Marshall said means they've both been lying to us . . . Ryder and Duckett. And still are."

"Do you think so?" The fire was burning up merrily now, but he shivered as he spoke, as though some of the damp chill of the street outside had invaded the warm office. "*I* think it's the boy who was lying."

Chris looked at him hopelessly. Bushey took his pipe from his mouth and said, mildly protesting, "The story had to be dragged out of him."

"Do you think so?" asked Maitland again. Bushey said, with unusual impatience,

"I'd have said it was obvious."

"Think a minute. Have you got the note? He was playing with O'Brien—oh, very cleverly!—every inch of the way; leading him on. From the first 'slip' he made (which I ought to have noticed, though I don't know what I could have done about it) to the final, damning revelation."

Bushey was gaping at him. "A boy like that!"

"I wasn't expecting it," Maitland admitted.

"No, but you did say that possibly Lawford—" Chris glanced uncertainly at Bushey, and let the sentence trail into silence.

Bushey said flatly: "If you mean he might have been suborned, what good could that possibly have done? He's our witness."

"So is Marshall. Lawford could have said he followed Beas and Mohamad when they left the pub, was still behind them in Badger's Way—"

"Be damned to that for a tale."

"Don't be so sure you could have picked holes in it. But this was better . . . foolproof, really. A clever boy, with a good deal of verbal dexterity, carefully coached—"

"He had his answers pat to all your questions, Bushey," said Conway slowly.

"That doesn't make me disbelieve him." Bushey's vehemence was uncharacteristic, he was obviously deeply

177

moved. "Look, I asked him if he could see through the car; he said he'd moved by then, was watching from an angle. That's reasonable, isn't it? And had he told his friend he was going back? No, he hadn't wanted to rub it in that Martin's parents were stricter than his own. At least, I suggested, he must have mentioned later what he'd seen—"

"He conveyed, very cleverly, that he was afraid of his knowledge," said Antony with a touch of impatience. "All those questions could have been foreseen."

"I don't believe it. Why should he care what happens to Ghulam Beas?"

"No reason at all. He might have been induced to take an interest. Not by Beas himself, of course."

"Who, then?"

"The man behind him, the man responsible for this prosecution." Bushey gave an incredulous snort. "I don't *know* who he is, but I do know he's prepared to go to almost any lengths to cover his own tracks. So it's quite reasonable that he took fright after Miss Garrowby gave her evidence yesterday, just in case the jury were influenced in any way by her confusion."

"The whole thing was cooked up last night, then?"

"Why not? I'm not saying that was the first time it was thought of." He shrugged and added, as though he were tired, "O'Brien didn't know what was coming . . . at least I don't think he did; but I wouldn't like to bet about Jones."

"Oh, come now, it would be highly improper—"

"Yes, I had thought of that," Maitland agreed, rather too readily. "So what do you suggest we do? I'm damned I'll ask our clients to change their plea. Do you want to withdraw?"

"No," said Bushey. "At least . . . no."

Maitland got up restlessly and began to move about the room. "You might do better to do so."

"Do you want me to?"

"Don't be a f-fool." He paused a moment, and caught his junior's eye. "I only meant . . . we're not going to make ourselves popular, you know. And as a member of this circuit—"

"Melodrama," said Bushey, with a half-smile. He seemed to have recovered his equanimity as his leader became more disturbed. "What about Conway? Does the gypsy's warning apply to him too?"

"Too late," said Maitland, and went to the window and back with long, impatient strides. "He's stuck with me now, sink or swim. You see, he's the junior partner . . . isn't that right, Conway?"

Chris was a little pale, but he looked back at Maitland steadily. "I'm with you," he declared, and Bushey threw up his hands in a gesture that disclaimed responsibility.

"I think you're both mad."

"Perhaps we are." Antony came back to the fire again.

"And as for this bogey-man of yours—"

"You don't believe in him? You may be right."

"Never mind about that," said Bushey illogically. "What next?"

"All I can be sure of is that O'Brien will give us hell tomorrow; he isn't loving me very much. And Gilmour will back him up. That unfortunate boy, Martin Ward . . . do you still think he'll come up to proof?"

"He's stubborn enough," said Chris, "but even so . . . will it do any good?"

"Not a bit, but at least we can make sure we don't reach a verdict. With the court adjourned till Monday—"

"Three whole days!" said Bushey.

"Precisely. In the meantime, I want to talk to Barlow."

"I'll take you there, after dinner," Chris offered. But he gave a sidelong, apologetic glance at Bushey as he spoke. "Only I don't quite see . . . he said there'd been something in the paper about his coin collection, so perhaps the theft was a straightforward affair after all."

"Perhaps it was," Maitland agreed; there was a flicker

179

of amusement in his eyes as he watched his young colleague struggling with facts that obviously seemed to him unreasonably contradictory.

"But then, he *has* mislaid those papers, and if those were what they wanted, I suppose knowing about the coins would make a good excuse . . . I don't know!"

"Don't worry about it," Maitland told him.

"And on Monday all will be well, and we shall convince the court of our clients' shining innocence," said John Bushey, apparently confiding in his pipe.

Maitland turned his head and looked down at him thoughtfully for a moment before saying in his gentlest tone, "You're not really very good at sneering, you know. If you mean to take it up seriously, you should practice in front of a mirror."

It was at this point that Conway, in some agitation, declared the meeting adjourned.

V

Sometime during the afternoon the rain had stopped, and down Market Lane the lights were blurred and softened by the mist. Maitland was walking quickly; he had refused Chris's offer of a lift, and was glad that John Bushey's way led him up the hill, away from the square, and the railway station, and the Midland Hotel. He was disturbed by the day's events, and angrier than he had been since he came to Arkenshaw; and he wanted to think, because if there was one thing he was more certain of than another, it was that these inquiries of Conway's wouldn't get them anywhere, though they had to go through the motions. But there must be some way . . .

He was passing through a district that seemed to be devoted to the wholesale stationery trade, small display windows with ledgers, and pencils by the gross, and graph paper, and various printed forms. *This is the last Will and Testament* . . . people really used those things, and a fine mess they often made of it, as he knew. There should really be a series of "hate" forms . . . how to disinherit your nearest and dearest without falling foul of the law . . . how to leave your money to a home for aging parrots, tying it up in such a way that no member of the human race should benefit therefrom.

The Imperial Insurance Company would have its literature printed privately, of course, and supplied from head office. Sam Barlow had lost a completed proposal form . . . surprising, because he seemed a careful little man, but what conceivable use could any unauthorized person have for such a thing? The person to be insured was a woman, an immigrant, but if she'd come into the country illegally she'd surely have known better than to hand over forged documents to support her application. Or would she?

Suppose the burglary was a fake, the theft of the coins and wallet merely camouflage for the recovery of some document that had been given, unwisely, into Barlow's care. Well . . . suppose it. So what?

In that case, why had the woman disappeared? Or had Sam Barlow merely "mislaid" her too?

Whoever was behind the illegal-immigration racket must have stacks of printed forms. On consideration, Antony found he was vague about what was needed, but one thing was certain . . . the vital documents couldn't be bought at the stationer's. You'd need special paper, presumably, and the right sort of type; given that, any local firm could do the job.

And keep their mouths shut?

Easy enough, of course, in these security-conscious days, for a company on confidential work to put a guard on the door and plead the Official Secrets Act. But none of his eagles was an industrialist (how Grandma's phrase stuck in his mind!), so that wouldn't wash.

One man, then, working overtime. Could it be as simple as that?

He came to the corner of Fellgate, and turned into it almost without thinking. There were more people about to-

181

night (yesterday had been early closing), and if they were going to have choir practice at the chapel it must be for later on. A big car was standing outside the club, almost blocking the narrow roadway. Maitland paused long enough to look up at the building he had taken for a warehouse, to note the brass plate that said only GREENHALGH & BLACKBURN, *Printers and Engravers,* to think . . .

Oliver Ward was honorary treasurer of the Arkenshaw Society. He'd be in touch with the firm that did their printing, even if it was only over the paying of bills. And Mr. Greenhalgh was at least so far amenable to influence that he had agreed to let Star Duckett keep her job when Frank Findlater asked him.

Of course, he may never have intended to sack her in the first place.

The car was a Cadillac. The same color as Findlater's . . . anyway, how many people in Arkenshaw were in a position to indulge themselves to that extent? Antony stopped again to watch a truck ease its way past, two wheels on the pavement. The chauffeur got out too, anxious about his paint, and he was more easily identifiable than the car, though today the distinguishing turban was turquoise instead of flame color. The truck got past without disaster, and he went around the car to open the nearside door as Frank Findlater came out on to the steps of the club.

"It's all right, Tom . . . why, Mr. Maitland! I've been meaning to phone you. Come and have a drink."

Antony crossed the road with a shade of reluctance, though it was ridiculous, he knew, to feel in some way compromised at being found staring up at a printing works. "I was just going back to the hotel."

"But you've finished for the day? How are things going, or shouldn't I ask you that?" He paused, scrutinizing the other man in the frugal light of the lantern outside the club. "I shouldn't ask you," he decided. "But a drink will do you good."

"Thank you," said Antony, making up his mind. But

Findlater had taken his acceptance for granted and was speaking to the chauffeur again. "Mr. Victor isn't here yet, Tom, so I'll have to wait for him. You'd better park the car."

The chauffeur saluted, flashed his teeth in a delighted grin, and shut the door again firmly but gently. "Another Pakistani," said Maitland with a question in his voice as he followed Findlater up the steps.

"In the circumstances, my dear fellow, I can understand your feeling haunted by them." This was said with such evident sympathy that Antony felt himself relaxing a little. "I don't know what I'd do without Tom. Smart, isn't he?"

"Very." He followed his host into the bar, where the sight of two more customers, far from depressing the ancient steward, seemed to have a livening effect. He hurried forward, beaming, and Findlater gave his order and led the way to a table at the other side of the room. There was a sprinkling of members here tonight, solid-looking citizens in more senses than one; conversations were broken off to greet the newcomer, and glance curiously at his companion. Findlater muttered a continuous " 'Evening, Joe . . . 'Evening, Bob . . . 'Evening, John-Willie" as they went, but returned as soon as they were seated to a subject that obviously interested him.

"It isn't only selfishness," he said. "They're better off with me than in the mills."

"All the same, their coming must have changed the district," said Maitland, stiffening his resolution. The club seemed a friendly place today, and the impulse to drop the reins, to let his host steer the conversation where he would, was almost irresistible.

"You've been listening to Fred Duckett," Findlater told him indulgently. "Well, it's natural some won't like it, and I'm sorry to see Fred in trouble now. But he's pig-headed, always was. Have you met Grandma?"

"I have." He smiled as he spoke, but he was feeling increasingly out of his depth in this town where everyone knew everyone else's business.

183

"Salt of the earth," said Findlater. "Still, fair's fair."

Maitland found this obscure, but decided not to prob his companion's meaning. He was glad when their drink arrived, giving him the opportunity of changing the sub ject, not too obviously. "O'Brien brought me here yester day," he said. "I'm beginning to feel quite at home."

"Ah, yes. An able chap, wouldn't you say?"

"Extremely."

"He's dining with us tonight. Now, there's an idea! Wh don't you join us? We shall be a small party, because th young people will be going to the bonfire."

"I'm afraid—" He couldn't say what was really in hi mind, that neither his amiability nor O'Brien's would b likely to stand up under so prolonged a strain, and a fire works display in his home circle was hardly what Findlate had in mind, even if it was Guy Fawkes' Day. "I hav some work to do," he said. The excuse sounded lame though it was true enough.

"At this stage?" said Findlater; and added apologeti cally, as he caught Maitland's eye, "I got the impressio from the papers that your case is almost over."

"Almost . . . not quite." He sat for a moment, sippin his sherry (which deserved, he thought, more attentio than he had to spare), and then went on, "I met a ma called Ward the other day, Oliver Ward. Is he a membe here?"

"Yes, I put him up myself a few years ago, but I don' think he comes in very often except for meetings." I Findlater thought the topic a strange one, he gave no sig "You've heard of the Arkenshaw Society?"

"Quite a lot."

"He's our treasurer. Invaluable."

"I heard mention in court of the scholarships."

"Yes, of course, Chakwal Mohamad. But you mustn' think that our only activity, Mr. Maitland, though Johnn is sometimes inclined to talk as if it was. The various clin ics do wonderful work too. And the special schools for im migrant children . . . it's odd, really, no one seems to think how difficult a new country will be for the little ones."

There seemed no valid reason why he shouldn't go on in this strain all night. "And the lawyers who give their services," said Antony, tossing the remark casually into the conversational pool.

"Why . . . yes." Findlater seemed to be wondering whether the interruption was due to an excess of interest, or just the reverse; he paused, staring at his guest, and then asked shrewdly, "Now, what made you bring that up?"

"Vulgar curiosity," said Maitland, smiling. But was he going the right way about it, after all? Suppose he asked Findlater, straight out . . .

"Of course, it's your own line, isn't it?" Findlater leaned forward eagerly, only too ready to share his enthusiasm. "There's been some really useful work done there, and I'm not giving away any secrets when I tell you it was our friend Jones who brought Ghulam Beas's problem to my attention." He broke off and gave his hearty laugh. "Am I being indiscreet? It can't concern you—can it?—how the prosecution is being financed."

"No," said Maitland, his eyes on Findlater's face.

"Fair's fair," said Frank, as he had done before. And then, obviously in earnest, "They needed my help, you see."

Oddly, it seemed as if all his values were being revised. He had thought once that if he knew how John Cadwallader Jones came into the picture, the way ahead would be clearer. Now he knew, and it didn't seem to help at all. "You'd know a good deal about the foreigners in Arkenshaw, I expect."

"Oh, yes, indeed. It has occurred to me once or twice, Mr. Maitland, that if you were aware of the problems . . . but I mustn't seem to be trying to influence you, must I?"

"Not everyone is so scrupulous. Some kind friend sent

185

me the newspaper account of another case in which Sergeant Duckett was involved with a Pakistani," he explained.

"Yes, I remember it. But why—?"

"An attempt, I suppose, to convince me that he is hopelessly prejudiced."

"Isn't he?" said Findlater, with some irony in his tone.

Antony's thoughts went back to his talk with Dr. Conway, and for a moment he did not answer. Then he said, "I wonder," and roused himself from his abstraction, to find Frank Findlater looking at him in a puzzled way. "Ahmad Khan," he added. "That case made a lot of talk, too . . . or so I heard."

"It certainly did." He hesitated. "Johnny acted for him too, but I remember he was by no means convinced of his innocence until the new witness came along."

"You didn't—?"

"No, Mr. Maitland. There was no question of funds being needed for the defense, and I shouldn't have thought it a worthy cause. Which shows one shouldn't judge rashly, because afterwards it was obvious . . . well, I tried to make amends by finding a job for him. I felt I'd been unjust, you see, if only in my thoughts."

"Had he been dismissed?"

"No, but Johnny told me he felt diffident about going back to his previous position. He went to Comstock's Mill, and I hear he's doing well there."

"But he was a skilled man in his own line, wasn't he?" said Antony. An idea had struck him, and for the moment he was hardly conscious of his surroundings . . . of the big room that was becoming uncomfortably filled with smoke, or the low growl of north-country voices, or the mingled smell of good drink and old leather . . . or even of Findlater's presence. "Someone said he was a printer, and I'm wondering . . . did he work across the road at Greenhalgh's, or am I all wrong about that?"

There was a politely veiled curiosity in Findlater's eyes.

"I don't remember that, I'm afraid. Johnny could tell you, if you really want to know."

Maitland came to himself with a start. "I'm sorry, of course you wouldn't know. I was only thinking aloud."

"You may be right, of course. The fact that he chose to work with machines . . . I could so easily have found him a domestic job."

"I suppose so."

"Most of us have some of them in our employ"—his gesture was wide enough to comprehend, perhaps, the entire membership of the Arkenshaw Club—"and I assure you, Mr. Maitland, such positions are very much sought after." There was a pause. "I wonder, now," said Findlater. "Johnny tells me you are showing an unusual amount of interest in this case . . . which I, in my ignorance, should have thought mere routine."

"I'm paid to take an interest."

"Even to the extent of having inquiries made about our poor Miss Garrowby? Don't tell me that was Chris Conway's idea."

This was plain speaking with a vengeance; he might have spared his efforts to be tactful, it seemed. "I wasn't going to tell you anything at all," he said honestly. And then, "Did Mr. Jones tell you that too?"

"Shouldn't he have done? Most of your questions could be answered openly, you know. I can quite see that to a stranger . . . but, Emily Garrowby! It's absurd."

" 'The heart has its reasons—' " said Maitland vaguely. "Why do you say that?"

Well . . . why? "Because . . . because I'm like you, I suppose. I can't believe her anything but sincere."

Findlater sat back. His hand holding the delicate stem of the sherry glass looked too large, too clumsy for so fragile a thing. Antony stared at it as though he were mesmerized by the play of color in the crystal, and was aware suddenly that he was very tired. Findlater's voice seemed to come from a long way away. "In that case, wouldn't it be easier to accept the obvious? It isn't for me to advise you, Mr. Maitland," he added apologetically, "but I can see you're worried."

He didn't want to look up and meet Findlater's eyes; the sense of defeat was strong, and instinctively he wished to hide it. (But suppose I told him, straight out, just what I suspect about his precious Johnny. Would he be quite so friendly then, so concerned? Or would he say I'm mad . . . as Conway did last night, and Bushey did just now?) Aloud he said, "There was a surprise witness this time, too."

"I thought when I saw you . . . I was afraid something had happened to upset you."

"To be exact, we knew about the witness; but we didn't know what he was going to say."

"I see."

"I wish I did. Still, it's a coincidence, isn't it?" He didn't wait for a reply, but dragged his eyes from the shining glass and added more briskly, "I've enjoyed our talk, but I ought to be going now."

"Can't you possibly change your plans for tonight? Well, then, perhaps tomorrow . . . that would be better, really. If I could help you in any way . . . set your mind at rest. I know this town very well, Mr. Maitland; and its people."

If Findlater weren't so close to old rat trap the offer would prove a temptation. (But in a way, it is he who has defeated me, because—more than anyone else—he is Arkenshaw, and it is the town itself . . .) "It's very kind of you, but I'm going home for the weekend," said Antony firmly; it was certainly time he was getting back to the hotel, while he could still call his soul his own.

"Tom will take you, if you really must go."

"No need for that, it's only a few minutes' walk."

But it was Findlater that got his way, and perhaps this too was characteristic. Tom brought round the Cadillac and received his orders with one of his brilliant smiles. An-

188

tony sat back and thought, only half-regretfully, that the walk might have done something to shake him out of this creeping depression. There'd be time to brood later; just now he ought to be making plans.

But when he got back to the hotel and ordered another sherry, unsociably, to be brought to his room, all he could think of was Frank Findlater and what it must be like to live under that benevolent despotism. For better or worse, the character of the town must be changed by his patronage . . . was it cynical to think that it could not be for the better?

VI

After all, Chris had offered to call on the Barlows on his way back to town. He reached the hotel about nine-thirty, with a page full of notes and an anxious expression, and by that time Maitland was ready for him. "Before we go any further, you'd better call off those bloodhounds of yours first thing tomorrow," he said.

"But I only just—" Chris was inclined to be indignant.

"I know. I'm sorry. But there's been a leak."

"You mean . . . they've told someone?"

"Findlater knew. I don't suppose he's psychic."

"But—" Chris said again.

"Well, he knew we were investigating Miss Garrowby. As for the rest, how did you go about it?"

"In a roundabout way. I don't know what else you expected." Conway sounded huffy. "Working backwards, if you like, from Beas and Ahmad Khan and the others . . . nothing they could think unreasonable."

"That's good. You warned me, didn't you, that in Arkenshaw—? Anyway, call them off."

Chris looked at him curiously. "Who told Findlater?" he asked.

"Jones. It's obvious when you think of it. I expect you

went to the most reliable firm of inquiry agents in town, it only needed one of their chaps to owe him a favor, and there you are."

"I never thought of that."

"Neither did I."

"And you think it was Jones who encouraged Beas to take this action."

"Yes, I do. Which is highly slanderous, considering there's no proof at all, and no likelihood of getting any."

"Then we might as well give up now," said Chris, suddenly angry.

"No. Oh, no. Tell me about Barlow. Had he recovered from his ordeal?"

"Just about."

"Go on, tell me, there's a good chap."

"The woman's name was Bhakkar . . . I've got the rest of it written down somewhere. He got on to her through the immigration people, so it doesn't look as if there was anything wrong there. Barlow says he's sure in his own mind about the address—which he's given me—but swearing's another thing."

"Very proper," said Maitland absently. "And did you ask Mrs. Barlow about the fireplace?"

"Yes, of course. They never use it . . . there's a sort of fan thing in front as a screen, and one of those electric affairs that pretend to be a log fire in front of that."

"There would be."

"Still, you were right about something having been burned. She said next morning she found the screen had been moved, and there were ashes in the grate, as if some papers had been burned there. She thought the police had done it, and never even mentioned it to Sam."

Maitland gave a brief but comprehensive summary of his opinion of Mr. Justice Gilmour that made Conway grin, though it should, more properly, have brought a blush to his cheeks. "But it wouldn't really have helped," said Chris, serious again, "if he had let you ask her about that in court."

190

"After the Marshall fiasco? No, I suppose it wouldn't. Is the fog very bad? Can we go and see this Miss—Miss Bhakkar?"

"Mrs. Bhakkar," Conway told him. "As for the fog, I got here, didn't I?"

But at 16 Wendover Terrace the landlady, Mrs. Gujranwala, denied that she had ever had a lodger of that name. "I am already telling the other man this, why are you not believing me?" Pressed, she admitted that she let rooms to single ladies—"rooms with facilities"; she seemed proud of the phrase. And she would have no objection to a married lady, provided no husband was in evidence.

"We'll try the grocer on the corner," said Antony, as they got back into the car.

"I thought you didn't approve of grocers," Conway commented; and disconcerted his companion by adding, "I wonder if this one 'keeps a lady in a cage.' "

"I shouldn't think he had room," said Maitland seriously as they drew up outside the shop. And he proved to be right; inside there was just about room for two customers, standing sideways and holding their breath, and behind the counter was just as bad, for though Mr. Grocer was a thin little man, Mrs. Grocer was extremely stout.

It was she who came to their rescue, when she had finished slicing bacon and ticked the item carefully off the order she was making up. Her husband had already been shaking his head for several minutes over the problem. "Well, I remember Mrs. Bhakkar," she said. "A nice, quiet body, for all she was foreign."

"Was she here long?"

"Round about three weeks, I'd say. In March, that was. Last March. I remember, because she felt the cold so, being just come from what I suppose is a warmer place."

"Had she come to Arkenshaw alone?"

"That's right. To find her husband, so she said. Which I suppose he'd left her," she added, and gave a jolly laugh and nudged her own husband so violently that he nearly

191

fell over. "There's some as would like the chance," she said.

"She did her shopping here, then . . . how was she placed for money?"

"Oh, she had a job. Do you think my lady down the road would have kept her if she hadn't?"

"She *was* staying with Mrs. Gujranwala?"

"That's right. And working in Brinkley Crescent, one of the big houses there."

"Do you remember the number?"

"I do not." She watched his expression until he registered his disappointment, and then laughed again. "But the name was the same as ours—see?—so I couldn't forget that, could I?"

"I'm afraid I didn't notice—" (Truth to tell, he'd been thinking of her as Mrs. Jack Sprat.)

"Jones," she said, and jerked her head toward her husband, who had retired to the other end of the counter and was rearranging a display of canned soup into which some tins of cocoa seemed to have infiltrated. "Fancy me, marrying a Welshman," she marveled. "But you could tell that, couldn't you, the daft way he talks?"

Conway muttered something under his breath, and Antony threw him a warning look. "You said she was here three weeks. Do you know where she went when she left?"

"Nay, that I don't. But they're secretive, you know. Why, some on 'em will hardly so much as tell you their name."

"She didn't tell you she was going?"

"Not a word. She was in here on the Monday, and then on the Wednesday there was that Mrs. Goodgy asking if we knew where she'd gone. Not that she'd owt to worry about, always being one for money in advance."

Antony asked a few more questions, but that was the sum of her story. "The thing is," he said when they were back in the car again, "whatever happened, it was all so quick."

For the moment, Conway seemed to have no attention

to spare for this aspect of the matter. "It's our Jones, all right," he said. "What do you suppose it means?"

"Summat and nowt," said Maitland.

"But, look here—"

"We'll have to find out, of course. Either she's still there or—or—"

"Or she isn't. In which case she may really have disappeared, and it does look as if you were right about the theft . . . that it was the papers they were after, not the money or the coins."

"Think of the time element," Maitland insisted.

"What of it?"

"She came into the shop on Monday; Tuesday, Barlow saw her, and the proposal form was filled in—"

"An endowment policy, quite a small amount," Conway put in. "But at least it means she felt sure of her job."

"I daresay she did. I wonder what time Barlow was with her."

"Early afternoon. She put down her occupation as 'domestic work,' and she told him Tuesday was her half-day. Her English was fairly good, but she needed a little help. And another thing, he said she was all ready to go out as soon as he left her."

Antony was thinking that the urge to play detective seemed to have taken possession of Conway to an unexpected degree; he seemed to have questioned Mr. Barlow with the same thoroughness he had used in preparing the brief. For some reason he was conscious of a lift in his spirits. "Quite invaluable," he murmured; and then, more soberly, "I wondered if she ever went back."

Chris was a little ruffled by Maitland's evident amusement, but his interest was caught as well. "I see what you mean about the time," he said. "Barlow left her at two-fifteen, and between then and ten-thirty something must have happened to make her want to get the proposal form back."

"It looks like that. Or perhaps it's more likely that some third party wanted it."

"Whichever way it was, it doesn't make sense," said Chris discontentedly.

"Yes, I thought you might notice that." He gave a sidelong glance at his companion, who was still looking affronted, and added with deliberate provocation, "Perhaps Jones went berserk and murdered her."

Chris smiled at that, though a trifle reluctantly. "It was her day off," he pointed out, and stretched out his hand to the ignition. Then he caught sight of Maitland's expression and added sharply, "You were joking . . . weren't you?"

"Yes. Yes, of course." He gave an odd, impatient gesture with his left hand, which Conway interpreted as an invitation to drive on. "She did disappear," said Antony thoughtfully. "Mrs. Goodgy was looking for her on the Wednesday, but afterward she denied she'd ever heard of her."

Chris had no attention to spare now for anything but the road. "You're going too fast for me," he said. And then, "Where do you want to go, anyway?"

"Back to the hotel, I should think. But as for the other . . . I can't be going too fast," Maitland objected. "I'm not getting anywhere at all."

"I'm surprised you're still trying," said Conway irritably, and Antony twisted round to look at him; because this was the second time that evening he'd said something of the kind, and it seemed a strange reversal of his previous attitude.

"Do you want me to stop?" he asked.

"No, of course I don't. Not that it would make any difference," he added disagreeably, but with a good deal of truth, "if I did."

After that they were silent until they reached the hotel. Conway declined an invitation to come in, but he still seemed to have their recent exchange on his mind, and perhaps he regretted it. However that might be, he twisted round in his seat as Antony stepped out on to the pavement, and said apologetically, "It's as I thought, they *are* going to move."

194

Maitland turned back with his hand on the door. "The Ducketts?" he asked, and Chris answered in a rush: "Star said her father talked to the estate agent before, and now he's told him to go ahead with selling the house."

So that was the explanation of Conway's mood. Antony was relieved to have one mystery at least cleared up, but his mind was occupied with other things, and he spoke absently. "Wouldn't she stay if you asked her?" he said.

"Well, I . . . no, she wouldn't," said Chris. He sounded surprised, but not particularly resentful. "She's said all along it wouldn't be fair, unless the case went the right way, you know. And that isn't as silly as it sounds, because in Arkenshaw—"

"Yes . . . Arkenshaw," said Maitland thoughtfully. And then, as though he had suddenly woken up to what they were discussing, "Grandma said they'd already had an offer."

"Yes, they have."

"A good one?"

"Not what I'd have thought . . . but the agent says it is. Good, I mean . . . more than the property's worth. He says the time isn't ripe for development yet, and I suppose he knows. After all, he must be interested in his commission."

"Or in his standing in the community."

"What does that mean?"

"I'm not quite sure. But tell Duckett he should get a second opinion," said Antony.

"*Now* what are you thinking?" said Chris resignedly.

"Nothing . . . really! I did have a vague idea at one time that there might be a plot to get hold of Old Peel Farm . . . well, you did say it was valuable. But I don't suppose it's any more than a bit of opportunism on someone's part." He was on the point of shutting the car door when he bent forward again to have the last word. "As for that lass of yours, you'd better start as you mean to go on," he advised. "After all, even a Yorkshirewoman has been known to change her mind."

195

VII

The lobby was quiet and almost deserted; he was surprised to find it was already past eleven o'clock, but of course the fog had slowed them down. He spared a thought as he went upstairs for Kevin O'Brien's engagement with the Findlaters. What sort of a woman would Frank have married . . . someone as assertive as himself? Or an echo, a sounding board for his own enthusiasm? And had Mr. Jones also been invited? *That* should have made the party go with a swing.

There was no real need to telephone home, when with any luck he'd be able to catch the five-thirty tomorrow. It was more because his tiredness had caught up with him again, his shoulder was damnably painful, and he didn't want to think, that he dialed the familiar number and sat listening to the ringing tone until he was quite sure that Jenny must be out. After a moment's indecision he tried Sir Nicholas' number instead, and this time he got through surprisingly quickly.

"I hope this isn't a change of plan, Antony. I want to see you." This might have sounded ominous, but it was obvious from Sir Nicholas' tone that he was on top of the world.

"No change. I couldn't get hold of Jenny."

"She went to see the Hortons, I think. Did you want her particularly?"

"Only to know how Pat and Mike are getting on," Antony explained.

"Pat and . . . oh, the plumbers. I don't expect you'll be exactly comfortable this weekend, but I daresay it will all come out right in the end," said Sir Nicholas optimistically.

"That's what I was afraid of."

"Never mind that—"

"I don't if you don't."

"What . . . oh, you mean this idea of Jenny's. We'll talk

about that when you get home," said Sir Nicholas. Obviously he wasn't lighthearted enough to have abandoned all sense of self-preservation, but the battle of "tenants' fixtures and fittings" would at least, Antony felt, be more amusing than his present preoccupations. "Meanwhile," his uncle went on, "I want to tell you about my discovery."

"What discovery?"

"You may forget about the totalisator," said Sir Nicholas kindly. "Its—er—its inner workings are not germane to the issue."

"Jenny told me you'd gone to the dogs," said Antony, enlightened. "I gather Derek was helpful."

"Stringer has an excellent understanding of these matters." This was said with a slight relapse into his normal, astringent manner. "It is all a matter of manipulating the balance of probability on the chances of a given animal—"

"Well, of course, if you could control the odds, you'd be on to a good thing. Can you?" he added with sudden interest.

"The operation requires a number of associates." Sir Nicholas sounded regretful. "If you can think of—say— half a dozen people who would be willing to take part in a demonstration—"

"Garfield," said Antony, naming the starchiest member of his own Inn that he could think of. "I'll come and see you on visiting days," he offered.

"I am not proposing actually to defraud anybody—"

"Thank goodness for that, anyway."

"—but in the interests of my clients it might be advisable . . . it is really quite fascinating," he added, suddenly abandoning his dignified tone and becoming human again. "As for the prosecution—"

"From the sound of it, you've got them cold."

"It is not precisely the phrase I should have chosen. However, there is a certain amount of truth in what you

197

say. Unless they are prepared to prove that my client acted in concert with a number of accomplices, and I don't think they are . . . but enough of that. How is that case of yours coming along, Antony?"

"It isn't. I'll tell you about it tomorrow," he went on hurriedly, but apparently he had already said enough to bring his uncle down from the heights.

"I knew how it would be," said Sir Nicholas testily; and could only be pacified by an account of his nephew's activities. Of these, he appeared to take a gloomy view. . . .

Ten minutes later Antony put down the receiver and wondered whether there was any encouragement at all to be found in the events of the evening. On the whole, it didn't seem likely. If he were to get up in court and say, for instance, "The issue between Ghulam Beas and the two policemen is relatively unimportant," would anyone believe him?

It *was* important, of course. To the Ducketts, and Constable Ryder, and even to Chris Conway, it was a vital matter. And now to himself, which was ironic when you came to think about it, because at the same time he had come to feel so much more sympathy for the plaintiffs than ever he would have believed possible.

Or perhaps . . . not for Ghulam Beas, who wasn't a babe in the woods by any reckoning, but eminently capable of standing on his own feet. He thought about Ghulam Beas for a while and decided his first impression still stood, he didn't like him. Which wasn't helpful either.

When he looked at his watch he was startled to see that it was now nearly ten to twelve. It might be as well to stop daydreaming and get to bed, though he had never felt less like sleep.

He had done no more than take off his jacket and loosen his tie when there came a tapping at the door, not very loud but curiously insistent. If he thought anything at all as he went to open it, it was that some member of the bar mess had heard a story that was too good to keep to

198

himself. He was completely unprepared for the sight of Chakwal Mohamad standing on the threshold and looking up at him anxiously.

"I am wishing to see you, sir," said Jackie, and slipped past him into the room. His eyes were overbright, and he was breathing rather fast, as if he had been running.

Short of using force, there was no way of stopping him. Antony turned, still holding the door ajar. "Mr. Mohamad, this is a most improper proceeding—"

But reason wasn't going to do any good, either; nor the assumption of his stuffiest courtroom manner. Jackie wasn't listening. He said in that soft voice of his, slurring the words in his haste, "Sir, I am begging you . . . you are not turning me away. There are things I must be telling—"

"Pull yourself together. You must know *I* can't talk to you." He spoke sharply, but there didn't seem much chance he would be heeded. Jackie's eyes were fixed on his face, but he was intent on his own story, not listening at all. There was something unnatural about that fixed stare. "If you have something to say, your own solicitor—" said Antony helplessly; and thought as he spoke that even in a different situation, Mr. Jones was the last person in whom he would choose to confide.

"Pardon me, but it is you I am wishing to see." His breathing got no better, but he didn't seem to notice that. "Ghulam Beas has said to me, 'Jackie, we only want fair play, but *he* is the danger.' Sir, it is you he is meaning." He stopped, and closed his eyes for a moment, and put a hand to his head.

"Mr. Mohamad, are you ill?"

"No, sir, that is not the case. I am hurrying, and that is not good, and I should like a drink of water, if you would be so kind."

Antony was still clutching the door knob; the corridor was deserted, the hotel uncannily quiet. "Help yourself," he said; "there's a glass in the bathroom."

"I am thanking you," said Jackie, and disappeared

199

through the half-open door. There came the sound of running water, the glass clattered against the tap. A young fellow like that shouldn't be so breathless, but at least this had given him a moment's respite. Antony glanced again at his watch. Too late to call old rat trap from his home, and in a way that was lucky; but O'Brien's room was only a few doors down the corridor, and surely he'd be back from the Findlaters' by now. "I'm going to call Mr. O'Brien," he said, as Jackie reappeared with a tumbler in his hand.

"But, sir, I am telling you—"

"Just a moment." He raised his voice in desperation, and gestured imperatively enough to stop Mohamad in mid-flight. "Your own counsel," he said. "If you must talk, you can talk to him."

Jackie said something that sounded like a protest, but Maitland was already in the passage. Three doors down . . . he knocked, and then knocked again more urgently. To his relief, he heard a sound he recognized; his own bedsprings creaked too; perhaps the hotel had them carefully tuned, a sort of trademark. . . .

"What the hell?" said O'Brien, pulling open the door. No lilt in his voice tonight, no friendliness in his eyes. He seemed to have been reading in bed, the clothes were thrown back, the bedside light was on, and a book lay open on the counterpane.

"There's one of your witnesses in my bedroom. He wants to make a statement, and I don't think I can stop him."

"Now, look here," said O'Brien dangerously. He was brilliantly attired in crimson pajamas . . . who would have thought his taste would run to the exotic? "What do you think you're playing at?" he asked.

"Have a bit of sense," Maitland urged him. "If I'd wanted to see him, do you think I'd be screaming to you for help?" O'Brien still seemed to be hesitating. "I do wish you'd come," he added, almost plaintively.

"Who is it?"

"Chakwal Mohamad. One of your clients, I should have said. And I don't think he's brought his sunglasses, so hadn't you better—?" He gestured apologetically, and O'Brien smiled for the first time, rather grimly, and turned to take up his dressing gown from the foot of the bed.

"I hope this isn't your idea of a joke," he said, and followed Maitland into the corridor. And then, when Antony had got no farther than the door of his room, "Good God, man, you never told me he was ill," said O'Brien, and pushed past him without ceremony.

Jackie was sitting on the edge of the bed, and he still held the glass, but in a slack grip; and he might have drunk the water, or it might have spilled out onto the rug. Before O'Brien could reach him, his hand opened slowly, and the heavy tumbler fell with a thud and rolled a little way, unbroken. Chakwal Mohamad looked up at his counsel; his eyes seemed to focus with difficulty, and then moved on until they met Maitland's and were lit by a spark of recognition. "We only want fair play," he said, as he had done before, but now the words were mumbled, barely audible. "I am telling you, sir, it is not right, what you are doing."

Antony moved then, and as he did so O'Brien released the grip he had taken on Mohamad's shoulder and stepped past him to pick up the telephone. He was already asking for a doctor when the sick man crumpled forward, and Maitland caught him and eased him back against the pillows.

Afterward he remembered the gasping breaths that tore through Mohamad's body as he held it; but most of all he remembered the look of appeal in Jackie's eyes and the sudden clarity of his voice as he said, "Too many people are telling lies."

It seemed as if the words had taken the last of his strength. He did not speak again.

VIII

The police arrived hard on the heels of the ambulance men and the doctor, and it was through them that the message was relayed from the hospital, about an hour later, that Chakwal Mohamad was dead.

I

Sir Nicholas, called from the breakfast table to the telephone at eight o'clock the next morning, was not quite so amiable as he had been the night before. "This is persecution, Antony. What do you want now?"

"I shan't be coming home tonight, Uncle Nick."

"But only a few hours ago you told me—"

"Yes, I know. Things have changed since then."

"Overnight?" said his uncle suspiciously.

"One of the plaintiffs died in my bedroom." There was no point, after all, in wrapping the matter up.

"One of the plaintiffs?" There was dead silence for a moment while Sir Nicholas worked that out. "You're acting for the defendants," he said, and the incredulous note in his voice made the words an accusation.

"It hadn't escaped my notice. O'Brien was there."

"I see," said Sir Nicholas in the ominous tone that meant he didn't. "Hadn't you better explain?"

"Chakwal Mohamad. He wanted to tell me something, so I fetched O'Brien. Mohamad didn't look well, but he wasn't ill when I left him; when we got back to the room he collapsed."

"Will there be an inquest?"

"I should think so, wouldn't you? O'Brien has been helpful," he added, and wondered at his own reluctance to make the admission. "I mean, he didn't stress it was me that Mohamad came to see. Which was decent of him, because he's rather hating my guts at the moment."

"I see," said Sir Nicholas again, this time with complete comprehension and a note of relief. "But they can't hold

203

the inquest before Monday, and I thought you wanted t
see Sykes."

"I think I can be more use here." The reply was evasive
and he knew it. "Look here, Uncle Nick, I've got to g
Will you tell Jenny?"

"What exactly—?"

"Give her my love," said Antony; and hung up withou
allowing his uncle time for further expostulation.

He breakfasted in his room, because he didn't feel lik
facing O'Brien until he had to. The phone rang just as h
had poured his second cup of coffee, and he was tempte
to leave it unanswered, but after a moment's hesitation h
picked up the receiver.

"Inspector Townsend would like a word with you, M
Maitland, if you're at liberty. He says—" There was
pause, while the clerk at the reception desk apparentl
turned his head away from the telephone, and then hi
voice came again more strongly, "He says he knows yo
have to be in court, but he won't keep you a moment."

"Tell him . . . you'd better tell him to come up, then.

Another big man. Remembering the officers he had see
last night, it was enough to make him wonder whether th
six-foot rule still applied in Arkenshaw. But Inspecto
Townsend was scrawny; his skin looked too big for him, a
though it had been made for a much broader man. "We
now, Mr. Maitland, I happened to be passing . . . no,
won't sit down, thank you, this won't take long. About M
Chakwal Mohamad."

"Your people have my statement, Inspector. I signed
last night."

"Why, yes, sir, all in order. If it were needed, which
isn't, you see."

Under the rather bovine stare Antony thought he sense
a watchfulness. He said, "But, surely—" and then brok
off and asked instead, "When will the inquest be?"

"I'm happy to tell you, sir, that won't be necessary." H
paused, but observing Maitland's expression of surpris
added with what seemed a rather heavy attempt at jocula

ity, "Now, what sort of an idea have you got into your head, sir? I wouldn't have thought it of one of you legal gentlemen, jumping to conclusions like that."

Whatever conclusions he had reached had been arrived at painfully in the dark hours before dawn. "He was under the doctor, then? Was anything like that expected?"

"Not as you'd say expected. He hadn't seen the doctor lately, which is why the coroner had to be advised. But he made no difficulties about the certificate being issued; there was a heart condition, you see." When Maitland did not reply, he added heartily, "Well, I thought I'd just let you know that. Set your mind at rest, as it might be. Then you wouldn't feel you had to be hanging about in Arkenshaw longer than you need."

"I shall have to stay until my case is finished, Inspector."

"Oh, yes, of course, sir." His smile had the effect of acknowledging a conspiracy: it wouldn't be proper for either of us to comment, but you know and I know that that's as good as over. "What will happen about that, do you think?"

If Chakwal Mohamad had died a natural death . . . "Actio personalis moritur cum personam," said Maitland abently, his mind on his problem rather than on the necessity of informing the inspector. Then, as he heard the question consciously for the first time, "There'll be an adjournment, I suppose."

"A mark of respect," said Townsend, as if approvingly. Well, I'll be getting along then, Mr. Maitland. Glad to ave met you."

In the circumstances, as was to be expected, the judge did not delay them long; he did not set a date for the fresh hearing, but intimated that it would not recommence until after the funeral. "Thinks we may change our plea if he gives us time," said Bushey, as he came out of the robing room with his leader.

"Out of the question," said Maitland abruptly.

Bushey's manner that morning had been one of careful

205

politeness, but his lips tightened a little at the brusquene
of the other man's tone. "Have it your own way," he sai

"I expect I shall." Maitland turned his head and ga
his sudden, disarming smile. "I'm out of temper," he sai
"Forgive me. Oh, there you are, Conway," he added wi
an air of relief.

"Have you a moment?" asked Chris. He seemed to rea
ize as he spoke that the question was a superfluous on
"It's Sergeant Duckett. I've explained the position, but
wants a word with you."

"Where—?" Conway gestured silently toward a doo
way at the other side of the hall from the court. "I'll com
then. What about you, Bushey?" But Bushey preferred
get back to chambers.

"Save me working over the weekend," he explained.

Sergeant Duckett was in no mood to mince matter
"That Jackie," he said, as soon as Conway had the do
shut, "how did he die?"

"Heart failure," Maitland told him. "Or so your frie
Inspector Townsend implied. Anyway, the certificate h
been issued."

"Do you believe that?" asked Duckett bluntly.

"On the whole, no. But it means there'll be no autops
no inquest, no investigation—"

"I'd rather it was investigated, if it's all the same
you," said the sergeant, at his most belligerent.

"It's nothing to do with me," Antony told him hastil
"But it may be just as well."

"Because you don't want it getting round that he died
your room?"

"That's an added advantage, of c-course." (No u
being angry; the poor chap was obviously half off his he
with worry.) "But I think I should explain that he said tw
things, in O'Brien's hearing as well as mine. One was th
'too many people are telling lies,' and the other, 'it is n
right, sir, what you are doing.'" Unconsciously he had r
produced Chakwal Mohamad's tone, as well as his word

206

ıd the effect in the quiet room was uncanny, as though
ıe dead man had spoken to them.

"Meaning?" said Duckett. His voice was gruffer than
ver.

"Meaning . . . oh, that his death was too convenient.
ut you could argue either way as to who would find it
o."

"If you think I killed him, you'd best say so and be done
ith it."

"What, in the presence of a witness?"

Conway, brought back into the conversation, moved
ırther into the room. "You don't think that, Maitland,"
ᵉ said, "unless you've been pulling my leg all along."

"No, of course I don't," Antony agreed, his eyes on
ᵘuckett's face.

The sergeant said uneasily, "I'm sorry if I spoke a bit
ıarp, like. But it's enough to rile a saint. They're talking
ready, if I know owt about it . . . unnatural, they'll say,
ım dying like that. And they'll say it's been hushed up."

"Isn't that what you think yourself?"

"Well then, I do. But I don't want people saying it was
ᵊr my sake."

Looking at him, Maitland was aware of a wave of emo-
on which he recognized after a startled moment as some-
ıing more than respect, if rather less than affection. Fred
ᵘuckett might be as stubborn as an army mule (a simile
hich seemed to keep recurring in his thought with regard
ᵗ the Duckett family) and as fixed in his ideas as the Rock
ᶠ Gibraltar; he might be full of prejudice, and as hard as
ıils, but he wasn't invulnerable, and under his stolid exte-
ᵒor he was just now going through hell. All the same,
ıere'd be no whining if things didn't go his way.

The silence had lasted a little too long. "Did Ahmad
han work for Greenhalgh and Blackburn before his ar-
ᵊst?" Maitland asked.

The unexpectedness of the question seemed to take Ser-
ᵉant Duckett off balance for a moment. "How did you
now that?" he growled.

207

"It's true, isn't it?"

"What of it?"

"You know perfectly well what of it." Antony was sud
denly indignant. "You worked out—didn't you?—just wh
he had to be saved. What I can't see is why you didn't te
me."

"Could you have used the information, in court?"

"No, but . . . well, never mind about that. The oth
thing I want to ask you is, is there a Pakistani quarter i
Arkenshaw?"

"Not exactly." Duckett was eyeing his counsel waril
but with a new respect. "But they do group together, i
three or four different parts, I'd say."

"So that you should have been able to find that 'goo
looking young chap' you spoke of—the one who might o
might not have been collecting hire-purchase payments–
if he'd been living with the rest of them."

"I should."

"But you didn't?"

"No."

"All right! You reached certain conclusions, didn't yo
Do you know anything else that tends to confirm them?
He saw the sergeant hesitate, and threw out his hands wit
an odd, extravagant gesture. "For heaven's sake, man, yo
can't think *now* I'll laugh at you."

Duckett looked at him in silence. " 'Appen you'
right," he said at last. "There is one thing, I didn't know
till the other day."

"Tell me, then."

"They send these booklets of theirs abroad, Gree
halgh's do." His eyes turned to Conway. "You'll know th
kind of thing, poetry and such. Our Star's brought som
on 'em home . . . well, you have to laugh. Better than th
wireless."

"Fragrant moments . . . today's great thought," said Con
way, by way of explanation.

"Yes, but—"

208

"I'm coming to that. So she happened to mention one day that some of the shipments went to Pakistan. She hadn't noticed the address, of course, but it was in Karachi, and that seemed to clinch it, like. Not that the lass thought owt of it, of course; it was just that she'd been down to the dispatch department on an errand—"

But Maitland was no longer listening. He said, "That does it!" and then, "Thank you, Sergeant. I'll see you later, I expect. Come along, Conway."

"Where are we going?" said Chris, who had been taken unawares and had to hurry to catch up.

"Do you mind driving me?" Antony paused, holding open the swing door. "The first place I want," he added, as they went down the steps together and turned along the wet pavement toward the place where the Austin was parked, "is a really good flower shop. Do you know one anywhere near?"

II

At the florists they were offered chrysanthemums, which Maitland rejected decisively. "Melancholy—" he said; his gesture seemed to Conway, who was beginning to feel light-headed after being rushed across town without any explanations at all, to be eloquent of all the sadness of autumn, of mist shrouding the river, and falling leaves. But then, he didn't like chrysanthemums much himself.

At this point the assistant lost her head and offered them lilies, which nearly made Antony lose his temper again. He said, enunciating each word very slowly and clearly, "Carnations . . . delphiniums . . . even asters if it comes to that. There must be something." And when the girl only shrugged helplessly he prowled to the back of the shop, where he came upon a massive stone jar filled with yellow roses. "Those will do."

"They're ordered," said the assistant sulkily.

209

"Yes, now . . . by me," he told her gently.

"And they're out of season, a special order. Very expensive."

"I'm sure they are," he agreed cordially. But he gave Conway a grin as they emerged from the shop. "At this rate I shall be borrowing from you before I get home."

"I can always rob the petty cash."

"At least I didn't give way to the temptation to charge them to Mr. Jones."

Conway gave a crack of laughter, quickly suppressed. "Are you going to deign now to tell me where we're going? It's a little difficult—"

"Didn't I tell you? Anyway, I should have thought it was obvious. To see Mrs. Mohamad, of course."

Chris didn't attempt to argue, but got into the car and started it obediently. "I'll have to go back to the office for the address."

"Never mind about that," Maitland told him, and produced a ragged envelope from his pocket with the information printed on it, quite neatly and legibly.

Conway glanced at it with awe, and then drove on in silence for a while. Then he said, as though he could no longer contain the question, "Do you think Jackie was really . . . really—?"

"Really what?"

"Well . . . murdered?"

"You heard what I said to Duckett. I don't *know*."

"And that the fact is being deliberately hushed up," said Chris, ignoring the rather vague nature of this reply.

"That's even more difficult." He sounded as if he was talking to himself. "Sometimes a mere suggestion is enough."

"But the doctor . . . the hospital?"

"I'm not suggesting a conspiracy; I'm sure they gave an honest opinion. Ask your father about that," Maitland added, seeing Conway's doubtful look. "There are poisons that produce an effect very like heart failure . . . no, that's

210

wrong, they do produce heart failure. If the patient is known to have a cardiac weakness and there is evidence that he had been subject to an unusual strain . . . it's all too easy, really."

"Yes, I see." Chris sounded subdued.

"Besides which, there is always the distinct possibility that they are right and I am wrong."

"I see that, too. But what I don't see," he went on with more spirit, "is why we're haring across town with a ruddy great bouquet in the back of the car."

"To express our sympathy," said Maitland. His tone was light, almost flippant, but when Chris stole a look at him at the next set of traffic lights, his expression was hard and forbidding.

Sunnyside Street, under a thin November drizzle, belied its name. "This part is better in summer," said Chris, as they cruised down slowly looking for number seventy. "You can't move for kids, it's a ghastly nuisance, of course, but it does cheer the place up a bit."

It certainly wasn't a day for playing out, but from behind the lace curtains of number sixty-eight two small, dark faces peered at them with solemn curiosity. Waiting outside the door of number seventy, Antony asked, "How many are there in the Mohamad family?"

"Four boys, four girls."

"All at home?"

"I think so. Jackie was the eldest."

The door was opened then by a girl of about twenty. "You are please coming in," she told them, when Antony had explained their errand. "My mother is not well to see people, but I shall be giving her the beautiful flowers and telling her you are being kind."

She was very like her brother, a slight, pretty child with the same grace of movement and a rather touching air of dignity. "I am Dera," she told them as they followed her into the parlor . . . not a Sunday or "company" room, this, but well used and untidy. "I am the eldest now, so I am staying with her; besides, I will be a nurse, so it is right that I should stay. The little ones will go to my aunt for their dinner."

"And Mr. Mohamad?" asked Maitland. He had a feeling this girl might help him more than her parents could but protocol must be observed.

"He is going to his work." She seated herself, and gestured gravely for them to follow her example. "A day's pay, you are understanding, he cannot be losing that unless he must. And next week will be the funeral." She said this very matter-of-factly, with no hint of self-pity or bravado, and then she turned to smile at Chris, perhaps sensing his discomfort. But Antony was in no doubt at all that she had been crying before they came. "I am telling him also of this kindness, Mr. Conway, and . . . I am sorry, I am not hearing your name."

"Maitland," he said, watching her.

"Then you are the man—?"

"Your brother was with me last night, when he was taken ill."

"The man at the court . . . the lawyer," she said quickly. "The man he is telling me he is afraid of."

Conway, his eyes on his colleague's face, saw him flinch from the word as he might have done from a blow. But Maitland said only, "He wasn't afraid of me last night," and his voice was steady enough, though perhaps a little too determinedly unemotional.

"No . . . no . . . I am sure he is being mistaken."

"He wanted to tell me something," said Antony. "Do you know what it was?" When she did not reply, he got up and began to move restlessly about the room. "If it wasn't important, I shouldn't be bothering you now. But please don't cry again . . . you make me ashamed." And this time when he stopped and looked down at her there was the same flickering smile she had given Conway a few moments before.

"I am sorry. I know only that he is being worried. First there is the—the arrest. That is terrible; it is as if we are all

212

ying, a little. And then all is well again, but I wish in my
eart that Ghulam Beas is not a revengeful man."

"It was Beas's idea . . . this prosecution?"

"Yes, but they are agreeing . . . Jackie and my father.
Vhen he is talking of our country, what else is there to
o?"

"But still Jackie was worried?"

"Worried . . . nervous . . . afraid. A little afraid," she
dded quickly, trying to soften the impact of the state-
1ent.

"And last night—"

"Jackie is never being angry, until last night."

"Did you ask him why?"

"Yes, but he did not tell me. So I am saying again, and
1en he is being angry with me, and he is going out."

"It was late when he came to see me. Do you know
here he went first, who he saw?"

"Not Ghulam Beas, for he is coming here at nine . . .
n o'clock."

"Did he stay long?"

"He is telling us about the court, that all is going well.
hen he is going away again."

"To find Jackie?"

"I am not knowing that."

"You don't know where your brother went, then?"

She frowned a little over the question, and he wondered
' he was being too persistent. But after a while, "Last
ight when I am in bed I am hearing a car, a big car, and
> I am thinking that Tom is bringing him home. And I
m feeling hurt, a little, because Tom is being my boy-
iend. But, after all, Jackie is not coming in."

Maitland, who had come to a halt near the window,
ame back a little way into the room. "I'm grateful to
ou," he said. Something of the intentness seemed to have
one from his bearing. He smiled at her and asked cas-
ally, "Is Tom nice?"

She had a shrug for that. "First I am finishing my train-
1g, and then I am making up my mind."

"He has a big car," he said, teasing her. Conway gave him a suspicious look.

"Oh, no . . . no. He is driving a gentleman, but sometimes he is letting him use the car." She paused a moment and then said confidingly, "Jackie is not liking it when he comes to see me. He is saying Tom has no right." She saw him frown, and added rather forlornly, "I am not understanding him."

"I've met someone called Tom who drives a big car, for Mr. Findlater—"

"Yes, that is Tom."

"—but I don't know his name."

"Bhakkar."

"Not so nice a name as 'Mohamad.' I should think twice before changing it, if I were you. Now, we ought to be going. Thank you for receiving us so kindly."

She came to her feet as Conway did, and turned to touch the roses, which she had set down on the table behind her. "It is you who are being kind."

"Will you tell your parents—?" He made his farewell gracefully enough, but he grimaced at Conway when they were back in the car again. "I wonder why one always say on these occasions 'If there's anything I can do—' "

"You said it very prettily," said Chris with a sour look

"Did I hurt her? I didn't want to, more than she's hurt already."

"I daresay you gave her something to think about," said Conway, relenting. But he went on, after a moment "You're giving me a headache, I can tell you that."

"What's worrying you? Bhakkar?"

"Findlater's chauffeur . . . Jones's maid."

"He may be her brother," said Maitland encouragingly

"Jackie didn't think so."

"He thought he was married, anyway. If Sergeant Duckett was here, he'd reprove you for jumping to conclusions."

"Who, me?" said Chris, surprised. "Well, if I am, it's because you're setting me a bad example."

214

"That's a pity. By the way, where are you taking me?"

"I don't know. I'm just heading downtown."

"We'd better have lunch, don't you think? Let's find a ub where they'll give us cheese and onions."

"All right," said Chris obligingly. "And after that?"

"John Cadwallader Jones." The car gave a lurch and teadied again. "I hope you'll wait for me, but I'd rather ee him alone."

"I don't think you should."

"Don't you?" He turned to look at Conway, and rinned when he saw his set expression. "You can watch ie window if you like, and I'll signal if he grows violent."

"Think I'd care?" Chris asked him coldly.

III

Mr. Jones greeted him with the same rather forced riendliness he had displayed on their previous meeting. You're wanting to get back to London, I suppose. I shall e in touch with Conway, of course, and he will advise ou—" But the atmosphere chilled perceptibly when Mait- ind interrupted him.

"I'm not leaving yet. I came to ask you to give me Mrs. hakkar's address."

"Mrs. . . . who?"

"Bhakkar."

"Why should you suppose I am able to help you?" And ien, with a burst of indignation that made him at once iore human, "What business is it of yours?"

Maitland ignored that. "You don't deny you know the idy. Is she still working for you?"

"Not for some time now." He began to get up, a sort of iken gesture; halted when his visitor did not follow his xample. "I must ask you to excuse me. I'm rather busy."

"I'll apologize, if you like, for disturbing you," Maitland ffered. The room was comfortable, too comfortable: a so- citor's office rigged out, without reference to expense, by the editor of the furniture section of a women's magazine. The hand of the unknown Mrs. Jones, perhaps? And what did it matter, except that it was such an unlikely setting . . . "I'm afraid it's rather urgent."

"Really, Mr. Maitland!"

"Yes, really."

"What possible business can you have with Mrs. Bhakkar?"

"I want to ask her why she never completed her application for an endowment policy from the Imperial Insurance Company." Seeing Jones's look of bewilderment, he added impatiently, "She's Barlow's disappearing prospect . . . as if you didn't know."

"I assure you—"

"Tell me about her, then."

"But what . . . what do you want to know?"

"When did she come to England?"

"I don't remember exactly. Early in the year."

"Well, did she come straight to your employment? How long did she stay?" (But old rat trap wasn't reacting as he had expected; he seemed genuinely puzzled, and if he was . . .)

"Yes, she came straight to us." With no change of expression he added, "I don't like your tone, Mr. Maitland."

"I'm not altogether surprised." Try it the other way, then. "Will you take my word for it that it's important?"

"Why should I?"

"No reason at all, unless you're interested in . . . justice."

"If you can explain to me—?"

"I think the motive for the burglary at Nineteen Badger's Way was to regain possession of Mrs. Bhakkar's proposal form. No, I'm not being controversial; we'll leave Beas and Mohamad out of it, for the moment."

"I don't understand," said Jones helplessly. But he relaxed a little, and gave Maitland a searching look. "I believe you're in earnest," he added. "Only I don't see how the motive can affect the issue at all."

216

"Let's just say it makes me interested in what happened to Mrs. Bhakkar. She came to work for you as a daily maid . . . charwoman . . . something like that."

"Housemaid," said Jones, but doubtfully; as a man might speak to whom the niceties of domestic organization were a mystery. "She didn't live in."

"No, she lived in Wendover Terrace. I think her reason for coming here was to find her husband."

"All this is very irregular."

"Yes, isn't it?" (On the whole, there didn't seem much likelihood of their ever becoming bosom friends.) "I'm only asking for confirmation."

"Very well." Whatever he thought of the vagaries of his visitor's conduct, he seemed to resign himself to some degree of cooperation. "She knew where her husband was, as a matter of fact; Tom has been here for three years, working for Frank Findlater. Unfortunately, as it turned out, he didn't want to be—er—to be caught up with."

"I see."

"She was very distressed about it, but the last time she came to work—I don't remember the date, but it was her half-day, when she only came in the morning—*that* day she told my wife that Tom had agreed to meet her. She was very optimistic, Dorothy said, quite sure that when she saw him . . . but unfortunately, things didn't turn out quite as she hoped."

"What happened?"

"They quarreled, I suppose. Anyway, he seems to have made it clear to her that there was no question of reconciliation. She agreed to leave him alone in the future and moved away from here . . . to Bradford, I was told."

"Didn't she tell you?"

"No. Frank Findlater spoke to me the next day. I suppose we're a couple of sentimentalists"—something very near a smile crossed Mr. Jones's features—"we'd been hoping for a happy ending. Well, I had a word with Tom myself, felt it my duty. He was sulky, but from what I gathered, he was making it worth her while to keep away."

217

Antony said slowly, "Did she come to say good-bye? Write to you? Ask for a reference?"

"None of those things." For the first time he sounded uneasy. "I imagine that Frank had found employment for her. He wasn't pleased with Tom, but he has a value for him."

"So has Dera Mohamad."

"Dera—?"

"Your late client's sister. But that *is* beside the point." And suddenly the anger that had been simmering in him ever since last night boiled up. He was angry with Arkenshaw, with charity gone sour and the futility of wasted endeavor. And beyond this, more bitterly, more deeply, he was angry with himself. He had thought himself free of prejudice, but that was what had blinded him . . . and he'd been wrong, all along the line. Strangely enough, though he had been so certain, he knew this without surprise. He didn't even have to marshal his arguments, he just knew. . . . "Did you tell Findlater that Conway was pursuing Miss Garrowby across the ice with bloodhounds?" he asked, incautiously presenting the thought as it occurred to him.

"You're not mad, you're drunk," said Jones. On the whole he sounded relieved.

Maitland stopped to ponder the justice of this. "On a pint of old and mild?" he said. "Surely not." His voice, at least, was under control. He didn't want to display his anger, and was quite unconscious that his sudden pallor and a rather grim look about his mouth made it obvious enough. "Are you going to tell me—?"

"I haven't the faintest idea what you're talking about."

"I wanted some inquiries made about Miss Garrowby. Someone told Findlater. I thought perhaps it was you."

"Most certainly not."

"I see." He sat a moment longer, and then got to his feet with an abrupt movement.

"May I ask you again, Mr. Maitland, why you have been interrogating me like this?"

218

Jones had made no attempt to rise, and Antony stood beside the desk and looked down at him. "It's a long story," he said, and smiled without any amusement. "I'm going now, I'm sorry to have disturbed you." In the doorway he turned. "When the trial starts again, we shall be introducing fresh evidence. I expect Conway will be in touch with you."

IV

He found Chris Conway, damp and cold and bad-tempered, glaring at a poster outside the Old Empire Cinema. "I didn't know your tastes ran in that direction," he said. Conway turned from the display of near-nude beauty that had apparently been engaging his attention, started to say something, and broke off to ask abruptly: "What's up?"

"Something," said Maitland, "has got to be done." He found Chris looking at him and added in a more normal tone, "I want to see Grandma."

"The stars again, I suppose," said Conway sarcastically. "All right, I'll take you."

"I thought I knew who she meant when she talked about eagles," said Antony; Conway was rather on his conscience, he'd been getting a raw deal, and some clarification was due to him. "Now I think I was wrong, and I want her to tell me—" He was quite unaware that the statement was in any way inadequate.

"So now it's bird-watching," said Chris, and got into the car and slammed the door. "Don't bother to explain," he added, as Maitland got in beside him. "You're welcome to the whole bloody aviary as far as I'm concerned."

"The trouble is, so far it's been mainly wild geese."

In the circumstances it says much for Conway's forgiving nature that he offered to wait to drive Maitland back from Old Peel Farm, but after a moment's thought Antony shook his head. "She might talk to *you* alone, or to *me* alone, but not to both of us together."

219

"I don't mind staying in the car."

"She'd see you through the window and insist on giving you tea and parkin, and probably make you take your socks off to dry. Don't you think?"

"I suppose she would."

"I'm going back to the hotel after this. Keep in touch, will you?"

"Right."

Maitland stood for a while, watching the receding car; then he turned and went up the path and rang the bell.

The kitchen looked unfamiliar by daylight. Grandma received him without comment; he even thought she might be pleased to see him, but it was hard to be sure. "Have there been any more anonymous letters?" he asked when they were settled by the fire to the old lady's satisfaction.

"One or two. 'Appen there'll be more after what came about last night." She looked at him keenly. "Is that what upset you?"

First Chris Conway, now Grandma. "It made me angry," he confessed. "He was a nice lad, in spite of everything. It seems such a waste."

"Aye, it does that. But you didn't come here for sympathy," she said robustly.

That made him laugh. "It's just as well, isn't it?"

"You'd get none," she told him. And then, "I suppose the case was put off, wasn't it? Fred hasn't been home yet. It was good of you to come and say good-bye. It doesn't mean you won't be coming back," she added, by way of anxious afterthought.

"I'll be back," he said. To take up the burden of my own incompetence. To watch the case move on to the inevitable verdict. Unless . . . "Will you tell me *now?*" he asked her.

"What do you want to know?"

"You said, 'Where the carcass is, there shall the eagles be gathered together.'"

"Aye, so I did."

220

"I thought you meant Jones. Because in a way he started everything . . . that's true, even if everything else was wrong." He hesitated. "I didn't like him," he admitted; "it was easy to believe—"

"Don't take on about it, lad."

"No . . . well . . . you see . . . something's got to be done," he said, as he had done to Conway. "Things have changed now, haven't they?"

"Fred says the case is over, after what young Jimmy Marshall had to say," she agreed. "But that doesn't mean it would be right for me to start slandering people."

"What about Star?"

"She'll get over it. We're flitting."

"Is she going to marry Constable Ryder?"

"Well, now, I hope not. They wouldn't suit."

"I wondered—"

"She's got this daft notion into her head . . . she's *sorry* for him," said Grandma scornfully.

"There's Chris Conway. His work is here, in Arkenshaw."

"I don't know as he wants to marry her."

"He wants to, all right. She agreed . . . on conditions."

"Nay!"

"If all this is cleared up; if we get a favorable verdict and you can all stay in Arkenshaw—"

"There's nowt I can do about that." She paused, and then added, perhaps a little less inflexibly, "I've no patience with such foolishness. Still, it's a shame, isn't it, wrecking her chances?"

"I thought you didn't approve of Conway."

"It's none of my business, is it," asked Grandma sulkily, "if t'lass has made up her mind?" She glared at him for a moment. "Not that I don't see what you're at," she scolded, "but talking behind people's backs is something I don't hold with."

"What about me? You've led me astray once—"

"I never!"

"All this talking in riddles."

"That's your own lookout." But he thought, just for a second, that . . . perhaps . . . she was wavering.

"I'm not asking for your conclusions . . . for what you only think you know. Just for your own impressions of one man, whom I will name to you."

She was silent for so long he began to wonder if she was ever going to reply at all. At last she said heavily, "I'm trusting you, Mr. Maitland." And then, after another pause, "Who?"

"Frank Findlater."

"He is governed by Saturn . . . you may laugh, young man. He is cold and cruel."

"I'm not laughing," Antony protested; indeed, he was more startled than anything. "I've a great respect for your wisdom, and you must have known him—or known of him—for a long time."

"I was his nurse," she said, and left him to work that one out. After a while she added, "That was after Fred's father died, of course."

"But what about Fred?"

"He stayed with my sister. He was at school already, old enough to understand—"

"Yes. I see," said Antony, abashed. And again he found her eyes fixed on him, but this time he thought their expression was kindly, perhaps even a little amused. "Tell me about Findlater, then."

"About his childhood?"

"The child is father to the man," said Antony sententiously, and risked a grin.

She wasn't the woman to allow this piece of impertinence to go unrebuked. "That's quite enough of that," she told him. "As for Frank, what else is there to say?"

"But . . . look here . . . I've met him. Well, I mean, I thought you might tell me he was proud, too proud to want it known if his financial position had changed . . something like that. Not that he wasn't kind."

"Proper mixed up, aren't you?"

"Of course I am," said Antony crossly. "Whose fault is that?"

She ignored the question. "He was a sweet-tempered child," she said. He had a sudden sense that she had withdrawn from him, looking back down the years. "Do anything for anybody, he would, so long as he got his own way. When he didn't . . . well, I don't know anything he'd stop at to be suited. Not the usual things . . . screaming . . . tantrums. You should have heard young Victor when he was in a temper. Frank was sly."

"Then you think . . . no, I promised not to ask you that, didn't I?"

"I think if things wasn't going well for him—if the money wasn't going as far as it used to, or if he found himself short—*then* I think he'd do almost anything to keep things as they were. And I know he'd put himself out for his own comfort, or even for that of his friends. But once he got a down on anyone—" She stopped there and scowled at her visitor. "I've said more than I should."

"Clogs to clogs in three generations," said Maitland thoughtfully.

"So they say." But she relented a little when he got up. "You haven't had your tea."

"I'll come again . . . may I?" He crossed the room quickly before she could struggle out of her chair, and bent to take her hand. "I'm going to gamble, Grandma. Will you wish me luck . . . or is that something else you don't hold with?"

"Come to a bad end, you will," she grumbled. But as she looked up at him he saw that her eyes were misty. " 'Appen I'd bet on thee, lad," she said, and he felt the faint pressure of her fingers before she released him.

He turned in the doorway to smile at her. "I'm glad I have your blessing," he told her, and was relieved to see the familiar scowl.

"Oh, get along with you," said Grandma Duckett gruffly.

223

V

He was far too impatient now to wait for a taxi; he made for the main road and got on a tram and sat staring blankly at the woman opposite until she got up in a huff and took herself and her parcels to the front of the car. It had come on to rain more heavily, and he got pretty well soaked on the short walk back to the hotel. He was mopping his face with his handkerchief as he spoke to the clerk, but he wasn't really conscious of being wet.

"Has Mr. O'Brien left yet?"

"Not yet, sir." And then, helpfully, "He mentioned a train at seven o'clock."

"Thank you." He went up the stairs two at a time, leaving the man staring, and thumped on O'Brien's door when he reached it without giving himself time for further thought.

Kevin O'Brien was packing. He held the door open when he saw who his visitor was, but nobody could have mistaken his expression for a welcoming one. He said "You'd better come in," and added as he closed the door again, "There's a towel in the bathroom."

Maitland gave him a vacant look. "Towel?"

"You appear to have been through a showerbath."

"Oh. I see." He became aware that the rain was trickling down the back of his neck and went away to fetch the towel and came back rubbing his hair. "I should have gone to my own room first, but I was so afraid I should miss you."

O'Brien laughed shortly. "This sudden desire for my company is very flattering, of course—"

"You're wondering why I'm here, and I don't blame you. But you don't have to be so stuffy," Maitland complained.

"All right, then; what *do* you want?"

"Your help."

"My . . . good God, man, wasn't what happened in court yesterday enough for you?"

224

"There is also," said Maitland, with a note in his voice that might have been taken for diffidence, "what happened in my room last night."

"I shouldn't have thought even you would try to make capital out of that. The boy told you quite plainly you were wrong."

"He also said, 'too many people are telling lies.' Don't you think he meant Jimmy Marshall?"

"No, I don't!" O'Brien paused, and quite deliberately looked his companion up and down. "I used to think I was a pretty good judge of character," he said.

"Yes?" Maitland's tone was rather too quiet.

"I've heard some pretty queer things about you from time to time."

"Yes?" said Maitland again. Perhaps it was his restraint that finally infuriated O'Brien, arousing him to plain speaking.

"I never believed . . . God help me. I thought you were sincere; at least, that you didn't try to raise the devil just for the fun of it."

"It isn't my idea of f-fun," said Maitland. He was still fairly well in control of his temper, and the tremor in his voice was of the slightest, but O'Brien heard it and laughed.

"Jones is more charitable. He just thinks you're insane."

"Or drunk," said Antony. And then, on a note of regret, "I wish I were."

"If that's all you want, I imagine it can be easily remedied."

"I shouldn't want your help for that," Maitland pointed out. "Won't you even listen to me?"

"What good will that do?"

"It might convince you. Unless you're too bloody pigheaded ever to believe you're in the wrong," he added, and watched the two telltale spots of color glow in O'Brien's cheeks.

"Why, you—you—"

"Don't mind me. Say it, if it'll make you feel any better." He paused invitingly, but O'Brien only glared at him. "You talked just now about 'raising the devil,' but do you think that was my doing . . . really?"

"The rights and wrongs of this business were obvious from the beginning."

"Not to me. I lost quite a bit of sleep deciding whether I should take it at face value, or whether there was something behind it."

"And the latter conclusion was more to your taste."

The ironic tone was more than Maitland could bear. "All r-right!" he said. "I'll let you h-have it s-straight. You're b-blaming me for exactly what you're d-doing yourself . . . only you're too b-bloody b-blind to see it."

"Indeed?" said O'Brien, on his dignity again.

"Y-yes, indeed," mimicked Antony savagely. "We both happen to believe in our clients, but at least I'll give you credit for being sincere about it. Don't you think you could do the same for me?"

O'Brien was very still now, and looking at the other man frowningly. "I don't understand you," he said.

"No, of course, you've h-heard things. Well, tell me this, O'Brien: believing as you do in Beas and Mohamad, if things had been going against you, wouldn't you have done what you could to prove they were in the right? Oh, I know you didn't have to; it was clear from the beginning to you and everybody else that the police had been up to some funny business. I nearly believed it myself at one time, only it doesn't happen to be true." He waited a moment, and then added angrily, "Answer my qu-question, d-damn you. Wouldn't you have tried?"

"I think perhaps I should," said O'Brien slowly. "But—"

"B-but when I try, it's d-different. Is that it?"

"Do you really believe that Beas and Mohamad were robbing the Barlows? That they weren't framed for the job?"

"I believe it absolutely, and utterly, and without equivocation."

"We'd better sit down," said O'Brien. "And for goodness' sake, take that coat off," he added irritably; "you're dripping all over the carpet."

Antony hung his raincoat on the back of the door, and stuffed the rainbow-colored scarf into the pocket; if he didn't remember to return it to Bushey soon he'd probably be saddled with it for the rest of his life. He turned and found that O'Brien had seated himself on the dressing-table stool, and, seeing the back of his head reflected in the mirror, noticed for the first time the slight thinning of hair at the crown. "They say it's bad for you, wearing a wig," he said vaguely; and Kevin obviously took his meaning, for he put up a hand to touch the offending spot, and grinned at the inconsequence of the remark in quite a friendly way.

"I'm damned if I know what to make of you," he said.

"Luckily that doesn't matter. I want to tell you a story—"

"Once upon a time," said O'Brien. His expression was serious, but when Maitland glanced at him, he did not think the remark was intended to be satirical.

"A fairy story, if you like," he agreed, and went to sit at the foot of the bed, ignoring the one armchair.

"Well, I've said I'll listen," O'Brien told him inaccurately. "But if it's this additional evidence you mentioned to Jones, why didn't you tell *him?*"

"It's more than that. And then I want to call on Mr. Greenhalgh, and I'd like you to come with me."

"Who the hell—?"

"He's a printer. I think he's been printing employment vouchers."

"Why shouldn't he?"

"Other things, too, for all I know. Whatever a Commonwealth citizen needs to get into the country. But I don't think the Ministry of Labor placed the order, and I'd like to know who did."

"Don't play the fool, Maitland." O'Brien was all set to

227

be angry again. "Whatever you think you mean, it ha
nothing to do with Ghulam Beas and those two bastard
you're defending."

"It has everything to do with them," Maitland asserted

"You're not telling me Beas came here illegally, with
forged papers?"

"No. But others have . . . a great many of them, ac
cording to my information."

"Even so, what has that to do with the burglary?"

"Nothing at all, but I think it has a lot to do with the
present case. Which, after all, is my main concern."

"Give me strength," said O'Brien helplessly.

"I'll try to explain." A moment ago it had been clear in
his mind; now all his certainty seemed to have vanished
and with it his confidence. "Before I start, there are a few
things I must ask you to recognize for the moment, beside
the fact that a great many foreigners have come to this dis
trict illegally. For instance, that Sergeant Duckett, who
was originally in charge of the investigation, is—and i
known to be—an extremely persistent man; and that there
is in Arkenshaw one person at least with a great deal of in
fluence and no scruples about using it."

"The first two points must be common knowledge. The
third I am willing to allow . . . for the purpose of your
argument only." His tone was stiff, and Maitland took
what comfort he could from the fact that at least he
seemed to be listening.

"I must admit that when I first talked to Duckett—and
to Ryder too, for that matter—I was very doubtful of the
truth of what they were telling me. I mean, Ducket
doesn't make any secret of his feelings about the foreign
ers, and the chance to shop Beas—who he says is a trou
blemaker—might have seemed too good to miss, even if i
meant taking some liberties with the truth. And then in
court . . . well, like you, I didn't really think it was likely
that either Beas or Mohamad was interested in Barlow'
coins, or his cash. Beas was doing quite well for himsel
financially. And Jackie just wasn't the type."

228

"No," said Kevin, watching him.

"But then there are the papers that Sam Barlow believed he had mislaid. The person concerned—"

"Jones told me about Mrs. Bhakkar just now on the phone. It seemed to worry him."

"But you don't think . . . no, why should you? There are one or two additional bits of evidence, however: some papers were burned in the grate at nineteen Badger's Way on the night of the burglary, *vide* Mrs. Barlow. And Mrs. Bhakkar really did stay for about three weeks in March of this year at the address where Barlow inquired for her; this on the evidence of the grocer's wife."

"And what does that prove?"

"Nothing, by itself. But let me tell you what I think happened on the day of the theft. Mrs. Bhakkar was at home that afternoon, and Barlow called on her at about two-fifteen and helped her fill in the proposal form for an endownment policy. She was dressed for going out, and was going to meet her husband if what she told Mrs. Jones is true. And I think the idea of the endowment policy may have been to give her confidence, to make her feel like a woman of substance—"

"But, damn it all, she hadn't even paid one premium," O'Brien protested.

"No." Antony waved the objection aside. "She hadn't seen her husband for three years at least, but things had changed in that time. She had a job, money of her own, and she had come to England, where even her status as a woman was different. I think perhaps she went to meet Tom Bhakkar with more assurance than was wise."

"All this is speculation."

"About her feelings . . . I'll grant you that. I've been giving a good deal of thought to Mrs. Bhakkar."

"So I gather," said O'Brien dryly.

"Yes, but don't discount the bits that aren't guesswork. That night—the night of the twenty-fourth—the proposal form disappeared, together with the certificates which accompanied it. Next day, Mrs. Bhakkar's landlady was ask-

229

ing for her at the grocer's shop; but later in the week, when Barlow called, she denied ever having heard of such a person. Nor did the Joneses see Mrs. Bhakkar again—all they got was a message that she was resigned to living apart from her husband and had gone to Bradford. All that is capable of proof."

"You're going to tell me the husband had killed her."

"At least, he had a motive. I don't suppose it was premeditated, but if she was persistent . . . You'll tell me I'm guessing again."

"Aren't you?"

Maitland let that pass. "I can't expect you to accept that part of the argument, because it's based on the assumption that the object of the expedition to Badger's Way was to remove any proof that Mrs. Bhakkar ever existed."

"I don't accept it," O'Brien agreed. "And even if I did, how are you going to bring in Beas and Mohamad?"

"Connect them with Tom Bhakkar, you mean? Tom is courting Mohamad's sister Dera . . . and I've her evidence for *that*."

O'Brien was frowning. "And you think that, just to oblige Tom, they broke into the Barlows' house to get the proposal form back. Knowing why he wanted it. I admit it's queer, but that's too much to swallow."

"No, I don't think it was quite like that. The trouble is, there are so many strands in this business, and all of them lead to a dead end . . . until you put them all together."

"Well, go on."

"The next strand is Sergeant Duckett's evidence, which he gave, I may tell you, most unwillingly. He was investigating the illegal immigration, as I told you, but after the first trial, he was instructed—quite understandably—to hand over the inquiries to his inspector. He says the inspector was doing nothing, but it's perfectly obvious he hadn't dropped the matter himself. Still, he felt sore about it, felt his superiors had been unreasonable, I suppose, and didn't want to say anything at all until he could offer proof. What he believed was that the racket was being run from Arkenshaw (it is at least certain that the printing was done in England), and one of his reasons for this belief was that some sort of—of tribute still seemed to be exacted from those Pakistanis who had no legal right to be here—"

"Blackmail?" said O'Brien, looking thunderous.

"In a way. There was one connecting link between the various cases that came to his notice . . . a good-looking young chap, a Pakistani, who was believed by the neighbors to be collecting hire-purchase payments, only for one reason and another Duckett didn't believe that."

"You say, the various cases—?"

"Where a chap had got into trouble, and then it was found his employment voucher was a forgery."

"And the 'hire-purchase' payments?"

"Duckett believes they were still paying for the documents that got them into the country. From what he told me, it seems a reasonable assumption. And that, though you may find it hard to credit, is the main reason he was so keen on finding who was behind it all." He paused, thinking of Dr. Conway, and then went on, almost in his words, "There have been cases of great hardship."

"This Pakistani—"

"There was a queer thing about that . . . he should have been easy enough to trace, but he couldn't be found in any of the foreign quarters in the town. When I heard that, I thought perhaps he was in service somewhere . . . someone's chauffeur, perhaps."

"And so we come back to Tom again. Don't you think someone would have recognized him?"

"He wears a turban on duty; not many of the foreigners do. That makes a difference, you know. I doubt if either of us would know him if we saw him without it."

"You may be right." O'Brien spoke quietly enough, but then he was suddenly angry. "This is ridiculous, Maitland. One minute you seem to be making sense, and the next you plunge into pure fantasy."

"I'm sorry you feel like that," said Antony, with truth "The third strand is the evidence of corruption in Arken shaw."

"Every town—"

"Yes, I know. I feel this goes further, but you may no agree with me. The case of Ahmad Khan, for instance, to which you alluded in such affecting terms in court—"

"It's nothing to sneer about."

"I'm not sneering. The point about Ahmad Khan is tha he was a printer by trade. He worked for a local firm called Greenhalgh and Blackburn—who, by the way, prin the Arkenshaw Society's annual reports. But the most in teresting thing about them is the fact (this is somethin, else that can be proved if necessary) that they have som dealings at least with Pakistan."

"You may be able to prove it, but what does it prove?"

"I should have told you that the person in Pakistan who distributes the forged papers is a bookseller. It's your own fault I forgot; you're making me nervous," Maitland com plained. "At the moment I can merely offer you the infor mation as suggestive, if only because it seems so unlikel, that the output of the local poets is being eagerly awaited in Karachi."

"So you think Ahmad Khan was the person who did the actual printing."

"Yes, I do. And I expect he was well paid, but it seem he was a chap with wide interests. Anyway, he got into trouble . . . don't you think it was worth someone's while to rescue him? After all, if he had been convicted, he migh have given the whole show away."

"And he was 'rescued' by providing perjured evidence," said O'Brien slowly. "We're back to the 'man with in fluence' now, who seems also—according to your readin; —to be the man behind the illegal immigration. I should hardly have thought the description fitted . . . Green halgh, for instance."

"No, I don't think it does." He got up with one of hi restless movements, but the room wasn't really big enough

232

permit him to prowl, so he gave up the attempt and stood at the end of the bed, leaning back against the high, old-fashioned footboard. "May I go back to the sequence of events, as I see them?"

"I suppose you're going to," said O'Brien humorously, "whatever I say."

"I think Tom Bhakkar is the good-looking young chap who was collecting among the Pakistani population. If I'm right, it means that, like Ahmad Khan, he is useful to his principal and must be protected . . . even leaving aside the possibility of his giving the game away. I think in his case there is an additional motive, but I'll come to that in a moment. I think he killed his wife."

"Accepting all this," said Kevin, "—not that I do, but *if* I did—"

"His principal stepped in and arranged that no questions should be asked about Mrs. Bhakkar's disappearance. Jones was given a story that satisfied him; Barlow had no longer any documentary evidence of her existence, and it was safe to assume that he wouldn't push his inquiries in face of the landlady's denials. And the landlady was squared—possibily that was a straight cash transaction—though not soon enough to prevent her asking at the local shop if they knew where her lodger had gone."

"You mentioned the grocer's wife. Did no one try to bribe her?"

There seemed to be some sarcasm there; better perhaps to ignore it. "I don't suppose anyone thought she'd be questioned. As a matter of fact, no one ever missed Mrs. Bhakkar—"

"Suppose she is in Bradford?"

"I might believe that if the landlady hadn't been told to deny she'd ever known her," Maitland told him.

"Yes, I think . . . it's certainly odd," said O'Brien. "But why not take your suspicions to the police?"

"Because Inspector Townsend's son has a scholarship from the Arkenshaw Society."

"But what has that . . . you think he's venal too?"

"Let's say I think most men are amenable to persuasio by somebody to whom they feel a sense of obligation, said Antony carefully. "A suggestion can be enough; it awfully easy to rationalize one's actions."

"Well, but, look here . . . the Arkenshaw Society?"

"I'm coming to that. You'll admit they dispense a goo deal of patronage."

"One man, capable of influencing their decisions," sai O'Brien reflectively, and looked long and hard at his com panion.

"Precisely." (Perhaps, after all, O'Brien was going to be lieve him.) "But to get back to the burglary—"

"Do you think that was a straight transaction too, i Beas's case?"

"No, I think it was more complicated than that. Rightl or wrongly, he's a chap with a grievance. I don't know i he knew about the illegal immigration already, or if tha was the first he heard of it; but I'm pretty sure he'd accep it as something laudable. He knew Tom; it wouldn't hav been difficult to find an argument to convince him . . perhaps that Mrs. Bhakkar had come in on forged paper herself and that the documents she had given Barlo might in some way reveal the fact."

"So far as I know," said Kevin, "a wife whose husban is already in this country is free to join him at will."

"Tom might not have said she was his wife. His sister in-law, perhaps, something like that. Give him credit fo some ingenuity."

"You've an answer for everything," said O'Brien, almos crossly. "What about Mohamad . . . did they threaten t take away his scholarship?"

"They might have done. But I think he was not a ver strong character, and to some extent under Beas's domina tion. Would you agree to that?"

"I would."

"And Beas, I am very sure, is quite clever enough t have persuaded him that what they were doing was righ

234

n the long run, I don't think it was very sensible of him to
se Jackie, but I expect he felt he could handle him."

"Very well, then. They decide to fake a robbery. I'll
dmit," said O'Brien generously, "I don't give tuppence
or the evidence from the pub. What I don't understand is
vhy they chose that particular time . . . but that applies to
vhoever did the job."

"It may have been just a reconnaissance; finding the
ouse dark and no car outside, they could have decided
he Barlows were out. The garage is some distance away."

"I see. So they did what they had come to do, collected
few souvenirs to make it look like an ordinary burglary,
nd walked out of the house into the arms of Duckett and
Ryder. But after that," said O'Brien triumphantly, "they
vere tried and acquitted on Miss Garrowby's evidence."

"I can't explain Miss Garrowby," Antony admitted.
I've a nasty feeling she's telling us what she thinks she
aw."

"You disappoint me. I was expecting something really
ancy."

"Nothing like that. What I do think is that there was
robably a witness lined up ready to do his stuff—"

"To commit perjury, you mean?"

"Exactly. Miss Garrowby was a piece of unlooked for
ood fortune, because I don't suppose they'd have risked
he wrongful-arrest charge on faked evidence, but now
hey had a witness who was manifestly honest. It must
ave seemed altogether too good an opportunity to miss,
f discrediting Sergeant Duckett, particularly if his con-
inued investigations were proving embarrassing."

"Yes, but what about Jimmy Marshall?"

"That follows the pattern . . . don't you see? First there
vas Martin Ward's father—"

"What did he want?"

"To tell Conway it wasn't any use calling Martin, be-
ause we were bound to lose anyway; he was full of fire
nd fury when Conway refused to dispense with the boy's
vidence."

"Of all the cheek," said O'Brien, genuinely outraged.

"He said one thing that was revealing. Something about having to consider his son's future. It might mean anything, or nothing. And I don't suppose it seemed too unreasonable to Mr. Ward, you know, if someone pointed out to him that Martin might be harming himself by giving evidence and not being believed."

"I'd like to have seen young Conway's face," said Kevin; and, surprisingly, he laughed.

"It was, as they say, a study. But after Miss Garrowby's evidence, they may have felt more desperate measures were called for. *We* know it wouldn't have made any difference—"

"Except to give me a bad half-hour. *And* infuriate me," said O'Brien, with unexpected amiability.

"—but a layman might have felt it introduced at least an element of doubt. Hence Jimmy Marshall . . . and I bet there was a *quid pro quo* there, all right."

"You think he was having me on?"

"Very cleverly," said Antony in a hurry. "Someone had coached him, of course."

"I see. So your case is that Beas and Mohamad had a better motive for the burglary than a simple shortage of cash; and you hope to demonstrate that they are proceeding against Duckett and Ryder with the intention of discrediting them."

"Exactly. And . . . that's about all, isn't it?"

"Except the identity of the man behind the scenes."

Having talked O'Brien into something like quiescence, it seemed a pity to rouse his anger again. What had he said himself? . . . when I see a dog sleeping . . . "it isn't really relevant as far as the trial is concerned."

"I think you'd better tell me," said O'Brien; he did not raise his voice, but his tone was insistent.

"All right, then." (You're not going to like this.) "Frank Findlater."

"*What?*"

"Frank Findlater," said Antony, with more assurance

"You're trying to tell me that Findlater—Findlater!—
as been running this illegal-immigration thing?"

"For a price."

"But he's a wealthy man."

"How do you know?"

"I don't, I suppose. But—"

"His grandfather was. That isn't the same thing."

"No, but he can't be penniless. He could economize,
ɔuldn't he?"

"Cut down on his charitable donations, for instance."

"Well . . . yes."

"He has a unique position in Arkenshaw; I've a nasty
·eling that means a lot to him. I also think he genuinely
kes helping people, but if that's true, only a psychologist
ɔuld sort out his motives."

"Robbing Peter to pay Paul!"

"Not a logical behavior pattern, certainly. If you're
ɔing to ask for that—"

"Now who's being stuffy?" asked O'Brien. "And even
ranting all that," he went on, "it doesn't make any sense
t all."

"He's Tom Bhakkar's employer. He's financing this trial
. . did you know that?"

"I didn't, but I don't see—"

"He is undoubtedly the most influential member of the
ɹrkenshaw Society, for the very good reason that he is its
ɹrgest benefactor. He knows Greenhalgh well enough to
ut pressure on him not to sack Star Duckett (that's some-
ηing else I forgot to tell you, but it's true). He busied him-
ɛlf with finding another job for Ahmad Khan after his ac-
uittal—"

"Why not just let him go back to his old one?"

"That wouldn't have been a very good idea, once he was
nown to be unreliable."

"You're assuming the police case is true. Oh, yes, I
now . . . the pattern!" said O'Brien irritably. "But
'indlater—"

"It was he who convinced Jones that Mrs. Bhakkar had

237

gone away; I don't imagine he'd have taken it just c
Tom's word. And the final thing is that when I saw hi
last night, I mentioned a surprise witness, and he kne
without being told that the evidence had been helpful
the plaintiffs."

"Jones might have told him."

"I'd only that moment come from the court, and he wa
at the club, not at home. Unless you postulate a quite e:
traordinary degree of urgency about the communicatio
he couldn't have known."

Oddly, O'Brien did not protest again. He said slowly, "
all this is true, what about Chakwal Mohamad?"

"Why did he come to the hotel last night? I think pe
haps when Jimmy Marshall was brought in it was tc
much for him. *He* wasn't the victim of an unfair syster
with a right—almost a duty—to use whatever weapo
came to hand. However Jackie himself had been pe
suaded (and I think his repeated words to me, 'it is n
right,' give us a good clue), he may have felt that bringi
Marshall in cheapened their high endeavor."

"Words!" said O'Brien. And then, quietly, "I mean
how did he die?"

"Convenient, wasn't it? I don't think we can say mo
than that. There is one thing, though: Dera heard a big c
draw up in their street last night and thought it was To
Bhakkar bringing Jackie home."

"I don't like it." He sounded more positive now, an
added when he saw Maitland looking at him inquiringl
"It may be a vicious circle you've drawn for me, but I'
got a feeling it *is* a circle."

"Well, thank goodness for that, anyway."

His relief was so heartfelt that O'Brien laughed agai
"All the same, I can't help wondering why you didn't wa
till the hearing resumed."

"I suppose I wanted to convince you . . . well, of cours
I did! You've been doubting my motives ever since the b
ginning, haven't you? I didn't like that much."

238

"I . . . see. And if I tell you I am now persuaded of their ιrity?"

"There's still Greenhalgh. You'll come with me, won't ɔu?" Antony urged. "It really would be better if you d."

"What's the hurry?"

"The rest can wait for the court . . . what do you sup-ɔse Gilmour will make of it? But if I'm right about reenhalgh, and Ahmad Khan, and the rest of it, there ust be some evidence on the premises. I want to make ιre nothing is destroyed, because after my talk with Jones won't be long before Findlater knows I've been asking ιestions about Mrs. Bhakkar."

"As long as you're not trying to start something?"

"I don't know what you mean."

"If you've an idea of forcing the issue in some way, of ɔing a bit further than just clearing your clients—"

"It won't be my fault—will it?—if Greenhalgh gets the ind up."

"You mean he might communicate with Findlater. ʹould that help?"

Maitland shrugged. "You never know."

There was a pause. "Very well," said O'Brien at last. 'm not saying I'm convinced, mind—"

"I realize you've only my word for some of the things ve told you."

"That wasn't what I meant." He glanced at his watch. ʹive-twenty. Do you want to go now?"

"I didn't know it was so late. But we might just catch reenhalgh . . . don't you think?"

"If that's really what you want." He got up and went to e wardrobe. "You've postulated a man who has a *habit* ` bribery."

"Yes," said Maitland doubtfully. O'Brien's tone was ɔmber, and he wasn't quite sure where this was leading.

"Findlater is a hospitable man; that's not unusual." It ·emed to be taking him an inordinate time to find what

he was looking for. "But now I'm wondering"—
dragged his raincoat off the hanger and turned at last w
it over his arm—"do you suppose he was trying to soft
me up?"

The idea obviously disturbed him. "You and me, both
said Maitland. "But in your case I expect it was just yc
fatal fascination."

VI

Chris Conway went straight to his office when
dropped Maitland at Old Peel Farm. There was pler
that needed attention, and he dictated a few letters to l
clerk, but broke off in the middle of a tortuous and lor
overdue explanation to an unsatisfied residuary legat‹
"We'll do that on Monday. Just bring me the Marsd
file."

The Marsden file was a refuge. You could spread t
documents over the desk and sit there looking at them, l‹
in thought. And no one could prove you weren't puzzli
over the complexities of the trust.

What he really thought about was Jimmy Marshall, a
Jackie, and Dera Mohamad, and that very unsatisfactc
fellow, Maitland, who inspired your confidence even wh
he infuriated you. From there it wasn't really a very l
step to Star Duckett, and her family; and their proble›
and his own.

He sat there till nearly five o'clock, and then he phon
the Midland Hotel. They thought Mr. Maitland had co›
in, but—no, he wasn't in his room. Nor anywhere e
where he could be reached, apparently. Chris put back t
receiver, sat staring vacantly at the topmost document
his desk until the words "NOW THIS DEED WITNESSETH,"
old-fashioned script, danced before his eyes. Then he bu
dled everything together in an untidy heap, fetched l
overcoat, and went out.

He turned into Fellgate from Moorfield Lane, and

ad to walk the full length before he reached the printing orks. It was obvious he wasn't too early; the men were aving already, surging up the cobbled street toward him ith no regard for possible traffic; hunched a little against e driving rain, but cheerful enough, by the sound of em. Then came a group of girls in brightly colored ackintoshes and a variety of rain hats—each, thought hris, more unbecoming than the last. And when he had assed them, he could see two other girls, who had turned the opposite direction. One of them was Star. . . .

He had to hurry, but he caught her up at the corner just fter her friend had left her. Star's mackintosh was a dark, by red, and her waterproof hood framed her face be-mingly; at least, so he thought, completely unaware that was exactly similar to one he had seen just now and con-emned as hideous. Her face lighted up when she saw him, ut she was very pale. He said, almost roughly, "I want to lk to you."

"Is there . . . any news?"

"Nothing. The case is adjourned until after Jackie's fu-eral."

"Poor Jackie," said Star. And then, "Poor Dad. Then or ow, it's all the same, isn't it?"

"That's what I want to talk to you about," said Conway. We'll get some tea." He took her arm, firmly enough to ve her no choice but to accompany him. "Come on."

Star gave a little skip, trying to adjust her step to his. "I ustn't be long."

"I'll run you home afterwards, before Grandma has me to get worried." But he said it absently, a routine as-rance that meant nothing. A moment later he steered er into the doorway of a brightly lighted tea shop. "Here. his will do."

"Well, you didn't have to drag me here as if you were— ere taking me into custody," Star told him, rubbing her m.

"I wasn't sure if you'd come quietly."

The room wasn't full yet, but there was enough chatter

241

going on to isolate them comfortably. The waitress car
and went, and Chris sat watching his companion with
rather grim air of satisfaction. Now that she had taken
the hood, her hair was curling up wildly, but there we
dark smudges under her eyes, and a curious air of lassitu
about her that he had never seen before. As if his ga
made her uneasy, she started to talk at random, somethi
about the rain and last night's bonfires; but perhaps s
saw he wasn't listening, because after a while her voi
trailed away into silence.

"About our getting married," he said.

"I'm not going to marry you, Chris. I told you that. N
now."

"You talked a lot of nonsense."

The word seemed to move her to a small show of ang
"I was only being sensible. One of us has to be."

"All right, then. Tell me again. Tell me exactly why–

Star turned her head and looked away from him acrc
the room that was already growing hazy with cigare
smoke. Anywhere, he thought angrily, so as not to m
my eyes. "People won't forget," she said. "Ask Mr. Bat
he'll tell you . . . it wouldn't do your practice any good

"Do you think I care about that?"

"No, but I do." When he did not reply, she looked ba
at him and said resolutely, "I suppose Mr. Maitland agre
it's hopeless now."

"I don't know what he thinks, and what's more, I do
care."

"That isn't a very nice thing to say."

"You know what I mean." He was glaring at her no
"I'm trying to convey to you that whatever the verdict
next week it makes no difference. Unless you tell me–
He broke off, and his expression softened. "Star, you
crying."

"I am not! It's just the rain, dripping off my hair."

"Drink your tea, and then we'll talk."

"No, I . . . I wish I could make you understand. I wo
spoil things for you, Chris."

"That sounds very fine. I suppose there's someone else."

"No. No!"

"Jim Ryder?"

"He's having a hard time," said Star defensively.

"Of all the slushy, sentimental—"

"I am not sentimental!"

"Oh, yes, you are. As sentimental as those ruddy poems ld Greenhalgh is always printing." (As he spoke, he re-embered Maitland's conversation with Sergeant Duckett at morning, but he hadn't time for that now.) "Are you ping to marry Ryder?"

"I'm not going to marry anyone." She looked down at er cup, and started stirring her tea as though nothing else terested her. "I wish you'd leave me alone."

He was almost angry enough to take her at her word. Imost . . . not quite. "Well, I will," he said, "if you'll ook at me—look at me, Star!—and tell me you don't want marry me, you don't love me at all."

"I don't—" she said. He saw her lip quiver, and thought, ith that odd detachment that comes sometimes in mo-ents of tension, that it might as easily have been for ughter as for tears. Then she raised her head until her yes met his. "I can't. I can't." The words were almost a hisper.

He did not pause to inquire more precisely into her eaning. "Then we'll be married . . . as soon as you like, soon as you can be ready. You may as well understand at."

"But, Chris—"

"I've stood just about all I can from you, my lass. After-ards we can decide whether to stay in Arkenshaw or not; e'll move, if you'd rather."

"I don't want you to have to give up anything."

"Then give me the thing I want most of all. Good lord, tar, I'm not a child, that you should have to decide what's od for me."

"I know." She set her lips, and then added with some-ing of her usual composure, "We'll not leave Arkenshaw unless it seems best for you. I mean, we won't be driven away."

He laughed, because that was Star all over. "Except for financial reasons," he agreed; and when she laughed back at him, he thought for one besotted moment that perhaps her name wasn't so dreadful, after all, the way her eyes lit up. . . . He leaned forward, suddenly suspicious. "Does that mean you will?"

"I didn't know you were giving me a choice," said Star demurely. But when he was helping her with her coat a few minutes later, he noticed that her cheeks were still wet.

Being a wise man, and content with his victory, he did not comment upon the fact.

VII

Maitland and O'Brien reached the corner of Fellgate about three minutes after Chris Conway had dragged Star into the tea shop. The street was quieter now, the workers from the printing shop had dispersed, and there were no late deliveries on Friday night to bring the trucks into town. One man was hurrying toward them, his head bent to the rain, but he turned into the chapel when he reached it.

"We've probably missed him," said Antony, frowning.

"It might be as well." Kevin O'Brien's tone was unusually hesitant, and his companion looked at him sharply.

"Having second thoughts?" he asked.

"Let's say I'm beginning to wonder if madness is infectious. How did you talk me into this, anyway?"

Privately, Antony thought that it had been O'Brien's own feelings about Findlater that convinced him, subconscious though they might be. But he had enough sense not to try to explain this.

There were two doors, both closed with what struck him as a look of finality. In the absence of a bell, Antony hammered on the smaller of them, but it was the right-hand

...f of the big door that swung open at his second knock-
...g. Against a dim light within they could see silhouetted
...e figure of a man.

He was of medium height, and slightly built, and his
...ice had the peculiar, high-pitched tone of some dales-
...en. "I'm afraid—"

"Has Mr. Greenhalgh left? We were hoping to see him."

"I'm Greenhalgh." But as soon as the admission was
...ade, he seemed to regret it. "It's very late."

"We won't keep you a moment." Maitland had been
...essing forward as he spoke, with that gentle insistence of
...ovement which it is almost impossible to counter with-
...t open rudeness; and a small part of his mind noted
...th amusement that O'Brien had kept with him, step by
...p.

Greenhalgh fell back a pace or two and said ungra-
...ously, "I was just leaving."

"Five minutes," said Antony. "It's quite important."
...'Brien had closed the door, and dropped the heavy latch
...at secured it. "My name's Maitland. This is Mr.
...'Brien."

It was obvious that Greenhalgh recognized the names;
...t the whole town was following the case in the newspa-
...rs, and anyway, Star might have mentioned them. "I
...n't see how I can help you." His eyes went from one of
...em to the other; perhaps he was wondering what possi-
...e connection . . .

They were in a large hall with a high ceiling. There was
...ly one light, over a door at the side that probably led to
...e offices, and the presses were dimly visible. Antony
...ought fancifully that the silence was unnatural, that at
...y moment the machines might come to life at the touch
...some unseen hand. Meanwhile, there was the smell of
...e place, a compound of printers' ink and hot lead, not at
...l unpleasant. "I understand you do some trade with Pak-
...an," he said. And saw, half-surprised, half-exultant, that
...e question had gone home.

"Well, now, really, Mr.—Mr. Maitland, offhand I ca tell you."

"Then perhaps . . . would it be too much trouble look it up?" This was said persuasively, and he added, w the air of taking Greenhalgh into his confidence, "T must seem a strange request, but circumstances ha arisen—"

"What circumstances?" The high voice was thin w fear. And then, as though he realized his reaction was in self revealing, "Of course, if I can be of any assistanc As he spoke, O'Brien found a switch near the door a pressed it, and with the lights the huge workshop spra suddenly to life.

The blaze of illumination startled all three of them; ev Kevin hadn't expected anything quite so dazzling. Gree halgh gave a cry, and retreated a pace or two, almost though his visitors had threatened him. He was a shif looking customer, Maitland thought . . . but then, th had him at a disadvantage. And his eyes were darting fr side to side, enough to give you the idea there was som one else in the building, someone who might interru them. . . .

It came to him then that Greenhalgh might not ha been expecting them, but he had a very good idea w they were here.

"The thing is, we'd like to know the name and addr of your customer in Karachi. A bookseller, isn't he?" B he was alert now to every detail of his surroundings. The were the machines, from the modern-looking affair Greenhalgh's elbow, which announced itself as *origin Heidelberg,* to an aged contraption in the distance th looked like something Heath Robinson might ha dreamed up at the height of his inventive powers; the was the office door away on the left, and another do labled DARKROOM beyond it; high windows, uncurtaine and dingy green walls, and a pillar decorated with brigh colored labels, designed to catch the eye . . . *Handle w care . . . 6d off . . . Do not disturb.* And on every availab

246

ace, on racks along the wall and on the high benches
at stood here and there between the machines, there
ere stacks of paper of every conceivable shade and
xture. And over all a sort of brooding silence that did
othing to allay his own growing conviction that they were
ot alone.

Greenhalgh was saying, "I'm afraid I don't under-
and."

"That's a pity. I thought I was being fairly plain. You'll
e asked to supply it in court, you know."

"In court?"

"Beas versus Duckett and another. We're calling addi-
onal evidence."

"But . . . mine? I know nothing." He had himself well
hand now; his bewilderment was no more than might
ave seemed natural.

"You know what you sent to Pakistan. You know who
aced the order. It would be simpler if you would tell us
ow."

"I'm afraid I see no reason—"

"You'd rather talk to the police."

Greenhalgh laughed. "To Sergeant Duckett, perhaps."

"You're well informed," said Maitland seriously. "But I
ink if Mr. O'Brien went to the police station—"

"There's nothing for them here."

"I can't help feeling they might find something to inter-
t them, and it seems a pity that you should take all the
ame."

"For what?"

"For arranging that so many foreigners should come
to the country with forged papers. I'm sure Mr. Findla-
r will find no difficulty in arranging for another printer to
ke over, when you're in prison."

"I don't know what you're talking about."

"Don't you? Ahmad Khan would know."

There was no mistaking it now; Greenhalgh had been
raid when first he heard their names; the mention of his
rmer employee made him almost blind with panic. He

said, very low, "What do you want?" And then, mo
strongly, "What do you know?" But before Maitlan
could reply two things happened.

From their right, from the direction of the chapel, a ba
voice, only slightly muffled by the distance, demande
abruptly, *"Why do the nations so furiously rage together"*
And on their left the office door opened, and Fran
Findlater came through.

He came toward them, threading his way between th
heavy machines as unconcernedly as he might ha
crossed the smoking room at the club. "I hope you'll fc
give me for butting in. I'm rather interested in the answ
to that question myself."

The only thing about him that might have aroused con
ment in a more public place was the service revolver l
carried.

As soon as he heard Findlater's voice, Greenhalgh ha
flattened himself against the "original Heidelberg," whi
formed one side of the aisle in which they stood. Now I
scuttled back, well out of range. Findlater gestured;
might have been by way of apology, it might have been
draw attention to the fact that he was armed. "I alwa
thought I'd find a use for this if I kept it long enough," I
said cheerfully. "Now I think if you'd come a little neare
gentlemen. Away from the door."

Antony strolled forward; after a moment's hesitatio
O'Brien came up to his side. His learned friend was gettir
more than his money's worth, Maitland reflected with d
tached amusement. This wasn't the way he'd thoug
things would turn out, but if Jones had talked to Findlat
since he saw him that afternoon, what more likely tha
that some sort of a council of war would be felt necessar

"I have been thinking, since yesterday to be precise, th
it might be useful to have a talk with you, Mr. Maitland
Findlater was saying. "I'm not altogether sorry to ha
this opportunity, though I hadn't thought to see you her
Mr. O'Brien."

248

"It's surprised I am myself," said O'Brien; the lilt—absent that day so far as Maitland had heard—was back in his voice again. "And if it's shooting us you're after, do you really think now it's a thing you can be getting away with?"

(*"Why do the people imagine a vain thing?"* asked the bass, who seemed to be of an inquiring turn of mind.)

"I'm sure it won't be necessary. I'm sure something can be worked out." There was a macabre quality about all this benevolence; Antony glanced at O'Brien, wondering if he felt it too. But O'Brien was scowling, his first light-hearted reaction to danger wiped out by the hint of bribery, and perhaps a little by the confidence of Findlater's tone. "Now, if you wouldn't mind waiting for me in the office, Mr. Greenhalgh," Findlater went on. (Greenhalgh was behind him, but he didn't look around.) "You'll find Tom there; tell him I may need him presently. I'll call when I do."

Greenhalgh slipped away between the silent presses; it was obvious that neither he nor Findlater felt any reply was necessary; his obedience was taken for granted. "That's known as tact," said Maitland to O'Brien.

Frank Findlater smiled at them both impartially. "I feel sure you would prefer that there should be no witnesses to any little arrangement we might make."

"Arrangement?" said O'Brien. His voice had a silky quality, but now no one in their senses could have mistaken it for anything but anger. (No finesse, thought Antony sadly.)

"Well, first, of course, I should like you to tell me: what *do* you know?"

"So far I shall be glad to oblige you." (O'Brien might be in a black rage, but he knew how to tear the guts out of a statement.) "We know why the Barlows were robbed, and why the robbery took place on that particular night. We know why the action against Duckett and Ryder was brought, and why it was necessary to discredit them."

"Do you indeed? What else?"

"Why Chakwal Mohamad came to the hotel last night—"

"And where he was before he came there," said Maitland clearly. (The voices of the choir shattered the silence that followed. *"Let us break their bonds asunder."* They had obviously been waiting all day for the chance to make a noise, and now were determined to make the most of it.)

"It seems," said Findlater, "that you are extremely well informed. What does surprise me is that you should have connected me—"

"But that was easy," Antony told him, "once I knew you were ruled by Saturn. It was different for O'Brien; he doesn't believe in astrology. I don't think he was really convinced until you came through that door."

"So you've met Grandma Duckett." For the first time the mask of benevolence slipped; there was an ugly look on Findlater's face. "You've been very sure of yourself, haven't you, Mr. Maitland? I wonder if we can remedy that."

"Well, I didn't hope for quite so much luck, you know."

"Luck?" For the first time Findlater looked slightly taken aback, and his glance flickered for a moment to the gun in his hand.

"Yes, but you don't mean to use it, do you? Think of the mess on poor Greenhalgh's floor."

"I should regret it, of course. However, I used to be considered quite a good marksman."

"In your army days?" said Antony, his eyes on the revolver.

"That's right. Now, this 'luck' you were referring to—"

"One or two things have been puzzling me. This seems a good time to clear them up."

"So long as you understand the position."

At this point O'Brien blew up again. "This," he remarked, with awful dignity, "Has Gone Far Enough." He turned to Maitland. "Are you ready to go?"

"And be shot in the back?" He saw the other man's disbelief and added more urgently, "He's quite serious, you know."

"I suppose this is your idea of a pleasant afternoon's entertainment." O'Brien's politeness had a searing quality.

"Not really. I could do with a drink, for instance. But I *am* curious," he admitted. "Besides, if you have patience, our friend here will have a—a suggestion to make."

"A proposition," said Findlater encouragingly.

"So I have gathered, but if you imagine for a moment—" He broke off, frowning; and then turned his head to look at Findlater, measuring the distance between them.

"That won't do, either. Not unless you feel like a martyr. Too far," said Antony. One thing was certain, the situation mustn't be allowed to endure too long; Findlater was safe enough as long as he had some hope of making a deal (I was right about that; his whole instinct is toward bribery), but with a hothead like O'Brien among those present there was no knowing how long that might continue. Kevin seemed to have retired for the moment; without prejudice, thought Antony with an impatience that didn't quite escape amusement, to his right to simmer gently in the background and erupt at any time. As if things weren't tricky enough already. He turned back to Findlater and said hopefully, "You're going to tell me, aren't you?"

"What is there left to tell you? You seem to know so much."

"All the important things," Maitland agreed.

"Some matters of detail, then. For instance—?"

"The newspaper reports of Ahmad Khan's trial. Did you send them to me?"

"I arranged for their dispatch."

"Why?"

"But, to help you, Mr. Maitland. I was a little surprised at your accepting the brief, and when I heard something of your reputation from Mr. O'Brien . . . well, let's say I felt it only kind to open your eyes to Fred Duckett's true character."

The queer thing was, he seemed to have persuaded himself in some way of the truth of what he was saying. And perhaps this was the secret of his power over other people, the reason he was able to convince them of the rightness of *his* point of view. "I suppose you don't know why Miss Garrowby told the story she did."

"Now, I thought from something you said to me last night that you understood Emily Garrowby."

Antony tried to think back to last night; it seemed an age ago. "*Le cœur à ses raisons que la raison ne connaît point.* I don't know, I just felt it wouldn't be right to call her a liar. And there was that queer phrase she used in court—you remember, O'Brien—'I have only borne witness to the truth.' That must have meant something."

"Perhaps," said O'Brien slowly, thinking it out, "she was quite sure Beas and Mohamad were innocent, and the rest followed from that. She worked out what she must have seen, and then believed she *had* seen it."

"She must have been damned certain."

"Now this," said Findlater in a pleased tone, "is where I have the advantage of you. You'd be too young to remember, Mr. O'Brien, I was only about fifteen myself at the time, but Emily was once engaged—or wanted to be engaged—to an Indian doctor. An 'eye specialist' as far as I remember; I don't know what his qualifications might have been. Anyway, her parents stopped it, but I remember my mother talking about the affair."

"You think, then, she had a thing about Indians . . . and Pakistanis now, of course?"

"I prefer your quotation, but I think that sums it up."

"It explains, too, that note of uncertainty," said Maitland thoughtfully. "I expect her subconscious was giving her hell."

"Poor woman." Even O'Brien seemed to be caught up in the interest of the subject now. "She must have been very fond of him."

"Oh, he was a handsome fellow; and he wore a turban, which all the ladies thought most romantic. You'll have noticed how well Tom looks in his. I remember my mother saying, 'They find fair girls so attractive'; and even then I thought how unjust it was, and that if ever I had a chance of helping—"

"I suppose that was why you suborned young Jimmy Marshall," said O'Brien, coming suddenly back to the present.

"Would you call it that?" Findlater seemed genuinely puzzled. "Really, the persecution the foreigners have had to put up with in this town is appalling, and if one can help to—to even things up in any way, it is no more than a duty." O'Brien gave an exclamation; it sounded as if he had lost his temper again, but at least Findlater's attitude seemed to have rendered him speechless.

The chorus had given way some moments before to a rather reedy tenor, who was proclaiming with admirable clarity and a good deal of repetition, *"Thou shalt break them with a rod of iron; Thou shalt dash them in pieces—"* He seemed to regard the prospect with enthusiasm. Antony raised his arm until he could rest his elbow on the high bench beside him; it was more like a desk really, of unfinished wood, but shiny with constant use. What you could see of it, there were the usual piles of paper. "I'm more interested," he said, "in this philanthropic scheme of yours for bringing them into the country. I understand it's still going on, in spite of the difficulties." He heard with satisfaction that his voice was steady, and he hoped he hadn't winced as he brought his arm up to the desk. It was too high for comfort, and with all his care the pain in his shoulder was sickening, but if he could stick it for a while . . .

What wasn't so good was that Findlater had been alert the instant he moved, his eyes sharpened to a new intentness. Perhaps he'd been underrating his ability, not as an organizer, of course—that was undoubted—but as a man of action.

"Oh, yes," Findlater was saying. (Had he really relaxed

again?) "They were tiresome, of course, but not insuperable. Once I could be sure of my man at the ministry . . .
well, you know, he quite saw my point."

This was too much for O'Brien. "What point?" he
snarled.

"That it is our policy at fault, not these unfortunates."

"And after you get them here—"

"I feel sure you must have misunderstood the position.
They don't like to feel beholden, you know, and it
wouldn't be good for them."

"Now, by the blessed Saint Patrick," said Kevin O'Brien
loudly, "I'll stand no more of this!"

Antony would have liked time to savor the oath, which
surely must have been dredged up from O'Brien's childhood memories . . . a reaction, perhaps, to the singing of
Messiah next door? (The tenor was still dashing them in
pieces, and with no less gusto than before.) But his learned
friend had to be calmed down somehow, if he didn't want
to see Findlater put a bullet in him. "Don't you find it interesting," he said, "to get another point of view?" and
O'Brien turned on him furiously, started to speak, and
checked himself, and at last remarked bitingly: "It would
be a pity, I suppose, if your curiosity went unsatisfied."

"Well, I think so." He had to fight against the feeling of
nausea; it seemed to be sweeping over him, wave after
wave. "Old Peel Farm," he said. "Do you plan to buy it?"

"Why, naturally. I shouldn't like Duckett to have to
worry about a thing like that."

Luckily, the implications of this were lost on O'Brien.
"That's about all," said Maitland, "except that I should
like to know what happened to Mrs. Bhakkar."

Findlater's eyes opened very wide at that; perhaps he
was surprised at the tactlessness of the question. "Tom is
such an impulsive fellow," he said.

"And Jackie? He was with Tom last night, wasn't he?"

"Really, Mr. Maitland, you make me wonder whether,
after all, I should be wise to have any further dealings with
you."

254

"Come now, you must have some safeguards in mind, or how could you trust us? Or wouldn't they cover . . . murder?" He shifted his position a little as he spoke, and set his teeth against the pain. "If the inducement was large enough—" he added, and completed the sentence with a gesture of his left hand. O'Brien growled something, deep in his throat.

"I'm beginning to doubt whether it could be."

"And I'm beginning to have a very lively interest in the alternative."

"I rather thought . . . the canal." Findlater's tone might have been an apology, but now Maitland could see, naked in his eyes, the truth of what Grandma Duckett had told him. Cold and cruel, she had said; and she might have added . . . dangerous. He might prefer to negotiate, but he'd kill without a second thought if it came to the point where his own interests were threatened.

"That doesn't sound a very good idea," he said; and again he moved his arm a little, a very little.

"Why not? It isn't a very nice night for a stroll," said Findlater, in so normal a tone that Antony wondered for a moment whether he had changed the subject altogether, "but everyone in Arkenshaw knows that Londoners are a little odd about fresh air, and if you should both be set upon and robbed . . . it would be regrettable, of course, but no one would be very much surprised."

"And how do you propose—? I forgot, you have your troops within call." His hand crept forward along the bench, inch by inch.

"I don't know that Greenhalgh will be very much help," said Findlater judiciously. "But Tom is extremely useful," he added more cheerfully, "and the plan has the added advantage that if I am compelled to shoot you—" He got no further, because the stack of paper from the end of the desk hurtled violently toward him with all Maitland's weight behind it. And as it came, the thin sheets separated, spread, and billowed about him as though rejoicing in their freedom; and just for a moment they formed a screen. . . .

Almost simultaneously four other things happened: the gun went off, which was only to be expected; the choir next door swept into the "Hallelujah Chorus" (Antony could never afterward decide whether he or Findlater found this, at that particular moment, the more terrifying); Maitland twisted around and grabbed at a tall, spindle-legged stool that was pushed half under the bench; and Kevin O'Brien, as though he had rehearsed the action for weeks, took Frank Findlater in a flying tackle.

Perhaps it was as well that the stool was heavier than he expected. Antony realized what was happening in time to stop himself from projecting it into the battle, which would have been a pity, because O'Brien was on top. He might be a lighter man than his adversary, but he had the advantage of surprise and was quite prepared to make the most of it. Before Maitland could intervene, his learned friend had quite deliberately raised Findlater's head and cracked it against what he thought at the time was a relative of old Heidelberg, but found later to be a Miehle press. Not surprisingly, Findlater lost all interest in the proceedings.

"*Hallelujah! Hallelujah! HALL-E-E-LU-JAH!*" sang the choir exuberantly. "Appropriate, don't you think?" said Antony, as O'Brien scrambled to his feet.

"They seem to me to have no restraint whatsoever," said O'Brien severely. "Do you—do you suppose I've killed him?"

"Not a hope."

"Well, in that case—" There might have been the faintest trace of disappointment in O'Brien's voice. He turned to pick up the gun, and so quickly had all this happened that it was only then that Tom Bhakkar erupted from the office, with Greenhalgh following reluctantly at his heels.

SATURDAY, 7TH NOVEMBER

I

So after all, he went home only a day late, though Saturday seemed about a week long because it was almost entirely devoted to making statements. "It's the last time I go adventuring with you," said O'Brien, when they were paroled briefly to get some lunch. "If you'd told me what you were up to—"

"I didn't know we were going to meet Findlater," Maitland protested. "But you did know what I was doing—didn't you?—at the end."

"I guessed," said O'Brien rather shortly. He knew better than to explain that it was the look in his companion's eyes that had alerted him, when he had turned to him in anger and found his mood changing all at once when he saw what Maitland was doing, and just how much the effort cost him. Seeking for a change of subject, he added, "I knew Greenhalgh would rat as soon as I saw him. At least, it will make things simpler for the police."

"And therefore for us. Do you think the coroner will demand an autopsy on Jackie, after all?"

"I rather think he will. But it doesn't really make much difference; they're bound to find some trace of Mrs. Bhakkar now they know what to look for."

"Yes, but that was Tom's show."

"Findlater was an accessory. And as for Jackie, there's no telling who was responsible."

"From what Findlater said . . . but that doesn't prove anything, after all. Have you seen Beas?"

"I'm leaving him to Jones . . . and the police, if they want him. I daresay we'll both have to come back to wind things up."

Chris Conway took Maitland to the station to catch the five-thirty; O'Brien, also a day late, was spending the rest of the weekend with friends in Baildon. Chris had been inclined to be indignant at being left out of things yesterday. "But I didn't know what was going to happen," said Antony again, more patiently than he felt.

"Oh, well, I suppose not." He did not sound convinced, but he grinned as he added, "You've left the police the hell of a lot of clearing up to do."

"Do them good," said Antony heartlessly.

"As for that, I shall be pretty busy myself. And I'm getting married next week," he added in a rush; and when Antony hesitated, wondering how to word his congratulations, he went on with a distinct air of belligerence, "If you're thinking it's because the charge against Sergeant Duckett will be cleared up along with the rest of it . . . it isn't that at all."

"No, of course not." He realized as he spoke that the words were meaningless, and Chris ignored them.

"I met Star last night; I must have only just missed you. I told her straight . . . come to think of it, that's what you told me to do, isn't it?"

"More or less," said Maitland, more happily.

"Well, she said then she'd marry me whatever happened."

"I knew you'd find something better to do with your time than coming with me to see Greenhalgh," Antony told him.

"Yes, I suppose . . . but I would have loved to see O'Brien jump on Findlater," said Chris a little wistfully. "I mean . . . O'Brien! You can't tell by looking at people, can you?"

"There's nothing wrong with his reactions," Maitland said. "And it wasn't only Findlater. He rounded up Tom Bhakkar and Greenhalgh too, and locked them in the office. All I had to do was phone the police." He remembered, as he spoke, the nausea that had finally overcome him as he put down the receiver, and thought it was decent of O'Brien not to have mentioned that part of the episode again. "About your wedding . . . shall I be here?"

"That's what we're hoping. There won't be time for proper invitations, but if you and Mrs. Maitland . . . I'll phone you."

"Good. What has Grandma to say about it? I hope to goodness the stars are favorable."

"Well, she doesn't really like the rush," said Chris. "She says people will talk, but life's too short to worry about things like that."

"Much too short."

"So she's buying a new hat for the occasion. I think that must mean she's reconciled to it, don't you?"

"That settles it," said Antony firmly. "I shall come to Arkenshaw for the wedding, choose how." Doors were slamming farther down the train, and Conway backed away a little to allow a porter to pass. "Give Grandma my love, and tell her not to buy anything Uranus wouldn't approve of. And be sure to tell Star—" A whistle shrieked, a hundred voices seemed to be shouting; he could see Chris's lips moving as the train started to move, but the words were lost, as were his own good wishes.

It didn't matter. He could deliver them himself next week. He'd get Jenny to come with him. . . .

II

"Of course I'd love to come," said Jenny. She was unpacking his case, and paused a moment to admire Bushey's scarf. "How . . . how magnificent, darling. Did Grandma knit it?"

"I might have known it would get in somehow," said Antony gloomily. "I don't suppose I shall ever be rid of it."

"Never mind, we can give it to the deserving poor," said Jenny lightly, and was surprised to see him frown. It might be just his shoulder, of course, it was obvious it was hurting him; or it might be what happened in Arkenshaw, she hadn't really heard the details yet. "I'd love to meet Grandma," she told him. "And as a matter of fact, I'm getting a *little* tired of Pat and Mike, they do seem to take so much looking after. But Mrs. Stokes would enjoy them for a day or two."

"Haven't they finished yet?"

"Well . . . nearly. Come and look." He followed her into the hall, and she pulled the bathroom door open and closed it again quickly, leaving him with a confused impression of enough pipes to serve a public swimming pool, and a gleaming porcelain bath, for some reason set on end like a mummy case in a museum.

"It isn't going to stay like that, is it? I mean, there are certain disadvantages—"

"We can use Uncle Nick's bathroom until they've finished."

"Thank you. We *shall* be popular. Isn't Uncle Nick tired of Pat and Mike too?"

"He was. But then he heard one of them calling Gibbs 'mate,' and that sort of reconciled him, you see."

Gibbs was Sir Nicholas' butler, a disagreeable old man with a strong sense of propriety. "Yes, I can see it might," said Antony thoughtfully.

III

He went down to see Sir Nicholas after dinner, and found him in the study with an evening paper prominently displayed on the table at his elbow. "I suppose you'll tell me right has triumphed—" he remarked when Antony had done his best to put the narrative straight.

"Nothing quite so trite, sir."

"—but why you had to turn the whole town inside out to achieve it," Sir Nicholas went on, ignoring the interruption, "I cannot think."

260

"Natural incompetence, I suppose," said Antony impenitently. "But there is one thing, Uncle Nick—"

"Well?"

"It's what Constable Ryder said to me . . . I saw them both for a few minutes before I left, but Duckett had gone by then. He said, 'I'm grateful, Mr. Maitland. Seemed like a shame to be broken for summat you didn't do.' And then he turned in the doorway and added as though it was the most natural thing in the world, 'Not but what I wouldn't have gone along, and willing, if Sergeant had said t'word.' " He paused, encountered a stony look from his uncle, and added in a doubtful tone, "There ought to be a moral in that somewhere, but I'm damned if I can see what it is."

"Your friend Mrs. Duckett could give you one," said Sir Nicholas, relaxing suddenly and giving Antony his blandest smile. "I think she would tell you, 'There's nowt so queer as folk.' "